MW00882174

REFUGIUM

RUINS
OF
TEMPTATION

USA TODAY BESTSELLING AUTHORS

C. HALLMAN
& J. L. BECK

Copyright © 2022 by Bleeding Heart Press

www.bleedingheartpress.com

Editing by Kelly Allenby

Proofread by Editing for Indies

Cover design by Opulent Swag and Design

All rights reserved.

No part of this book may be reproduced in any form or by any electronic or mechanical means, including information storage and retrieval systems, without written permission from the author, except for the use of brief quotations in a book review.

TRIGGER WARNING

This is a dark romance containing various tiggers. We will not list triggers specifically due to spoilers, but if you have any concern about a certain trigger you can reach out to us any time at read@ bleedingheartromance.com

Thank you!

Josi & Cassy

BLURB

I've spent years trying to be someone I'm not. Controlled and humanized.

Still, the darkness lurks inside me, waiting for a chance to break free.

As the headmaster at Corium University, I must maintain professionalism and keep myself in check.

I manage to do that until the day I discover I have a daughter, and all the carefully constructed walls I've built around myself start to crumble.

I know I need an outlet, a way to shut it off, and then she lands in my lap.

Delilah.

I want to punish her, humiliate her, and hurt her in the best ways.

It's nothing but a game of cat and mouse till I discover the secrets she's hiding...

PROLOGUE
LUCAS

I tighten my grip around her slender throat as I fuck her wet cunt without restraint. Confusion flashes over her face a second before her baby-blue eyes go wide, searching mine for my intention. I wonder what she sees or what she thinks I'm doing. I don't really know myself.

Whatever she sees has her frantically grabbing at my arm holding her in place. Her mouth opens, but nothing besides a strangled gag comes out. The sound has me pumping faster, and the way her skin is turning a hue of purple has my balls tightening. Tears form in the corner of her eyes. Fascinated, I watch each one roll down the side of her cheek, wishing she was wearing makeup just so I could see it smear all over.

Of course, Charlotte doesn't need to wear anything on her face. She has the kind of skin other women pray for.

Panicked, she starts fighting me in earnest, trying to push me off by bucking her hips and digging her sharp nails into my skin. Her fight only makes her pussy tighter and gets me more excited.

I'm holding her life in my hand. I could end it now, snuff it out and watch the life drain from her eyes just like I do with the poor guys who dare to step in the ring with me.

But this... this is different. Charlotte is an innocent woman who hasn't done anything. She didn't ask for this, nor does she deserve it. Maybe that's the reason my usual numb self is so fucking excited. I've killed so many men that it barely scratches an itch anymore.

Smiling, I fuck her as hard as I can. Sweat drips down my forehead, and my own breath is labored from exhaustion. Charlotte is still scratching my arm like a wild cat, scratching me so deeply that I know it's going to leave scars.

Her face is turning deep blue, and a small vein in her right eye has burst, filling the white part with an angry red. Grinding myself deep inside her until I finally blow. My vision blurs, and my whole body shakes from exhaustion.

Releasing her throat, I collapse on top of her just as she struggles to suck in a breath. She immediately throws herself into a coughing fit while shoving at me, trying to push me away.

"What the fuck is wrong with you?" she creaks, barely getting out the words between her efforts to suck in air.

"Everything," I whisper against her skin.

"Get off me, Lucas!" she yells in my ear, making my brain hurt.

I roll to the side and onto my back. Charlotte scrambles off the bed and gathers her stuff in a hurry. I watch her get dressed frantically as big tears roll down her beautiful face. Her cheeks have returned to their normal color, but red-bluish spots remain on her delicate neck.

"You came inside me. " Her hoarse voice cracks at the end. "I told you I'm not on birth control."

"Take some money from the dresser." Money fixes everything.

"I'm not a prostitute."

"You oughta be with that pussy."

"You're a fucking psychopath!" She leaves the room, slamming the door shut behind her before the only two words that come to my mind leave my mouth.

"I know."

1

DELILAH

I pull back the curtain covering the window, peering out of it and into the parking lot. I've been hiding in this hotel room for days now, trying to build up the courage to leave town. I know I have to. It's no longer a *should* scenario. There's no other option.

The buzzing of my phone has my heart racing in my chest. I fish it from my pocket and smile when I see his message light up the screen.

Nash: You okay?

Me: Yes, still at the motel, but I'm thinking about leaving.

Nash: That's probably a good idea. I'm telling you fucking Rossi is taking out your family.

Family. Ha. I don't give a shit about them. The only person I care about is Nash.

Nash: Go to the place I told you about. You remember?

How could I forget? He has made me memorize the address, telling me to go there if I need to lay low.

Me: What about you? Can't you come here and get me?

I stare at the screen, hopeful. I wish he would just come with me.

Nash: No. I'll meet you there. No matter what, you go there. Even if you don't hear from me, you'll be safe.

Me: Why wouldn't I hear from you.

Nash: I might be next.

Me: Don't say that.

Just the thought of losing him has my chest aching.

Nash: Don't worry about me. Just go to the place and clear your phone.

Me: Okay.

I let the drape fall closed after staring into the mostly empty parking lot for another few seconds. I'm afraid to leave this room, but I'm more afraid of what will happen if I don't. Just like Nash taught me, I reset the phone to manufacturer settings, deleting all calls, messages, and phone numbers saved.

Mustering as much courage as I can, I tighten my hold on the strap of my backpack and walk toward the door. All I have to do is leave the room and start walking toward the train station.

Once I'm out of North Woods, it'll be easier for me to blend in, but until then, I need to put as much distance between me and this town as possible. I open the door to the hotel room and step out into the empty hall, checking both directions for any possible assailants.

With a person like Quinton Rossi after you, you can't ever be too sure. Once I feel certain the coast is clear, I start my walk toward the stairwell. I force myself to ignore the loud voice in my head telling me to turn around. No matter what, I'll never be safe here again—not after what happened.

I descend the stairs and make my way through the hotel lobby, where the woman behind the front desk smiles at my appearance. I look away, and my stomach churns as I reach the doors, which open automatically in my presence.

No going back after this.

It's all running until I get somewhere I can never be found.

Against my better judgment, I leave the protection of the hotel and walk toward the train depot. I follow the directions on my phone, my legs moving quickly and my heart galloping in my chest as I peer over my shoulder every two seconds to make sure I'm not being followed. A van drives past slowly before coming to a stop on the road. The windows are blacked out, but that doesn't matter. I don't need to see inside to know who's inside that vehicle.

Fear ripples down my spine, and my fight-or-flight instincts kick in as soon as the door slides open, and Quinton Rossi's form appears before me. I pedal backward and whirl around, prepared to take off at a dead run, only I'm not fast enough. *Fuck.* Quinton grabs me by the back of my shirt and hauls me toward the van.

Panicking, I twist in his grip, trying to escape him. His piercing blue gaze collides with mine, and the coldness freezes me to the bone.

"Let's have a little chat..." He snarls, and before I can comprehend what's happening, he's shoving me into the van, my ass landing haphazardly on the seat while the door slams, closing me inside.

My hands tremble as I slowly adjust myself in the seat. I can feel Quinton staring at me, and I keep my eyes trained on the floor. The van starts to move, and I wonder where he's taking me? Not that I plan to ask him. I'm going to keep my mouth shut as long as possible.

"Who is Nash Brookshire to you, and how do you know him?" His voice is sharp, but I ignore his question, almost as if I didn't hear it at all. "Or maybe Matteo Valentine. Does that name ring any bells in your head?"

I swallow around the lump of fear forming in my throat. I know the power that Quinton has and what he'll do if he ever finds out that we're related. Nash, on the other hand, is a different story.

"Silence won't save them. Hell, it won't save you, either. One way or another, you'll tell me what I want to know. Everyone does." His warning is clear. He'll do anything to get revenge. Anything.

Even though I'm trembling, I somehow manage to keep my composure. "I have nothing to tell you."

"Sure, you don't." Quinton hisses through his teeth. "I know you're connected to them, and I'm going to figure out in what way, even if I have to torture you until you give me the answers I want."

The van makes a sharp turn, and I find myself pressed against the window, my stomach churning, bile rising up in my throat. Shit, I think I'm going to be sick. Silence follows the rest of the ride, and the silence is almost worse than the repeated questioning because silence means he's thinking, and if he's thinking, I'm as good as dead.

I'm not sure how long he has his men drive us around in the van, but once we come to a stop, my fear rises exponentially.

"Where did you bring me?" I ask, trying to hide the fear in my voice.

"Now she wants to talk. Nah, I don't think so. That's not how this works. I ask the questions, and you provide the answers."

Grabbing me by the wrist, he pulls me out of the vehicle as soon as the door slides open. My legs are jelly, but somehow, I manage to keep myself upright as he drags me toward a building that appears to be a warehouse. I look around, trying to figure out where he's brought me, but it appears we're in the middle of nowhere.

Ahead, a door opens, and Quinton's grasp on me tightens. We enter a hallway, the lights flick on as we walk inside, and I spot a couple of men following us; their heavy footfalls filter into my ears.

I don't even attempt to make a run for it. I'm many things, but dumb is not one of them.

Quinton stops and opens a door to the right, pulling me inside with him, none too gently. Again, I barely manage to stay upright with the sudden movements. He's dragging me behind him at this point. The room illuminates with a dim light that shudders on above us.

I squint and notice the chair in the center of the room. Quinton releases me, giving me a shove toward it.

"Sit and get comfortable because you won't be leaving until I get the answers I want."

"I already told you..." My words are halted by an even harder shove toward the chair. I take the seat because I'm not sure what he's willing to do to get me to follow his orders, and I don't particularly want to find out. Sitting, I now face him, his face half shadowed in the dark.

"Get the rope," Quinton tosses the words over his shoulders.

"Rope?" I croak. Now I regret sitting down even more. Stupid me walked right into the lion's den.

"Yes. I'm not going to risk you escaping. You'll be tied to this chair until I'm satisfied with the information you provide me. From there, we'll see what happens to your pathetic life."

I bite my tongue, the coppery taste of blood filling my mouth. Nothing I say to him will get me out of this room faster, and I'm not giving him the answers he seeks because I know he'll kill all of us. One of his men walks into the room, and my gaze catches on the rope in his hand.

Even in the dim light, I still catch the slimy smile on his lips. He's a sick fucker, I just know it.

"Tie her up and make it quick," Quinton orders.

A shiver ripples down my spine, and every instinct I have tells me to move, to try an escape, but I resist. I don't even so much as glance at the man as he ties my legs to the chair, his touch lingering longer than necessary. His rough fingers running down the inside of my thigh makes me want to vomit. All I want to do is shove him away, but with my hands behind my back, I'm helpless to his assault.

"That's enough," Quinton growls, and I almost forgot he was still here. "I want her tied up, not groped."

I'm surprised that he seems to have a sliver of care for what happens to me. Or he just wants to be the one doing this to me. Yes, that's more like it. I've heard stories about him, and I know what he's capable of. He probably wants to break me himself.

Time moves at a snail's pace for the next few hours as he starts questioning me. Minutes tick by, but it feels like hours. I want this to be over, but to end it, would mean I'd have to give him what he wants, and I'll never do that.

"This could all be over if you'd tell me what I want to fucking know!" Quinton yells, his voice piercing my ear drums. My stomach clenches, and my throat and tongue are so dry that it feels like I've been chewing on cotton balls.

"Please, I'm hungry and tired and have nothing to tell you."

Rushing forward, he gets in my face and growls, and spittles of saliva land against my cheek. "You're a fucking liar, and we both know it. Tell me what I want to know, and this can all end."

Tears prick at the back of my eyes, and I'm so close to exhaustion that it's not even funny. No matter how much I blink back the tears, they still somehow escape and traitorously slide down my cheeks. I hate, with every fiber of my being, that he gets to see me so weak, but I'm past the point of caring.

"Your tears don't do shit to me, so if you're trying to get me to feel bad for you, maybe try harder?"

"I already told you half a million times that I don't know who they are. I know nothing and have no information for you." The tears become bigger, and my pain and exhaustion rush to the forefront of my mind. It's all I can feel and see.

Quinton is resilient and refuses to show remorse. As soon as I start to give in to the exhaustion, he has one of the men toss a bucket of water at me. It's cold and soaks me to the bone until I'm a trembling mess, and my body is ready to give out completely.

"Please, I can't do this anymore. I don't have any information. Please, I'm begging you." Maybe I would tell him what he wanted if I knew it wouldn't get me killed. I value my life more than giving in.

He leans in close, filling my field of vision. There's nothing in the world but exhaustion, hunger, and cold. I can't stop shivering. I can hardly keep my eyes open to look at him.

He takes me by the chin and jerks my head up. There's no light in those eyes. No soul behind them. Just endless black pits. "You're going to tell me what I want to know."

"H-how can I?" My teeth are chattering so hard that I can barely speak. "W-when I have nothing you want?"

"Come on. We both know you're lying. You'll lie to your dying breath to protect those fuckers. Do you honestly think they would do this for you?" He shoves my head away before backing up. "They would sell you out in a heartbeat. There's no such thing as honor or loyalty for heartless fucks like them. Are they worth this?"

I don't have the strength to hold my head up anymore. It hangs low, my dripping hair falling on either side. "I don't know anything. Please, stop this. You're wasting your time."

"Me? I have all the time in the world." His heavy footfalls pace back and forth, but I can't lift my head to look at him. I'm too weak and sore. I don't want to see him, anyway. I don't want to look into his soulless eyes.

The footsteps come to a stop in front of me. "You're going to see what a patient person I am. I can wait forever. The question is, can you?"

There's so much evil in his voice. Cold, hard, inhuman. I raise my head slowly, still shivering, my eyes burning from the effort of holding them open. "For the last time, I can't help you. I don't know anything."

The smile he gives me balances on the edge of a serial killer smiling at you before he kills you. "We'll see if a few weeks of solitude will loosen your tongue a little bit. Help you see things in a different light." I don't have the chance to ask what he's talking about before he motions to one of his men. He springs into action, untying me, his hand firm around my wrist as he forces me to my feet. My wobbly legs barely keep me upright, and then we're moving. I don't bother looking up because I know where he's taking me.

My nightmare is just beginning.

2

LUCAS

*M*y footsteps echo down the large empty castle halls as I walk Aspen and Quinton to the meeting room. The only other sound is the rapid beating of my own heart, pushing blood through my veins at an irregular speed. My hands are shaking, and my gut feels like more acid than usual is swirling around in my stomach.

It's been so long that it takes me a moment to recognize this foreign feeling. *Fear.* I'm afraid, which is a notion I am not very familiar with.

I'm never scared. I used to step into a steel cage willingly, knowing only one person would survive the fight. At first, I did it because of the money, then I did it merely for the fun of it. Yes, fun.

So why do I feel afraid now? Maybe it's the fact that it's not my life in danger. It's the girl walking a few steps behind me. The girl I didn't know was my daughter until earlier this morning.

My daughter. Fuck.

I still can't wrap my mind around it. Me, a father. To Aspen of all people. Guilt swirls into my fear, making the useless thing in my chest ache. I can't be a father; a father is supposed to love his child, which is something I'm incapable of.

The only thing I can give her now is protection. No matter the outcome of this meeting, I will not let her die.

As we get closer to the room, I shove all those pesky feelings, doubts, and fears deep down and put my well-rehearsed game face on. I won't let her die either way, but the best-case scenario would be a unanimous vote. So for now, that's what we are going for.

We enter the meeting room a moment later. In the center of the space sits a giant oval table that looks like it's been a part of the castle since it was first built. Around the table are all the founding members, including Xander and my brother, Nic. Also here are our friends, Julian Moretti, Lucian Black, Adrian Doubeck, Enzo King, and Dr. Lauren.

Alessio Bianchi is a wild card for me, but hopefully, Quinton got through to him, like he said. Nathaniel Brookshire and Katharina Ivanov are no friends by any means, but at least Katharina agreed to vote in our favor. Now we only have to convince the Brookshire prick to do the same.

Nic's eyes find mine immediately, searching for any kind of hesitation. As always, he is the concerned older brother. I guess that will never change. He is the only other person who knows about Aspen, though I think Xander probably knows as well. At least that's the feeling I got at the wedding earlier.

Looking around the table, I find Brookshire staring daggers through Aspen, and his beady eyes only narrow further once I open my mouth.

"Take a seat," I order, and we all sit down at the end of the table. "As requested, you may ask any questions now."

"So it's true. You did marry? Is that why you killed my son? Did you think you'd simply get away with it because you are a Rossi?"

"I killed him because he attacked me."

"Sure, he did, and do you have any proof of that?"

"Her word is enough proof," Quinton interjects. "Nash had been trying to get to her for months, and he knew she was under my protection. There was no reason for him to be in her apartment."

"Maybe she invited him? Who knows, with how many guys she slept with behind your back."

Quinton looks ready to slam Nathaniel's face into the edge of the table, which I wouldn't mind seeing myself.

Unsurprisingly, Aspen speaks up for herself. "I didn't invite Nash in. As a matter of fact, I asked him to leave. I told him to stay away from me multiple times. He wouldn't. Then he admitted to drugging me. He gave me a drug that led me to have a miscarriage."

Brookshire shakes his head. "You are lying. Many words and no proof."

"She is telling the truth. I examined Aspen myself," Dr. Lauren announces.

"I also had my personal doctor examine her right after the attack, and he agreed. Furthermore, we have a video taken with Nash's phone that proves he was there when Aspen was attacked. All of that leads me to believe it was your son who killed my grandchild."

For the first time since we entered this room, Nathaniel looks a little pale. Xander's comment seems to have ruffled his feathers. "Those are all speculation, and even if there was some truth to that, Corium rules are clear. No death to any student can take place on school grounds."

"Of course, you are right," Xander offers. "But these are very special circumstances, and of course, we would offer your family something as a gesture of goodwill."

"Did you make that same offer to the Valentine family? Is that why they are all dead? They wouldn't take your deal?"

"We are here to discuss Aspen. The Valentines have nothing to do with this."

Nathaniel's eyes become slits as he glares at me with nothing but hostility. "Sure, they don't. I wonder if the rest of Corium agrees with that. Not to mention everyone we work with." He turns back toward Xander. "Your family might be powerful, but there is an end to your reach, you know."

"Are you threatening me?" Xander raises an eyebrow.

"Of course not. Simply pointing out the truth." Nathaniel's slight backpedaling almost has me cracking a smile.

"Good thing our family just expanded, solidifying one of our allies with a marriage." Xander grins, his eyes landing on Aspen and Quinton.

"Ally? Even if Mather wasn't dead, he would have hardly been of any help to you."

Nic gives me a nod so slight that most people would miss it, but I'm not most people, and I know exactly why he is getting my attention. This is it. The time I need to speak up. I didn't think it would be a big deal, but now that the moment has come, I have to force the words out. Not because I'm ashamed of Aspen being my daughter. I'm ashamed of myself. Of failing her.

"Clyde Mather wasn't Aspen's biological father," I glance around at everyone's curious expressions until I finally say the last two words. "I am."

"You are her father?" Nathaniel sputters, looking just as shocked as the rest of the founding members.

I look over at Aspen to find her staring at me with her mouth gaping open and her eyes wide as can be. For a second, I regret not telling her in private, but the truth is, I didn't know how, or maybe I was just too much of a coward.

"Yes. Aspen is my biological daughter," I state firmly while looking into pale blue eyes so similar to mine. "Nic is her uncle, and though we agree she has broken the rule, we are also willing to rectify her action in another way. My family is willing to offer you part of our territory."

"That won't bring my son back."

"Neither will killing her," Nic speaks up for the first time, his voice deep and penetrating as always. His dark hair is slicked back, and his features weathered, but still, he looks as dangerous as ever. They don't call my brother the devil for nothing. "But letting her live will give you and your other children peace of mind."

"Peace of mind?" Nathaniel scoffs.

"Yes, because it means that I won't come after your family for killing the heir of the Rossi empire," Xander adds casually, though everyone knows his threat is taken very seriously.

"And what about the rest of you?" Nathaniel addresses the founding members. "Do you think we should let her live? How would that look to the rest of the students and their parents?"

"This is a blind vote," I explain. "No one has to tell you what they are voting for."

"I guess then there is only one thing left to do. Let's vote." Nathaniel leans back in his chair, crossing his arms over his chest.

"Let's begin." I nod and push myself up from my chair. I grab the large metal bowl from the display case hanging on the wall. "If you agree to let Aspen live, simply write an L on the paper. If you think her punishment should be death, write an X on the paper."

Walking around the table, I let each founding member pull out a piece of paper to write their vote on. When I move around the second time, everyone throws their folded-up paper back in. With each step, the bowl feels heavier in my arms, though I know its weight is insignificant. The papers inside should add no weight, but each feels like an extra twenty pounds.

Returning to my seat, I dump all the papers out, showing everyone the empty bowl. One by one, I unfold each paper, and with each sight of the L scribbled down, I can breathe a little easier.

By the time we have only two left, sweat drips down my forehead, and it takes all my concentration to go at an even pace and not tear the last papers apart.

The ninth paper reads an L. Only one left. This is it. The last vote.

I unfold the tenth paper, holding my breath.

L, it's an L.

I huff out the air in my lungs as relief crashes down on me like a tidal wave. We did it. Aspen is safe.

The room clears quickly, with Nathaniel practically running out like he can't get away fast enough. He throws one more glare at Aspen, but she looks too much in shock to notice.

"Aspen." Quinton takes her arm gently.

"I think I might be in shock." Aspen gasps softly.

"You're safe now. It's all over," Quinton assures her, but she doesn't look convinced yet.

"Aspen. Are you all right?" Xander steps next to Aspen's chair, handing her a glass of water. "I suppose anyone could be excused for feeling overwhelmed at a time like this."

"Thank you." She grabs the water with a trembling hand.

"We do what needs doing for one of our own," Xander tells her.

I give Aspen a few more minutes to gather herself while I run through the speech I have been memorizing all day.

I'm just about to get her attention when she looks directly into my eyes. Determination forms in her gaze, and she suddenly stands. Quinton wraps an arm around her waist like he wants to lead her away. That's my cue. I clear my throat. "Can I have a minute with you?"

Aspen exchanges a look with Quinton and nods. "Go ahead. I'll catch up to you."

Then we're alone. It's not the first time we've been alone, but today feels different because today is different. She takes a seat again. I choose to stand for a little bit longer. I don't know where to start, whatever I had thought about before is gone, so I say the only thing that comes to my mind. "I hope you don't hate me for blurting that out in front of everyone."

"I don't. You probably saved my life."

"Not entirely. You did a lot of that on your own."

"So it's really true?" She searches my face, looking for a lie or maybe some kind of resemblance she missed before.

"I want you to know I had no idea there was even a child." I pace the room, unable to sit still for another moment. "Not until we watched that video together. I can't tell you how shocked I was. Because I did see a woman named Charlotte, and the time we were together lined up with roughly the time you were born. Last I heard, she passed away a few years ago, I'm sorry to say."

I rub my hands together nervously. "It was enough to make me want to look deeper into the situation. I had your DNA tested against mine. The results came in earlier today and confirmed our connection."

"Earlier today? Before the...?"

I stop pacing. "Yes. Before the wedding. I had the honor of walking my daughter down the aisle and giving her away." Again, I regret not telling her sooner. I should have, but I didn't know how she would react. I draw in a deep breath. "I'm sure you have plenty of questions."

"Only about a million. The one that stands out is why was my birth mother so afraid of you? I don't understand."

Straight to the point. She's the one subject I don't want to talk about, but more than anything, I owe her the truth. "Honestly, sometimes I feel like I used to be a different person back then. I was young and hurt and so fucking lost. I was reckless and didn't care about anything. I'm sorry, Aspen. It's probably not what you want to hear, but I'm glad you didn't meet me then." So fucking glad. Charlotte did the right thing by hiding our child from me.

"I'm glad I met you now." Aspen's words hit me with more force than a fifty-pound weight on my chest.

"I'll tell you everything you want to know. We have all the time in the world now that you're safe. For now, you don't want to keep your in-laws waiting too long. Xander's patience is not legendarily generous."

A tiny smile crosses Aspen's lips. She looks hesitant about leaving as if she would rather talk more, but she also knows I'm right. If she doesn't leave the room soon, one of the Rossi's is going to march in here regardless.

"Thank you for speaking up when you did."

"It was only what was right," I assure her, keeping to myself just how far I would have gone to keep her safe.

3

DELILAH

"Oh, god, no! No, please, stop!"

No matter how hard I press my hands against my ears, it's not enough to block out the screams. I've never heard screaming like this before. I didn't know human beings could make such sounds. Like an animal, desperate, in pain to the point where they lose their humanity.

"Please!" I squeeze my eyes shut and curl into a tighter ball on the corner of the cot. Why won't they stop? When will they stop? They're going to torture him to death.

The question that looms larger than the others: who is it?

I have a feeling I know. I've never heard Matteo scream like that before, but when he sounds human, the voices are similar enough. If Quinton has Matteo, why am I still here?

I can't let myself start asking questions like that, or else I'll go crazy. Not that I'm not already halfway there.

Another wordless shriek tears through me. I clench my teeth and rock back and forth, humming in a vain attempt to block out the horrors happening on the other side of the wall at my back.

I'm reminded of how cold and hungry I am then; the shiver that racks through me is almost as painful as the ache in my stomach.

Quinton is doing his damnedest to break me. I don't want to give him that satisfaction. I can't.

I have no idea how long I've been here. There's no way of telling how much time has passed. If this was a normal situation, I might mark time by the number of meals I ate. That's not going to work here. If I went off that, I'd say it's been maybe three days. But I know it's been a hell of a lot longer than that. My clothes are the same clothes I was wearing when they picked me up—I'm practically swimming in them now. I can smell myself, and I hate it.

At first, I was determined. Yelling, screaming, spitting in the faces of the assholes Quinton left to keep watch over me. But over time, I've quieted down. It takes too much energy to do that kind of thing, and energy is one thing I'm pretty low on. That's been the plan all along, obviously. To starve me and keep me weak and docile. I hate letting him have that small victory over me, but there's only so much my body can handle.

I lower my hands just long enough to draw the thin blanket tighter around my shoulders when I hear what has to be the sound of a fist meeting flesh. Matteo, if it is Matteo, lets out a strangled grunt. It's better than the constant screaming. Maybe his vocal cords are too fucked up for him to scream anymore.

That's okay. They'll give him just enough time to heal up before starting it all over again.

I should feel sorry for him, and in a way, I do, but it's the same way I'd feel sorry for anybody being slowly tortured over the course of days, maybe even weeks. It's nothing personal. There's no deeper feeling. I should probably care more about my brother's life, but it's not like he ever gave a shit about me.

There he was, living in a great, big house with all the money in the world. He could do whatever he wanted, could have whatever he wanted. That's what you get when your father actually acknowledges and cares about you. Our father treated him like his flesh and blood.

Me? I only deserved a trailer park with my aunt. I wasn't even allowed to live with my own family. I wasn't allowed to have their name attached to my own.

I don't think anybody who hasn't been through a situation like that could understand what it's like. Nobody had to come out and tell me I wasn't good enough. They didn't have to sit me down and explain all the reasons I couldn't live in the big house. Why I couldn't participate in family events like birthdays.

Nobody had to come out and say those things to my face. I figured it out over time, day by day. It's stuff like that which slowly whittles away a kid's sense of worth. It makes a kid wonder what's wrong with them. Why they aren't good enough. Loved enough. Why no one gives a shit about them.

Then they might go out of their way to be better. Like I did. What a waste of time that was. I told myself if I got perfect grades and always behaved and never did anything that could embarrass anybody, they would finally see how worthy I was.

What happens to a kid when that day never comes? When they try, and they try, and it still isn't good enough? What happens when they finally realize nothing will ever be good enough for the people they want so much to please?

They get hard. They shut down. *You can't hurt me if you can't reach me.* That became my motto.

And that's why I'm able to curl up in this corner of my pathetic little cot, wearing these filthy clothes that stink worse than anything I've ever smelled on myself. How I can sit here shivering, covering my ears, drowning in the darkness but not shed a tear.

If Rossi expects me to beg and wail for mercy on my brother's behalf, he's going to be waiting a long time.

Lost deep in my thoughts, it hits me that the sounds around me have grown quieter. I lower my hands slowly, just in case this is nothing but a momentary break in the action. The only thing I hear is my heart pounding in my ears. The silence is unnerving. For all I know, that might be another part of the torture. The sense of being so disconnected from everything else in the world.

I rest my head in the corner, closing my eyes to shut out the bleak cell around me. What's Matteo going through? What did they do to him? I don't hear him weeping, not this time, but I have before. A memory pops into my head and reminds me why I haven't shed a tear.

The day my father told me they finally found something to prove myself useful—him and my brothers. I guess it was a joint decision. Who knows?

"It's very simple." My father leaned back in his chair, holding a glass of liquor in one hand. My brothers were drinking, too. None of them offered me a glass of my own, even though I could more than use one now.

"We've been working on this for a long time," Matteo informs me, standing at our father's right hand. *"So you could at least muster a little enthusiasm. Perhaps a thank you?"*

Enthusiasm? I was still trying to catch up with what they were telling me. They acted like I was supposed to be on the same page when I couldn't remember the last time I saw any of them.

"Or gratitude if enthusiasm is beyond you." My father laughed with Matteo.

"It's just I'm not sure what I'm supposed to do? Why do you want me to meet that person?"

"Stop asking questions. No one cares about your opinion." Matteo rolled his eyes, lifting his glass. "You'd better shake it off before you meet Brookshire. He doesn't have much patience for stupidity, and we don't need you ruining this before the final details are ironed out and the contract is signed."

"I won't ruin anything." I feel like I'm drowning, flailing around with nothing nearby to grab. I know there has to be a huge reason for them to invite me up to the house, but I can't have imagined it would be this, not in a hundred years.

"We finally figured out a way to make you worth something." My father —my very own father—lifts his glass and laughs at his own pathetic joke. "So you'd better not disappoint me."

"We'll probably have to buy her some new clothes." Matteo looks me up and down, disdain etched over his face. "We don't want the Brookshires thinking we're welfare recipients. They won't like being involved with a piece of trash."

"That's a good point." There couldn't have been a bigger difference between the way the old man looked at me and how he beamed at Matteo. "Way to think things through. I can't imagine she has much of a wardrobe."

Matteo burst out laughing. "Who needs formal wear when you live in a trailer?"

I wonder if he thinks about that now when he's screaming and throwing up from the pain. Does he ever wish he had made different choices?

The familiar sound of a lock disengaging startles me into sitting up straight, eyes wide open. The pitiful blanket isn't much protection, but I clutch it closer to my shaking body just the same. Like armor against whatever is coming next.

It's not so much the sight of my guards that twists me up inside and makes my bladder suddenly feel much too full. It's the blood on their hands, coating their knuckles, flecks of it on their wrists and forearms. I can even smell the coppery tang in the air when they step closer to the cot.

"What are you doing?" I hate the weakness in my voice. The fear.

"Taking a break." The one I've heard Quinton call Bruno laughs and elbows his buddy, Rick. I'm pretty sure there aren't more than three brain cells between the two of them, but they don't need to be big thinkers. They only need to follow orders and be complete, merciless thugs.

Rick sneers, looking down at his swollen, blood-coated hands. "Nothing like a good day's work, right?"

The way they laugh about it stirs whatever is left of my sense of self to life. I don't care that they probably beat my brother half to death and laughed about it while they did.

It's the way they laugh about it now. It's a joke to them. They don't even know him, and they don't care to. They don't even have the decency to act like they regret doing what they're paid to do. Fucking pigs.

"So what?" I whisper. "You wanted to come in and show off? Congratulations."

"She's still got that smart-ass attitude," Bruno remarks, flexing his hands.

"It's a shame we can't beat it out of her," Rick replies.

"Or fuck it out of her." They share a cold, nasty laugh, and revulsion makes me shudder until I think about the way he said it.

They can't beat or fuck it out of me? Hmm, interesting. Quinton must have given them an order. Not that it makes him a good guy or anything like that, but at least I know what I can expect and what probably won't be happening.

There's no guarantee they'll obey orders, but I doubt Quinton is the kind of boss who likes finding out his orders were disobeyed. And I'm sure they know that.

It gives me the strength to sit up straighter and look at them without ducking my head or acting like a weak, pathetic captive.

"It doesn't seem like such a shame from where I'm sitting."

Their laughter cuts off abruptly. Rick steps up closer to the cot, and I don't like the look in his eyes. The look of a man who's about to say fuck it, let's spit roast this little bitch anyway. "You know, there's other stuff we could do." *Like what?* I don't dare ask. I don't want to know. I can only hope he's bluffing.

Bruno nods a second before his hands move down to his belt. My heart starts hammering, and every instinct tells me to run like hell, but how? And where to? I couldn't get away if I tried. I don't even know if I'd have the strength to make it out of here, much less make it to safety.

"Take off your shirt," he orders. "I've been wanting to see those tits since you got here."

Oh, no. Not this. I remain still, staring at him, silently begging him to laugh at his joke. But he doesn't. His eyes hold no humor, only a sick and twisted desire.

He grabs his zipper, opens his fly, and digs around in his shorts before pulling out a thick, stubby little dick. My stomach clenches and would probably force anything inside back up out of my mouth if it wasn't completely empty.

"Yeah, I want to see. Show us those tits, bitch. Or we'll make you, and we might not be able to hurt you, but all we'd have to do is tell Quinton you tried escaping."

Rick's dick is slightly bigger than his buddy's but just as disgusting. I wouldn't touch either of them with a gun to my head. I'd rather take the bullet. As I stare at them a moment longer, I know they're not kidding.

If I don't do this willingly, they'll tear the shirt off me—and worse than that, I might not get it back. As bad as things are now, I can't imagine going through it with no clothes. That would be one humiliation too many. My resolve breaks, and I lower my gaze to the floor while lowering my hands. I grasp the hem of my shirt, my fingers trembling while pulling my arms over my head to show them what they want.

Even now, dehydrated, tears threaten to well up in my eyes. I can't let them. I don't want these pigs to see me cry.

"Oh, yeah. Fuck, those are nice tits. Touch them," Rick grunts. I don't want to look up, but from the corner of my eye, I see the way they move their hands up and down, jerking themselves off to the image in front of them.

"Play with the nipples," Bruno adds.

My teeth sink deep into my bottom lip, and I focus on the pain rather than reflecting on what's happening right now. My chin quivers before I can help it while I take my tits in both hands and hold them up a little, then use my thumbs to roll circles around my nipples. They're hard as bullets, thanks to the cold.

"Squeeze them." Rick's breathing becomes faster now; soft grunts escape his parted lips as I do as he says.

It makes my skin crawl, and I want to scream. I turn my face to the wall and close my eyes. A single tear leaks out and cuts a trail down my dirty cheek.

"Moan for me." When I don't do it right away, Bruno shouts, "I said moan!"

"Oh, yeah..." It's barely a whisper, but it seems to satisfy them. They're both breathing heavily, grunting like animals, and I tell myself at least it's almost over. *It'll be over soon.*

Until Rick grabs me by the hair and twists my head around so I'm facing him, his dick maybe six inches from my face. A whimper escapes my lips. What's he going to do? I wince and struggle to get away, but all he does is pull harder, my scalp burning as I hear some of the hair tear from it.

Bruno steps up beside him. *Not my face, please, God, not on my face.* I squeeze my eyes tight and press my lips together. A silent prayer fills my mind.

"Oh, fuck, yes! Yes!" I don't know who comes first, but the warmth of spilled cum on my chest is a twisted relief. I can't believe I'm actually glad. That's how fucked up and sick all of this is. I'm actually grateful they're coming on my tits and not on my face.

By the time they're finished and Rick releases me, I'm coated in their cum. The sight of it, the smell, makes me gag, and then I gag again at the realization of what just happened. I think I'm going to vomit.

"There. They look even better coated in our cum." Rick laughs at his little joke, and Bruno joins him before sneering at me while tucking himself back into his pants. Neither of them says another word, leaving the cell and locking the door behind them.

I almost wish they would kill me and get it over with.

4

LUCAS

Over the years, I have stepped into Lauren's office more times than I can count. Sometimes willingly, but almost always with dread following me like a shadow. That dread has never been more overwhelming than today. Today. I feel like I'm the shadow.

Without knocking, I shove the door open and march in.

"You're late." Lauren scowls me like I'm a misbehaving child. She sits on her sofa, wearing a casual pale blue sweater and black slacks. Her legs are crossed, and a notebook is lying on her lap. Her brown hair is pulled into a neat bun, completing her textbook therapist look. "Good thing I freed up two hours of my afternoon for you."

"Of course you did." I flop down on the couch across from her, getting comfortable.

"I know my patients well, and you've had a lot to deal with over the last few days. Tell me how you feel about it all."

"You know I don't do that shit… *feelings*." Lauren has been my therapist for many years, but we rarely talk about feelings, mostly because I don't have any. At least not usually.

"Things have changed. You have never been emotionally responsible for another person."

"I'm still not."

"You are. Don't downplay your relationship with Aspen, and don't forget she is my patient as well. I need to consider her well-being too, and I will do so more than yours."

"Harsh, but okay. I'm pretty sure that's against some kind of doctor code, not to mention being extremely immoral." I can hardly get the words out and keep a straight face. As if I care about morals.

"Lucas, everything I'm doing within these walls is against the law and extremely unethical."

"Fair point, but you have known me for a very long time."

"Which is exactly why Aspen is my priority. I barely like you."

"Pffff. Lies. You love me. Why else would you have moved to Alaska with me?"

"I moved because you basically forced me to."

"I prefer to look at it as giving you a nudge."

"If getting me fired and packing up my apartment behind my back is a nudge to you, then maybe we need a three-hour session today."

"An extra hour for fucking?"

"Lucas," she warns, her cheeks turning a hue of pink. "We don't do that anymore. I'm your therapist now; no more fucking."

"But I do think busting a nut would be very beneficial to my mental health."

She rolls her eyes. "I'm sure you are very capable of busting a nut on your own."

"Yeah, but having a woman involved is more fun."

"Are you done trying to avoid talking about your feelings?"

"Never!" I huff, sinking back into Lauren's leather couch and propping my feet onto her coffee table.

Lauren leans back, mimicking my movement. Then she simply waits for me to say something. Her patience is endless. I know because I've tested it extensively.

"I'm angry," I finally say.

"That's nothing new." She is right about that.

My anger is the reason I started seeing her in the first place. I was tired of being so fucking angry all the time. Angry with my parents, my brother, the council, and angry at the world. Maybe that's the only feeling I'm actually capable of.

"Yes, but this is different."

"Because this time you are angry with yourself."

"Sometimes, I really hate how smart you are."

She shrugs. "Wouldn't do you any good if I was dumb."

"I need a drink," I say more to myself. Getting up, I walk toward the wet bar and grab a bottle of scotch. I don't even bother with a glass. This is a bottle kind of session.

"How do I fix this?" I ask after taking a few long sips.

"You start by telling me about it. What's going on in your mind right now?"

Too much. Which is the problem. I sit back down and drink a little more, simmering down the fury inside. "I want to kill someone, preferably Matteo or Nash, but they are already dead. All the Valentines are dead, which means there is no one left to kill."

"Why do you want to kill them?"

"Because they hurt Aspen." I want to do more than just kill them. I want to make them suffer, draw out their pain until they rot, and die an excruciating death.

"And you feel responsible for that?"

"I know it wasn't my fault," I lie. I could have stayed with her or taken her with me. I just left her at her house unprotected. I could have stopped it.

"Are you sure you know that? Or do you blame yourself?"

"What if I do?"

"Then you need to learn how to forgive yourself, which is often much harder than forgiving someone else."

Great. "I'm done talking about this."

"That's fine. Let's talk about something else." She pauses, waiting for me to suggest something. When I stay quiet, she continues. "Do you want to talk about Aspen's biological mother?" I shake my head before she finishes the sentence. "How about we talk about the future instead of the past? Tell me how you see the next few years panning out."

"I guess not much will change for me. I'll still be here. Aspen is returning to her regular class schedule, but I think she still wants me to give her self-defense lessons."

"You think, or you hope?"

"Both. I want to spend time with her." I equally enjoy and hate drinking during a session. Yes, it calms the raging storm inside my head, but it also makes me say things I wouldn't admit so easily sober. I'm guessing that's the reason Lauren lets me drink during therapy.

"That's good. That's very good." She taps her pencil onto her notebook. She always has it in her lap when we talk, but she never actually writes anything inside.

"You sound surprised."

"Because I am. Normally, your favorite thing to do is to push people away." Yeah, I notice that too. Aspen is far from my norm. Everything involving her is upside down.

"I don't know why things are different with her. They just are."

"Are you happy about her being with Quinton?"

"Yes, she's safe with him, and I'll know where she is even after she leaves Corium." Most parents would probably despise the thought of their daughter marrying into the mob, but I'm not most, and though the Rossi family is known for being ruthless and cold, I know they treat their women well.

"Have you talked to Nic about Aspen?"

"Yes, he was the first person I told. He was surprisingly... happy." But no one was as ecstatic as Celia. She was annoyingly excited about the news. "Celia wants to meet Aspen and spend some time with her. The problem is, I don't know if that's a good idea."

"Because Celia met you at your worst?"

"I guess." I take another long sip of scotch, letting the alcohol settle in my empty stomach before continuing. "I don't want Aspen to know how fucked up I am."

"*Was*," Lauren corrects.

"We both know I'm still fucked up. I'm just better at hiding it. I fit in now, thanks to you. I'm able to control myself enough not to let people see the real me. That doesn't mean he isn't hiding underneath, ready to come out and play."

"You don't have to be that person."

"I am that person." Deep inside, I have always been the same. Even now, I can feel him right beneath the surface, scratching at my insides, begging to be free.

"Let's say you're right, and you are that terrible person you think you are. The real question is, do you want to be him?"

"Yes," I say without hesitation. I want to be him because he doesn't care about anything.

The corners of Lauren's lips pull down into a frown. "Then *that's* the real issue."

Don't I fucking know it!

5

DELILAH

The walls of my cell are thick, but not thick enough to lessen the agonizing screams coming from the other cell, and definitely not thick enough to hide the gunshot from me.

Pulling my legs to my chest, I lay my head on my knees and place my hands over my ears. I'm not sure how much more of this torture I can take, but giving up is not in my nature. To give up would be giving Quinton the gun and bullet he needs to end my life, and I'm not dumb enough to do that.

Finally, silence falls upon me, and my worries become gnawing. Is he going to come for me next? Will my death be fast or slow?

The rattling of keys at my door sends me into a frenzy, and I try to make myself smaller on the bed. The air in my lungs stills as the door unlocks and swings open.

Quinton Rossi steps into the cell. His usual anger-stricken face has softened as if he is happy about something. If it wasn't for the murderous glint in his eyes, I would call him giddy. Or maybe that's exactly why he looks so cheerful. The psycho is about to kill me.

"Come on. There's something I want to show you." He closes the distance between us, and his hand circles my arm so quickly that I can't even think about pulling away. Not that there is anywhere I could escape to.

Trembling, I dig my feet into the concrete, trying to stop him as he drags me from my cell, down the hall, and into the next cell, where he releases me with a shove, and I lose my balance, colliding with the cold floor.

My knees land on the concrete, and pain radiates through my thighs, causing me to wince. I squeeze my lids closed, refusing to see the bloodbath he wants to show me.

"Look at him," Quinton growls, but I refuse to lift my head.

A moment passes, and I can barely get air into my lungs. Unhappy about my defiance, he crouches next to me and grabs a fistful of my hair, twisting my head in what I assume is the direction of Matteo.

"I said, look. Look at what's been done to him." His grip on my hair tightens, and I whimper. "This could be you. And it will be."

I open my eyes slowly, taking in the gruesome scene in front of me. Matteo is lying in a puddle of blood, only inches away from me. He is naked, his face almost unrecognizable, and his eyes open wide and vacant.

There is so much blood. I'm not sure where it's coming from, and I don't want to find out either. Blinking the tears away, I look up at the ceiling, saying a silent prayer, hoping my death will be quick.

"Who is this?" A female voice startles me. I turn my head as much as I can with Quinton gripping my hair tightly.

"This is Delilah Wallace. Delilah has ties to Matteo and Nash, but she refuses to say exactly how they're connected. Or *were* connected,

I should say. When speaking of Matteo, one needs to use past tense from now on."

He finally releases me, and I slump back forward. The smell of blood and urine is overwhelming, and my stomach churns even though it's something I'm used to now.

"What do you think, Delilah?" Quinton asks. "Does this convince you I mean business? This isn't a game. Who was he to you? What did you have to do with his family?"

Everything and nothing.

"He was my brother," I finally admit. Whatever he is going to do to me, he will, regardless. I should have realized that sooner. "Satisfied?"

"Your brother is dead now," he states all matter-of-fact.

"No kidding. I thought that was paint on the wall behind him."

"You have more spirit than he did, that's for sure. So you're a Valentine?"

"I'm a Wallace. I might have shared blood with Matteo, but I was never allowed his name." I wasn't allowed anything.

"And it means nothing to you, seeing him like this?"

I wish I would feel nothing. He never deserved my love, but the naïve little girl inside me always looked for his approval. I just wanted all of them to accept me, to love me. I know they never did, but that didn't make them less of my family.

On the plus side, they have taught me to hide my feelings well, so it doesn't take me a lot to reply without a lick of empathy. "He played with fire. When you play with fire, do you cry when you get burned?"

"Most people would puke their guts out seeing someone like this, not to mention a family member. You know what your reaction tells me? That you are not innocent. You are more of a Valentine than you claim."

I turn my head away, not wanting him to see my reaction.

"Delilah's number was in Nash's phone. He called her quite a bit after your attack."

At the mention of Nash's name, my head snaps up to take a better look at the girl in the room.

Fuck. It's her. I recognize her right away.

I'll never forget what I saw.

"I had nothing to do with that. I'm not an animal." I turn my attention back to Quinton. "Is that what this is about?"

He crouches down beside me again, wrinkling his nose at the smell. "You mean to tell me you knew nothing about it? Matteo's own sister?"

"We shared blood, but that's about it."

"Were you close with Nash?" My throat tightens at the mention of his name. I have no option but to lie to them.

"Not very. I heard about what they did to you." I glance up at Aspen. "I was disgusted, and I told him so."

"Nash is dead now."

I'm deadpan. No. No...

Nash. No, he can't be dead.

I don't have time to even process that, so rather than flinch, I force a snort. "So he got burned, too. They took it too far."

Apparently, my act isn't enough to convince him because he reaches for the gun anyway.

"Shall I do the honors?" he asks Aspen.

"I told you. I didn't know anything about it." My desperate pleas fall on deaf ears. My whole body is shaking, and if I wasn't on my knees already, I'd probably be by now.

"You're a part of the family. And they're dead now. I don't like leaving loose ends."

"A family that wouldn't let me share their name. They kept me a secret because I was a girl. Do you think I give a shit whether they're alive or dead? I couldn't care less. And I don't deserve to die for what they did."

Aspen exchanges a look with Quinton. Does she believe me? "I'm tired of death," she announces. "She wasn't there that night. That's good enough for me. And if she was guilty of anything..." She shivers, looking around. "I think she's paid her price."

"Do you hear that? My wife is granting you mercy. If it were up to me, your brains would join his on that wall." He points at the grotesque splatter as if to remind me. "But Aspen is compassionate enough to let you live. She's endured far worse than you have since you got here, and she wants to let you go. Every morning you open your eyes, I want you to remember that, and I want you to be grateful to her. Do you hear me?"

"Yes," I manage to whisper, then look up at Aspen. "Thank you."

Quinton pulls out a cell phone and types a message into it. "They're going to take you home," he announces. "And if you say a fucking word about this, so help me God, you won't live to see tomorrow. I'll be watching you. Got it?"

I'm too scared to ask who *they* might be. I just hope it is not those two goons from before. "Understood." A single sob bursts from my lips as I fight to get back up on my feet.

Quinton motions for me to wait here before taking Aspen's arm and leading her away. He doesn't close the door behind them, and for a moment, I'm thinking about making a run for it.

I take a single step toward the door when two large figures appear in my way.

"Well, hello there, sugar. Looks like we're getting to spend some more time together."

I swallow the lump forming in my throat. "Quinton said you are taking me home."

"Welcome home, baby." Rick grins. "You didn't actually think he was going to let you walk out of here, did you?"

"Back to your cell, stupid bitch. Unless you want to stay here with your dear brother. We'll even let you use the ten-inch dildo we shoved in his ass." They both start laughing at their sick joke, and the image makes bile rise up in my throat. My heart sinks into my stomach. I can't believe I thought I was going to get to walk out of here. Part of me hoped he would let me go, but I should've known. I'll never be free of Quinton, his family, or my father's namesake.

I'm forever trapped with no escape, and with that knowledge, a sliver of me wishes Aspen had let him kill me because, at least in death, I'd be free.

6

LUCAS

*L*eaning forward, I set my elbows on my desk, curling my hands into tight fists in front of me. "You did what?" I'm pretty sure I heard every word Quinton said, but my mind is still fighting belief.

"I kept Matteo alive to torture him and give Aspen a chance to kill him herself." The way he says it all nonchalantly makes me want to shove my fist into his face. I can't believe this.

Fuck.

I don't know what bothers me more, knowing he's been alive when I was dreaming about killing him in indescribable ways or knowing he's now dead, and I missed another chance.

"Did she do it?"

His lips curl up into a satisfied grin, and I know the answer before he opens his mouth. "She did. Shot his dick off first, though."

"Nice." I nod, pride filling my chest at the thought of her pulling the trigger. She deserved to be the one to end him. After all he did to her... my blood starts to pump through my veins faster, and the thundering of my heartbeat fills my ears. I can't think about it because thinking about it makes me murderous.

Quinton stretches his arms out and interlaces his fingers behind his head. "But now we have this other problem."

"*You* have this other problem," I correct.

"Yeah, I fucked up. I shouldn't have lied to Aspen, but at the moment, I didn't know what else to do. I can't let this chick just go, but I can't kill her either."

"How old is she?"

"Nineteen."

"Well... I guess we could enroll her as a student."

"That's a terrible idea."

"You have a better one? You said it yourself that you can't just let her leave, and if Aspen finds out you are keeping her locked up somewhere, she's not going to be happy about it. At least we can keep an eye on her here."

Quinton rubs at his jaw, his eyes narrowing. "We can pay her tuition with what Valentine paid for Matteo."

"We could, yes, and we do have a few rooms empty." Really, this is not a bad idea. I like it more by the second. I missed my chance at killing the rest of the Valentines, and though I won't be able to kill this one, I can still make her life hell in every way possible.

Maybe that will satisfy me? The longer I think about it, the more I enjoy the idea. I'll never get revenge for Aspen. I'll never be able to ease my guilt for not walking her up to the house that night, but I can use Delilah.

"Yes, I like it," Quinton announces. "Do you mind getting her? The place I've been keeping her is close by. Just twenty minutes with the helicopter. I'll talk to Aspen while you're gone."

"Sure, I'd love to."

Quinton raises a questioning eyebrow at my answer but doesn't question my sudden interest in this girl. "Okay then, I guess I'll see you later." He pushes himself up from the chair, giving me a final nod before turning around and leaving my office.

I'm out of the chair the next moment, suddenly excited about my new task. I grab my winter coat from the closet and pull it over my normal clothes. As I walk out of my office, Lea—my new assistant—looks up from her desk in confusion.

"I'll be out for the day," I say before she can ask. "If anyone needs something, tell them it's going to have to wait until tomorrow."

"Of course!" She nods eagerly... a little too eagerly. I haven't figured out why, but I don't like her. Something about her is rubbing me the wrong way. I make a mental note to look into her and ask Nic why he sent her here.

When I get upstairs to the helipad, one of our helicopters is ready and waiting for me. Quinton must have called ahead. I climb in and buckle up just as the pilot lifts us off the ground.

Twenty minutes later, we land in front of what looks to be an abandoned hangar.

"Wait here," I tell the pilot, who points me to the door at the side of the building. The place is covered in snow and barely visible from the sky. Even walking up to the building, it's hard to make out how big this place is because it blends in so well with its natural surroundings.

The freezing wind whips around my head, ice particles settling on my skin and hair. The inside of the hanger isn't much warmer, but at least there's no wind.

I walk through the large empty space that used to hold planes. A small dim light comes from a hallway toward the back of the building. It leads me to a row of doors; the first one is wide open, chatter coming from inside the room.

As soon as I step inside, the two men stop talking, their heads turn toward me, and they drop the playing cards in their hands onto the table.

"Mr. Diavolo..." One of them clears his throat. "We didn't expect you to be here so soon."

"Where is she?"

"Down the hall, last door. I'll show you." One of the goons jumps up, eager to show me what a good employee he is. The other one is less worried about crawling up my ass and stays quiet instead.

"I'm Rick," the one leading the way explains. Then he points at the guy following us. "That's Bruno."

I simply nod, not caring what their fucking names are the least bit. Rick stops in front of the last door, fumbling with the key to unlock it.

"What condition is she in?" I ask while he tries out three different keys as if he forgot which one to use.

"She's fine... I mean, we roughed her up a little when she was mouthy, but there's no permanent damage."

"Did you fuck her?"

"No." Rick shakes his head. "Boss said not to."

"And you always do what the boss says?" I challenge. "After all, you're all alone in the middle of nowhere, nothing to let some steam off while a girl sits right under your nose. Seems like a waste not to fuck her."

"That's what I said," Bruno chimes in. "She's a pretty little thing too. It would have been fun to break her in and see what she was made of."

Turning my head, I cast a look over my shoulder at Bruno.

With a grin, I say, "Maybe I'll give you the opportunity to fuck her after all. Let's see how well behaved she is today."

"Let's see." Bruno smiles widely, showing off a set of uneven yellow teeth. With a creak, the door swings open, and my eyes come to rest on her small frame curled tightly into a ball on a filthy cot.

If I had a heart, I might give a shit. No. If she was someone else, maybe I'd be inclined to care about what she's been through but knowing she is Matteo's sister. Knowing she is the last person I can hurt when it comes to righting my wrongs with my daughter. Nothing she has been through matters to me. She might as well be invisible to me, and by the time I get through with her, she'll wish she was.

7

DELILAH

My head falls forward, then snaps back, my good eye open wide. I have to force myself to stare at the light on the ceiling until purple spots dance in front of me. It's the only way I can keep from falling asleep. No matter how much I want to, I can't risk it.

Aspen should've killed me. One of them should have. If I could go back, I would beg for a bullet to put an end to all of this. Anything, so long as it was over.

Every time I close my eyes, I see Matteo in front of me. That splatter on the wall. His brains and fragments of skull mixed with the blood.

Though it isn't Matteo who makes my heart hurt. The gory memories of the way he died aren't what make me wake with a scream stuck in my throat.

It's when I see Nash's face instead of his. My twisted nightmares blend their deaths together into one endless horror.

I force a deep breath into my lungs to take in all the air they can hold. It's stale, stuffy air, but my brain needs oxygen if I'm going to stay awake—my dreams aren't the only thing I'm afraid of here.

I lift a shaking, filthy hand to my lip and wince even at the gentlest touch. I don't know how long it's been since Rick split it open.

At least it doesn't throb so much anymore. I'm glad I can't see it myself. The sight of my bruised face, the filthy matted strands of hair, and my sunken cheeks might be too much.

It might be what finally breaks me. I'm that close to the edge. I feel it. I know it. All this fighting was for nothing. I might as well have given up that first day when Quinton took me off the street.

What was it all for? I told him what he wanted, he got his revenge, and I'm still here. It didn't mean anything. I didn't save myself. All I did was elongate the pain.

"I'm sorry," I whisper. It's a little slurred, thanks to my busted lip, but it isn't like there's anyone around to hear me. No, the person I said it to is far away—if there is such a thing as an afterlife, anyway.

I never was sure. Now I don't know what that means for Nash. Where did he go when he died? Is he hovering over me somehow? Watching me? I hope not. I wouldn't want him to see me like this.

He was the only one who gave a damn about me. And he wanted me to get to safety. I failed. Him. Myself. "I'm sorry," I say again, though I'm not quite sure what I'm sorry for anymore.

Not being fast enough? Even if I wasn't, I never betrayed him. I need to believe that counts for something.

I always stood by his side, no matter how much easier it would have been to talk. I owed him way too much.

"Where are you taking me?" My words are just a whisper, but my father hears them even over the humming of the engine.

"I told you, I have a friend who would like to meet you."

When he first told me about it, I was so thrilled. He has never introduced me to any of his friends. Hell, he has never called me out of the blue, either. My excitement faded as soon as he told me to put this weird outfit on.

I look down at the school outfit that fits about two sizes too small for me. The skirt is so short I have to pull on the hem as I sit just so my underwear is not showing. The blouse is missing a few buttons, making it dip too low for my liking.

I'm only sixteen, but my breasts have developed early. For the last few years, I've been trying to hide them from the guys my aunt brings home sometimes. There is no hiding in this getup, though.

Shifting uncomfortably in the passenger seat of my father's car, I wonder where exactly he is taking me. A few minutes later, I get my answer. We pull up to a large fancy estate, much like my father's place. He parks the car right in front of the door and kills the engine.

Up until now, I was simply uncomfortable, but as the seconds tick by and my father gets out of the car to open my door, that feeling turns into fear. Something is wrong, very wrong.

"Get out," my father orders. "Nathaniel is waiting."

On shaky legs, I climb out of the car and follow my father to the front door. It opens before we get a chance to knock.

"Ahh, there you are," a man about my dad's age greets us. "I've been waiting all day for my new girl." His eyes move up and down my body, scanning every inch of me besides my face. I immediately try to cover myself with my arms, feeling dirty and exposed in this outfit.

"She is untrained... but she'll do. I'll just have to use the cane on her until she knows not to cover up," the man says with a sly grin.

My fear turns into heart-pounding panic. This has to be a mistake. My father wouldn't leave me here.

"Dad, I want to go back home." I turn to my father, begging him with my eyes to take me with him. I reach out for his arm, but he simply slaps my hand away as if I am nothing but an annoyance to him.

"I told you not to call me that. She is all yours, Nathaniel. Use her as you see fit."

My heart shatters into a million pieces. No matter how hard I press my palm against my chest, I can't stop falling apart. A single tear rolls down my face as I watch the man I call my father walk away from me without remorse.

"Don't worry, sweetheart. I'll take good care of you. And if you behave, I'll even let you call me daddy."

A shiver runs down my spine at the memory. Nash saved me that day. He saved me from a fate I don't ever want to think about. Now he is dead, and I can never repay him.

Did it hurt? Was it slow or fast? They never told me. I don't know if that's a good thing or not. After the endless living nightmare I've been through, one thing is for sure: the anticipation of pain can be worse than the pain itself. The mind can come up with a lot of ugly ideas if you give it enough time—and I've got nothing but time.

I only wish I could have seen him again. Just once more. You never think the last time you see someone will really be the last time.

I try to open my right eye, and the lid lifts a little more than it did yesterday, but it's still swollen half shut. Another gift from Rick. What I wouldn't do to pay him back, to pay them both back. Filthy bastards. Nothing better to do than terrorize me. They're the other half of the reason I'm afraid to sleep.

Now I know for sure they're watching me. There have to be cameras in here somewhere. It seems like whenever I finally doze off, when I can't possibly fight it anymore, that's when they choose to open the door and barge in and fuck with me. Taunting me, slapping me around, even pushing me to the ground threatening to rape me.

Sometimes, I think about maybe pushing them back. Maybe I'll force them into taking things too far. Pushing me too hard, slamming me against the floor instead of shoving me down. Maybe I can put an end to this myself. Go out on my own terms, at least. Because what else is there? I'd rather die than live the rest of my days like this. An animal in a zoo for them to take out their aggression on.

My head is swimming, my thoughts murky and mixed up. I'm not sure if I'm asleep or awake anymore. I tilt my head back, blinking with my good eye, and the overhead light sways back and forth.

Only it's mounted flush with the ceiling. It shouldn't sway. Is it my head swaying?

The door slams open, startling me into scrambling across the cot until I'm curled in a tight ball in the corner. I brace myself. They like to get right down to it usually. Throwing water at me when I fall asleep, hauling me to my feet, shoving me back and forth like I'm a ball they're playing with. I wait, anticipating what might happen next. Instead, it's nothing I would expect, just footsteps before a deep voice rings out. "She smells like shit."

I turn my face away from the corner, squinting up at the mysterious man now standing at the foot of the cot. He's never been here before. I know because I'd remember a man like him.

Tall, imposing, he stares down at me, wearing a nasty smirk. What is he here for? Is he the man who's finally going to show mercy and put an end to this? I don't even care how he does it. So long as it gets done before I start to beg. That's the one thing I haven't done yet, but every day that passes, I get a little closer to begging. For mercy, for my life... For them to end my life.

He turns his head toward the doorway, where Rick and Bruno are waiting. "How long has she been here?"

"A long time." Yes, if I had it in me, I would point out how unlikely it is for either of them to be able to count.

The man snorts as he turns his attention back to me, shaking his head slowly. "Well done. I don't know that I could have shown such restraint."

Restraint? What the hell is he talking about? I look up at him again, focusing harder this time. Who is he? Better yet, who does he think he is? What would he have done differently?

He walks around to the side of the cot, and I flinch before I can help it. He only chuckles, reaching out. I try to turn my face away, but he's too quick, taking me by the chin, yanking my head around, and tipping it back so he can look me in the eye. "You understand you deserve everything you've gotten, don't you?"

Am I supposed to answer that? I wouldn't know how. I don't even know who he is.

"What, did they cut your tongue out? Answer me." His fingers bite into my flesh. "You deserve all of this, don't you? Tell me."

Before I can say a word, he shoves my head away. I recover in time to see him wipe his hand on his pants like I've soiled him. Maybe I have. I'm filthy, after all.

He takes a step back. "On your feet. Now."

What fresh hell is this? I'm so weak and sore, but something in his voice gets me moving. It has to be the fear of what he'll do if I don't give him what he wants. This isn't Rick or Bruno. I feel something totally different coming from him. They're mindlessly cruel, a couple of bullies who get off on hurting people.

But this guy? This guy makes me feel like there's something personal going on. He isn't nasty. He's hateful, the way Quinton is hateful.

I sway on my feet but manage to stay upright. The little bit of strength still inside me won't let him watch me crumble.

"You're coming with me." Before I know it, he's walking through the door, and my two keepers step aside to give him room. Is this really it? Am I leaving? Just like that? Part of me is afraid to follow him, afraid of where he's taking me. Will it be worse than this?

Move your feet, stupid. If I didn't know better, I would think I was already brainwashed or something. One of those people who ends up siding with their captors after being kidnapped. No way. I glare at Rick and Bruno as I pass. They only roll their eyes and snicker.

This new guy, whoever he is, isn't slowing down or waiting for me. I follow him at the fastest pace I can manage, my bare feet slapping against the cold floor. I'm really leaving. I'll never have to see that cell again. I've told myself so many times not to have hope, but now that the prospect of breathing fresh air is right in front of me, I can't help it. And it gives me the strength to keep moving, staring at the back of the man's head.

That hope lasts about as long as it takes him to open the door to the outside, and a fierce gust of wind slams into me, almost knocking me on my ass. He notices the way I wrap my arms around myself and hunch my shoulders against the cold, but he doesn't so much as offer me his coat. He keeps moving, not even looking over his shoulder to make sure I'm following. He crunches through the snow, and for a second, I think this has to be a cruel joke. I'm supposed to walk barefoot in the snow now? He can't mean it.

"Move your ass!" he barks, the sound of it almost lost to the wind. So he does expect me to do it. It's either grit my teeth and get it over with or stay here. I know what I'm choosing.

Even so, the first touch of my bare skin against the snow is horrifying, sending pins and needles up my legs. A silent sob tears from my throat, but I keep moving, almost running, even though I'm barely strong enough to stay upright. The faster I move, the sooner this will be over. In the swirl of snowflakes, I can make out lights up ahead and soon the outline of a helicopter. I focus all my willpower on it, determined to get there even as my feet go numb. Maybe that's a blessing.

By the time we reach the helicopter, and I somehow climb inside, they're frozen, my toes caked in frost. My new captor, whoever he is, glances down at them before turning his face away to look out the window. I rub my feet together, grinding my teeth against painful sobs that threaten to tear their way out of me once the feeling starts to come back. Now they're on fire, my nerves sizzling. But at least I still have feeling in them.

Once we're in the air, he sees fit to speak again. "My name is Lucas Diavolo." The name sparks recognition in the back of my mind, and I clutch it tight to me. It's something to think about besides the agony of my feet. "I am taking you to Corium University."

Corium. That's where Nash and Matteo went. The thought of walking the same halls Nash walked when he was alive makes emotion swell in my chest, even if I'm not quite sure why. I guess it's one final thread connecting us.

But it's not all sunshine and roses. Corium isn't a sanctuary. It's a school for the children of criminals—mobsters, murderers, thieves. The rich and powerful make their money the way my father made his. Which was why Matteo was a student.

What do you think about that, asshole? Your forgotten sister attending the same school? I almost wish he was alive to see it, even if I know he would've made life miserable for me there.

Maybe it's finally breathing fresh air or the way the snow startled me back to my senses, but whatever it is, it gives me the strength to speak. "But why? Why would you take me there?"

He doesn't bother looking my way. Instead, he stares out into the darkness, where I'm sure he can't see anything. "You'll be taking classes there soon. And I'll be keeping an eye on you."

I might be close to starving to death and exhausted, but I'm not stupid. He's not doing this out of the kindness of his heart. Hell, he won't even put his coat over my shoulders. He'd rather have me sit here with my teeth chattering, half freezing to death.

He's out of his mind if he thinks he's going to keep me there. I've been a prisoner long enough. I'll bide my time for as long as it takes me to get my strength back. I mean, I hope he'll at least let me eat and sleep.

But then? I'm out of there. I don't care what it takes.

I catch sight of the school before we begin our descent. It would be difficult not to, the fortress rising up from the snow and sprawling outward in all directions. A castle for the wealthy and powerful.

A far cry from a double-wide in a trailer park. Of course, when we land, I'm given no greater consideration than before. Lucas descends from the helicopter and begins walking toward some kind of tunnel without offering me a hand down.

I follow him, once again willing myself to ignore the shock of the snow on my bare feet. At least it keeps me moving fast. By the time we're inside, I could weep with relief. It's warm, at least once the doors are closed. It's also quiet as a graveyard.

Everybody must be asleep; perhaps it's the middle of the night? I don't know why I feel like I have to tiptoe as I follow Lucas down a long, wide hall. It's not like anybody would hear us.

As I trot behind him, I try to remember anything I've ever heard about Corium, but it's not like anybody wanted to have a conversation with me about it. I heard the building was originally some kind of castle or fortress or something, and there's a lot more going on under the surface, but that's it. I guess I'll have to learn what I can as I go along.

Like how to get out without anybody seeing me.

We take an elevator down below ground level. Never once does Lucas look at me, not even standing together in a little box. I can tell from the way he wrinkles his nose that my smell disgusts him. How does he think it makes me feel?

"You'll be staying in my apartment so I can keep an eye on you." He opens the door but doesn't let me take more than two steps inside before holding up a hand. "Don't touch anything, and for the love of God, don't sit down. Not until you've had a shower. I won't have you ruining my things with your filth."

A shower. Oh, thank God. Not even his nasty, condescending attitude can ruin my relief. Once I'm clean, rested, and fed, I'll be in better shape, and then, I'll get the hell out of here and never look back.

8

LUCAS

I didn't know where else to bring her, not with her looking the way she does. If Aspen sees her like this, Quinton is gonna be sleeping out on the helipad for a week.

But having her in my own apartment is probably not a good idea. No matter how rough she looks at the moment, she is still a woman, and I haven't had sex in way too long.

Leaning against the doorframe, I huff out a breath. This is the worst idea I've ever had. I listen to the sound of the shower running, wondering how much longer she is planning on being in there.

I'm just about to knock on the door when the water shuts off. My hand is still raised, my knuckle hovering inches away from the wood as I listen to her get out of the shower.

The room goes oddly silent. Tilting my head, I rest my ear right at the door. The low creak of the cabinet meets my ear, followed by the sound of her rummaging through my stuff, most likely looking for a weapon.

Not wasting any time, I grab the handle, turn, and push my way into the bathroom. She shrieks in surprise and jumps up so suddenly that the towel wrapped around her loosens. I watch the fluffy white fabric slide off her wet body, exposing every inch of her skin to me.

I'm not sure if it's a second or an hour, but I spend every moment of it scanning the soft curve of her naked form. Her breasts are more than a handful, perky, with light rose-colored nipples. Small bruises and cuts mar the otherwise smooth skin of her flat stomach and long legs. But her feet seem to look the worst from walking barefoot in the snow.

Her high-pitched scream still echoes through the room when she quickly kneels and grabs the towel. But she isn't fast enough, and I get to sneak a peek at the curly tuff right above her pussy. My cock stirs, pressing against my jeans, begging me to let him out to play.

She doesn't wrap the towel around her like before. Instead, she holds it in front of her chest like a curtain to cover her most private parts.

"Get out," she demands with a shaky voice, clutching the fabric like it could possibly protect her from me.

"You are in my apartment, using my bathroom, rummaging through my stuff. You don't tell me to get out."

"I was just looking for a hairbrush." The lie rolls off her tongue so smoothly that I almost believe it. Her wet hair is plastered against her skin in silky waves that look a few shades darker now.

Forcing a smile on my lips, I step farther into the bathroom. The closer I get, the more her bottom lip quivers. The grip on the towel tightens to the point of her knuckles turning white. Her breathing quickens, but when I'm close enough to smell the citrusy scent of my soap on her skin, she holds her breath altogether.

The tips of my boots are less than an inch away from her toes. Her ass is pressed against the sink when I lean into her, eating up all the space between us until my fully clothed body is flush against her wet naked one. She tilts up her head, and I lower mine. Our faces are so close, the tip of my nose almost touching hers. I can see every freckle on her nose, every speck in her emerald green eyes, and every long dark lash framing them.

My cock is standing at full attention now, and I make certain to press my hard length against her softness while I reach past her. Lifting my arm slowly, I grab the brush sitting at the top of the cabinet.

Her heart beats so rapidly, I can hear it, and if her hand wasn't between us, I could probably feel it against my chest as well. A shiver runs through her body, and I wonder if it's only because she is cold and scared.

Straightening myself up, I take a small step backward and hold the brush out to her. For a few seconds, she simply stares at it like it's a foreign object she's never seen before.

"Thanks," she whispers a moment later, reaching for the brush. "I-I don't have any clean clothes. Do you mind if I wash these in the sink?"

"I'll have some clothes delivered for you in the meantime..." I trail my eyes down her body, her exposed hips and thighs, imagining holding her down while fucking her in long deep thrusts. *Fuck, I need to jerk off.*

"I don't need much. An old shirt would be great. Or maybe you have a lost and found box or something like that?"

"Or maybe you sleep naked?" I say before I can stop myself.

"I'd rather sleep naked than get back into those filthy clothes," she quips without missing a beat.

"Then you'll sleep naked."

Confusion flashes over her tired eyes. She isn't sure if I'm joking or not. She's about to find out I'm dead serious.

"Come with me. Walk ahead." I point toward the hallway but leave my eyes on her. A hue of red spreads over her cheeks as she readjusts the towel to wrap around her body, giving me another glimpse of her tits before being covered once more.

She walks ahead of me back to the kitchen. I can't take my eyes off her ass swaying, especially knowing she is bare under the fluffy fabric. I could take her so easily; one tug of the towel, and she'd be naked, ready to take my cock.

I know I'm only attracted to her because I haven't been with anyone in so long. Still, the thought that she has any kind of hold on me has my stomach in knots.

"Wait," I order when we get to the kitchen. Grabbing a granola bar from the cabinet, I throw it in her direction, almost wishing she wouldn't catch it. To my disappointment, she does, grabbing onto the bar like it's some priceless artifact. "That's your dinner, so eat up."

She doesn't waste any time, ripping the paper open and shoving the granola into her mouth as if she is worried I'll take it away from her.

Pointing at my bedroom, I motion for her to go in, and she obeys quickly. Her cheeks are still full of food when I take one of my shirts from my dresser and hand it to her.

She takes it, holding it in one hand while awkwardly holding that now-empty wrapper in the other. Her eyes scan the room, I'm assuming for a trashcan. Instead of letting her throw it away herself, I snatch it from her fingers and growl, "Put the shirt on."

"I thought—"

"I changed my mind." Letting her sleep naked is a terrible idea. Not that I care about her comfort, but I don't want to go to bed with blue balls, either.

Turning my back to her, I give her a few seconds of privacy while I throw one of my pillows on the floor and take the rope from my closet.

Wide, fearful eyes stare me down when I turn back to a now dressed Delilah. She quickly covers her discomfort with a remark. "I didn't know you were into rope play."

"Get on the floor." My voice comes out a little gruffer than needed, but it gets her moving. She gets on the ground in a hurry, lying flat on her back with her head on the pillow. Her slender fingers cling to the hem of my shirt, holding it in place.

With the rope in my hand, I kneel next to her and snatch her wrists. "I'm going to tie them together in the front tonight. If you try anything stupid, and I mean anything, I will make sure to restrain you in the most uncomfortable position possible. You got that?"

"Got it." She nods rapidly while watching me curiously as I wrap the rope around her wrists and secure them with a knot that will be impossible for her to untie on her own.

I repeat the process with her ankles, noting that her feet are still cold to the touch. Her toes are slightly blue, and the bottom of her feet are scratched up and red. I guess making her walk barefoot wasn't such a great idea after all. Aspen is not going to be happy if Delilah loses some toes, but it's not just about what she wants. It's about righting my wrongs. Delilah is a reminder of how I failed Aspen.

Pushing off the ground, I stand over her for a few moments, admiring my own handiwork. I could offer her a blanket; it would be the responsible thing to do, the kind thing, seeing as she is tied up on the floor, her small frame shaking, and her toes still blue from walking in the snow. I shake away any inkling of remorse. She deserves to suffer.

Forcing my raging hard-on down, I get undressed down to my boxers and crawl into bed. I hate the reaction my body has to her presence, but I am a man, after all. Still, if I'm going to fuck someone, it isn't going to be her.

Before switching the light off, I glance at Delilah's form one more time. Her eyes are closed, but I doubt she is sleeping. Not with the way her entire body is shaking. All I can do is smirk, swallowing down any feelings of remorse or kindness for her. She's part of the problem, part of the people who hurt Aspen, and if she thinks it's all going to be fun and games from here on out, she's dead wrong.

I'll make her wish Aspen had chosen for her to die that night.

9

DELILAH

It might have taken forever to fall asleep, but even with my wrists and ankles tied tight enough to turn them numb, I somehow slept better than I have in weeks. I still don't know what day it is. All I know is that sleeping on the floor of Lucas's bedroom was more comfortable and more restful than that stinking, filthy cot, even without the blanket.

My arms are sore from being in this position for hours, and my legs are stiff, but I'm clean and wearing clothes that aren't covered with filth.

It's the little things. I'll never take clean clothes for granted again as long as I live.

It finally hits me that there's something about this room that reminds me of the cell I just left: a lack of windows. Because we're underground, there's no natural sunlight or anything. It's disorienting, but I'm used to that. It's like the torture I went through prepared me for this.

Movement from the bed makes me freeze up. I hold my breath, waiting to see what will happen. From my vantage point, I can just see him under the blankets. A soft snore tells me he's still asleep. How can he sleep soundly, seeing what he did last night?

Knowing what I went through? He must be a soulless bastard to rest soundly after tying a girl up and forcing her to sleep on his floor, knowing she's already been through hell.

He shifts again, leaving me to wonder just how soundly he's actually resting. Now he's on his back, one arm flung over his head. It would be so easy to kill him. He was smart to tie me up.

The old me would never have thought about doing anything like that. I'm not a violent person; at least, I wasn't before. But time and torment have a way of doing things to a person's mind. They teach you how far you're willing to go to survive, and that's what this is really about at the end of the day. Survival. If you want to survive, you have to get the people who would rather destroy you out of the way. The law of the jungle or whatever.

He stirs on the bed, then clears his throat, and I know he's awake without having to see his face. I have to do something to get on his good side. I need him to start looking at me as a person. The more I can get him to like me, the more freedom he'll give me. The more freedom I get, the better my chances of escape. Now is as good a time to start as any.

Especially when I see what's sticking straight up under the covers. From the looks of it, my host has a respectable dick, which I guess makes sense seeing as how he's so tall. It moves back and forth a little as he stretches and sits up.

His gaze immediately falls on me. Even with sleep still heavy in his eyes, I don't miss the deep-rooted hatred for me. I don't even know why he hates me so much, but I'm certain he does. I only have to find out his reason. And the best way to get the truth out of him is to be unexpected. Be blunt, shock him, and keep him on his toes.

"Morning wood is a bitch, huh?" Somehow, I manage to sit up, ignoring the stiffness in my legs and hips. "What do you usually do? Do you jerk off, or do you ignore it and wait until it goes down on its own?"

"What kind of question is that?" he sneers.

A snort escapes me. "Sorry, I didn't get a chance to read the chapter on approved conversation topics in the captor-captive handbook."

He still can't tell if I'm serious or not. I wonder if he's used to being off-balance like this. I can't imagine he would be. Not a man who practically exudes strength and control like he does. He didn't even hesitate to bind me up before making me sleep on his bedroom floor. Like his conscience didn't get in the way at all.

He murmurs something I don't understand, but his eyes slide over my body the way they did last night when I was getting out of the shower. That gives me hope, too. He's only human, nothing more than a man, no matter how much power he has over my life right now.

"How about you let me take care of it for you?"

"Excuse me?"

"I think you heard me," I murmur.

When he swings his legs over the edge of the bed, I have to fight off a triumphant grin. It's almost too easy. Here I was, thinking I'd have to come up with some big, elaborate scheme. All it takes is the offer of a blowjob, and he's putty in my hands.

"You know what. That does sound kind of exciting," he rasps, standing, and now his erection juts out in front of him like a flagpole. "I could keep you tied up the way you are. Fuck your face a little. And there's nothing you could do about it."

"I'd be at your complete mercy," I tease, my heart hammering as he crosses the room to stand in front of me. I clasp my hands together so he doesn't see how my fingers shake with each tiny step he takes toward me.

I get on my knees, a little awkwardly, considering I can't use my hands, but something tells me he doesn't care much about me moving seductively. He's too busy imagining getting his dick sucked.

My heart sinks. I haven't done this with anyone since Nash, and I didn't plan on it either. I know he is gone, but this still feels like a betrayal of sorts.

Lucas stops in front of me, and I have to lift my head to be able to see his face. He glares at me with hate and disdain, which has my stomach in knots. This is going to be rough. He hates me, and he is going to let me feel that hate.

Instead of dropping his shorts, he drops into a crouch, his face inches from mine. He is so close now I can smell his minty breath when he talks. "Like I would ever let you get close to my dick," he snarls, his lip curling in an ugly sneer. "What, do you think I'm some horny teenager? Like I'm as stupid as those assholes I took you from last night? You're way out of your league here, Delilah. Keep that in mind."

Disappointment and relief settle into my bones. I didn't want this, but it would have helped me, and I was so close, at least I thought I was.

But here's the thing about me: I've known nothing but disappointment my whole life. And when you've been knocked down more times than you can count, you learn real fast how to disguise your true feelings. That's why I can grin while looking him dead in the eye. "We'll see about that."

He responds by untying my ankles, then hauling me to my bruised and aching feet. I hate that I have to lean against him for a moment to catch my balance as my stiff muscles come back to life. There isn't much time to recover before he shoves me toward the bathroom, where he unties my wrists immediately before leaving me alone. "Don't take long," he barks from the other side of the door. "I have a schedule to keep."

I'm not sure exactly what that's supposed to mean, but right now, I'm just glad to have a moment's privacy. Even peeing in an actual toilet rather than a bucket is almost a joy. So is washing my hands and face. "I could use a toothbrush," I call out. There's a bottle of mouthwash on the sink, so I use that for now.

"Yeah, no kidding. Like I said, I'll take care of that." He opens the door before I tell him I'm ready, taking me by the arm and pulling me out.

"Where are you taking me now?" I try to twist my arm free of his grip, but it's like trying to fight through quicksand. The more I struggle, the tighter he squeezes until my eyes start to water.

He leads me from the bedroom through the main room, which I don't have time to look at before entering a smaller bedroom. He lets go of me, flinging me toward the bed. "Here. You'll stay here while I go to work."

"You didn't have to break my arm." I rub the place where he gripped me, soreness radiating through my arm.

"Trust me. If I wanted to break your arm, it would be broken." Now I notice what is in his other hand: a key ring. "I'll be locking the door behind me."

Panic flutters in my chest, and before I can stop myself, I blurt out, "Do you have to?"

"Do I have to lock you in this room to make sure you don't find a way to attack me once I come back?" He speaks slowly, like he's addressing a small child. "Yes, I do have to. What's more than that, I want to. Some people don't deserve freedom."

I'd love to know exactly what the hell that's supposed to mean. What does he think I did? There's no time to ask—not that he would answer. All I can do is stand here, helpless, rubbing my sore arm while he closes and locks the door.

"When will you come back?" I finally think to ask, but I guess that doesn't warrant an answer. All I get in return is silence.

My eyes dart around the room, searching for something I can use to pick the lock. The problem is, while there's a small dresser and a table by the bed, there's nothing in them. This is only the guest room, after all, but I was sort of hoping for something. Anything. A hairpin, a nail file. But even when I get on my knees and search under the bed, sweeping my hand back and forth, I come up empty.

No windows, which is something I'm going to have to get used to. There's a small vent in the ceiling, but no way I'd be able to fit up there if I wanted to crawl through the ductwork.

What the hell am I thinking? Who do I think I am? I'm not some action movie hero. I'm not anybody. I don't even know why he has me here. Not really. I only know he hates me. There's not much I can do with that.

Finally, I sit down on the bed. At least it's soft, and the sheets are clean. Maybe the best thing to do right now, since I'm clearly not going to eat this morning, is get some more sleep. I need to sleep if I'm going to heal up.

And obviously, Lucas Diavolo isn't going to fall for a scheme I come up with off the top of my head. He's sharper than that and more distrusting.

I'm sharp, too. And if there's one thing my life trained me for, it's to never trust anybody.

If he thinks it's going to be easy to break me, I can't wait to prove him wrong.

10

LUCAS

*L*ifting my mug, my lips are already touching the rim, I'm ready to take a sip when my office door suddenly flies open. I set my mug back down on my desk and frown at the intruder.

"Is it true?" Aspen basically yells at me.

This is definitely one of the moments I regret telling my secretary to let her through whenever she likes.

"Yes. Yes, it's true. I am incredibly handsome."

Aspen gives me an over-exaggerated eye roll. "I'm talking about Delilah. Is she really here?" I figured that's what she was referring to, but I was hoping it would take a little longer for word to get to her. Turns out I was wrong.

"That is also true, yes." I motion for Aspen to sit down, and she takes the seat in front of my desk.

"Where is she? How is she doing? Is she going to start classes?" She bombards me with questions, not even giving me the chance to answer one before she fires off the next.

"She is in her room right now." It's not a complete lie, but also not the total truth. "She needed a few days to recover and wrap her head around everything before starting classes." Again, not technically a lie but not the whole truth either.

Aspen huffs, sagging into her chair. "I know I shouldn't care about what happens to her, but that's just not the kind of person I am. What if she just got roped into all of this, but really, she is completely innocent."

I want to snap and be the authoritative father figure but hold myself together. Delilah is not Aspen. She is not innocent. She is a reminder of everything I failed to be for Aspen.

"She is not you, Aspen. You realize that, right?"

"Maybe not..." She nibbles on her bottom lip nervously.

"Delilah will start attending classes as soon as her clothes are delivered." *And I'm ready for her to go to classes.*

Aspen's eyes light up. "Oh, she could have some of mine. We should be around the same size."

"I don't know." The thought of Aspen's clothes on Delilah leaves an unsettling feeling in my gut. "I'm sure she is okay waiting for her own, plus pissing off Quinton isn't really that high up on my priority list."

Aspen snorts. "I think you underestimate the amount of shopping Scarlet and Ella made me do and overestimate Quinton's ability to tear apart clothes. There are boxes full of outfits I haven't even worn yet."

A smile tugs on my lips at the mention of Ella and the way she has been spoiling Aspen. "If you say so."

Aspen might've had a rough start with the Rossi's, but since they realized who she was, they have taken her in as one of their own, and I know they would do anything to make her happy.

I will never be able to offer Aspen the kind of family she deserves, but knowing Xander has accepted her into his gives me a sliver of peace.

"So..." Aspen clears her throat. "Since I'm here... I was wondering if you wouldn't mind telling me..." She looks around the room to avoid my eyes. "A little more about... well, you."

"As I told you before, I'll tell you anything you want, but my past is not pretty, Aspen. There is a reason Charlotte was scared of me. I treated her terribly. I was selfish and cruel. I didn't care about anything then, not even my own life, which made me a very dangerous person to be around. When you don't care if you live or die... it's a place in your mind you never want to be."

Aspen swallows down her disappointment at my confession but not before I catch a glimpse of it. "I remember you telling me about how you used to fight for money. Was that the same time you met her?"

"Yes, it was. That's actually how we met. She saw me at a gas station and asked if I was okay. She was worried about me, and she didn't even know me. I thought she was cute, and I ended up going home with her so she could wrap up my broken fingers."

"That sounds like something I would do too." Aspen grins, her shoulders sagging like she was worried the story would be much worse. "So you kinda dated?"

"I wouldn't call it that. I was very clear in my intentions. I told her from the start I didn't want to do *feelings*. I just wanted sex." I'm not ashamed of telling Aspen the truth, but I'm still relieved when she doesn't seem to judge me for it either.

"So why did you stop?"

"It was a rough time in my life. I was still dealing with the aftermath of my parents' murder. I was so angry, so out of control, and one night, Charlotte saw that part of me. I scared her away, and she never looked back."

We sit without saying anything for a few moments. I can see on Aspen's face that she needs a little time to process it, and I'm happy to give it to her. "That's in the past." She finally breaks the silence. "You're not that person anymore."

"You always see the good in people. You have that in common with your..." Shit, I don't even know what to call her.

"You can say mother. I mean, that's what Charlotte is. She did give birth to me, and if what Quinton has told me is true, she gave me away to protect me, not because she didn't want me."

"She was a good person. I can tell you that much. And like you, she always saw the good in everyone, even when they didn't see it themselves."

"She saw the good in you."

"Yes, but in the end, it wasn't enough." Desperate to change the subject, I steer the conversation toward my brother. "Nic and Celia would like us to come for a visit soon. Especially Celia."

"Really?" Aspen perks up at the idea. "I'd love to!"

"I'll talk to them and plan something." Although thinking about it now, I'm sure Celia has already planned a vacation with a full itinerary.

"See. You couldn't have been that bad in the past. Your family loves you."

All I can muster up in response is a tight smile. Yes, Nic and Celia somehow stuck by me all these years, but there used to be no love at all between us. As a matter of fact, the first time I met Celia, I loathed her so much that I wanted to kill her in the most gruesome way I could imagine.

"Do you even know what your family has done? I guess the better question is, do you even care?" I spit the words out with so much venom I can almost taste the bitterness on my tongue. Her whole body is shivering, recoiling from me in fear. She looks so small and vulnerable, and I relish knowing how easily I could kill her right now. How easily I could wrap my hands around her slender neck and end her miserable life. Maybe I'll fuck her dead body after, just for fun.

"I don't know what you're talking about," she tells me in her small, meek voice. Fucking liar.

I charge forward, crossing her small cell until my boots kiss the edge of the mattress. She scoots away as far as she can, cowering in the corner like a trapped animal.

"You're part of that disgusting family. The only one with decency was your sister, who knew when it was her time to die."

Celia flinches at the mention of her dead sister, and the pain in her eyes only gets me more excited.

"I should kill you right now. Slit your throat and send your body back to your daddy."

That's just one of the many memories that haunt me. Sometimes, I still can't believe she forgave me for the way I treated her. Then again, my brother did worse, and she married him anyway. I suppose real love is seeing the worst in someone and still choosing to stay.

Aspen sighs. "I guess I'll go meet Quinton for dinner before he comes looking for me."

"I'll have to grab some dinner myself soon. Maybe we can meet up at the gym this weekend. I need to teach you some more moves just in case you need to kick Quinton's ass."

"Yes, please, teach me. I can't wait to see his face when I take him down."

"I wouldn't mind seeing that myself." I chuckle.

Aspen gets up from her seat, giving me one more big smile before she leaves my office. Every time I see her, I can't help but think about how much I have missed, and all that time I will never be able to get back. I try not to dwell on it or let the guilt from that night when she was taken eat away at me. All we have now is the future, and I'll do whatever it takes not to fuck it up like I did my past.

11

DELILAH

*T*oday, boredom has been my biggest problem. Boredom and the countless questions I have about the elusive headmaster of Corium and what he wants with me.

Is this more of Quinton Rossi's doing? Does he want to keep me close, just in case? At least being locked away means he can't get to me.

Unless Lucas gave him a key.

And they want me to take classes here? There has to be a catch, an alternative motive. He wants me for something. Why else would he keep me alive? No matter the reason, I'll have the possibility of running into Quinton and his little girlfriend—no, wife, he called her his wife. Plenty of stuff to look forward to.

I hope Aspen doesn't expect me to be thankful that she let me live. Or worse, wants to be my friend. I'm not the giggly girlfriend type, for one thing. And I don't need her holding it over my head. How could I be friends with somebody out of obligation?

I must doze off at some point because the sound of a door opening and closing makes me jump. What time is it? How long have I been here? Yet another way for a mind to be tortured: the absence of a way to mark time. No windows, no clock, no way of knowing where I sit in relation to the day or even the week. When the hell is it?

That'll be the first thing I ask when he opens my door. I mean, he has to. He can't leave me here to rot, or can he? Was that the idea behind this? To change my location, but not the torture and isolation?

For the first time today, I start to pace the room. All things considered, I'm surprised I didn't start before now.

Maybe I'd better stop and conserve my energy. Who knows how much longer I'll be in here.

There's a lot of movement going on out there. Enough to send a flood of ugly images rushing through my head. What is he doing? What if it isn't Lucas at all? What if he really did give Quinton a key?

Dammit. How deep inside my head did that guy get? I figured surviving without turning into a raving lunatic meant I won. He didn't break me. Now I'm starting to wonder.

When a familiar humming noise starts out there, I let out a sigh. The tension drains out of my muscles, all thanks to a vacuum cleaner. It must be the staff taking care of Lucas's apartment while he's busy.

For a moment, I wonder if I should knock on the door and let them know I'm here. No, that would be stupid. No way would they be willing to help me, even more so knowing their job depended on it.

I lose track of how long I've paced in front of the door when I hear the front door open and close. Once again, I hear movement coming from the living room area of the house, but nobody comes for me.

Dropping to my hands and knees, I peer out from under the door. There's only a slim gap, but it's enough for me to see two pairs of feet walking around a table.

The unmistakable sound of silverware clanking on the table tells me they're staff, too, setting up dinner. I guess guys like him don't have to do their own cooking?

The sound of Lucas's voice makes me jump up, my heart in my throat. "Thank you," he says, and a few seconds later, the door closes.

He's back. I can handle this. Whatever he throws at me, I can take it. I'm not going to let him win whatever game he's playing with me.

I back away from the door when a key slides into the lock. A moment later, the door swings open. "Were you planning on jumping me when I came into the room?" he asks, scowling, once we're eye-to-eye.

"If I was going to do that, I would need a weapon, wouldn't I?" I hold up my hands, shrugging. "Nothing here."

"Because there was nothing in here for you to use. Don't think I would ever give you the opportunity. I'd snap your slender throat before you even had the chance."

"I mean, I could always *jump* you in another way." I lift a shoulder and grin at the way his features darken. Yes, this is working. "You know, that offer is still on the table. After a long day of work, I'm sure you could use a little help unwinding." I finish with a pointed look at his crotch and dart my tongue out over my bottom lip. I'll play whatever part I have to if it means I get out of this place alive.

He takes a menacing step toward me, and I can feel the heat from his body radiating into me, but I can also feel his rage. Like the wind picking up right as a storm moves in.

"Didn't you listen last night? I'm not like other men, Delilah, and I don't just think with my cock. I'm not as simple-minded as the idiots you've fucked in the past. I mean what I say, and I will follow through with my actions. Do not cross or try to bait me because I promise you..." He leans in closer, and I can smell his cologne; it's spicy and intoxicating, though I will never admit that out loud. "I'm not as forgiving as Aspen. I'll kill you if you try to fuck with me." Without warning, he grabs me by the wrist and pulls me from the room, giving me only a moment to pull myself together, his words frazzling me, making me wonder if he's bluffing or telling the truth? Could he kill me? Does he have that power? Of course he does. Everyone wants me dead, so he'd only be doing them a favor.

I can just about weep when he stops at the door to the bathroom. All day, I haven't been able to go. Then again, it's not like I had anything to drink, did I? He releases me and gives me a shove inside.

"If you want to piss, you better go now," he orders gruffly.

A response sits heavy on the edge of my tongue, but I bite it back, not wanting to press my luck too hard. I take a moment and rub at my tender wrist, the flesh aches where he grabbed me.

"Hurry up, or you won't get to go at all, and no, before you say something smart, I won't care if you piss yourself. In fact, I'd make you sleep in your own piss."

His cruelness isn't shocking to me. In fact, it's expected. He thinks I'm the bad guy, but he doesn't have a clue. Instead of arguing with him and asking for a little privacy so I can go to the bathroom, I quickly use the bathroom, trying to appear unaffected by his presence.

When I'm finished, he proceeds to drag me back out into the living area. Any harder, and he'd be pulling my arm from the socket. I bite my lip to stifle a cry of pain. I don't want him to know he's hurting me, even if I'm sure he knows.

On the table, I spot two lidded plates set out. One has silverware, and one doesn't. I guess I'm not to be trusted with cutlery.

It hits me, then. There are two plates. *Thank God.*

"Sit," he orders, and I take a seat in front of one of the plates before he has an excuse to shove me into the chair. A bottle of water sits beside my plate, and it takes me all of two seconds to uncap it and gulp down almost half of it.

If he notices, he doesn't mention it. I guess he doesn't care. Anybody with a soul would think to themselves, huh, maybe I should leave her with at least something to drink if I'm going to be out of the apartment for hours at a time. Not him. He doesn't give a shit, and it'd be best to realize that now.

"I was afraid for a minute there that you weren't going to let me eat." I watch him lift the lid of his plate and barely stifle a moan of pleasure.

Steak. Baked potato. Asparagus.

Forget moaning. I might cry at this point.

"I'm not interested in starving you to death. That would be too easy of a death." He doesn't waste any time cutting into his meat.

Eagerly, I lift my own lid from my plate. With all that savory smell around me, I have to struggle against the impulse to shove my face into the plate and not come up for air until it's empty.

Staring down at my plate, that impulse momentarily fades away when I see nothing but some soggy old French fries and half a hot dog. Yes, half. He brought me someone's leftovers.

Any other day, I wouldn't touch this with a three-foot pole, but today, I'm so hungry that I decide to pretend I already ate the other half myself.

Mind over matter.

Using my fingers, I pick up one cold fry and pop it into my mouth. It tastes even worse than it looks, so I swallow it down as fast as I can. The hot dog tastes slightly better and is less dry, so with the next bite, I combine the two. Then wash it down with another sip of water.

Just when I thought we were going to spend the entire dinner in awkward silence, Lucas starts asking me questions. "Where did you live before you were locked away?"

I glance up at him with a grin. "Big castle, up on a hill."

"Do you think this is funny?" The sternness of his voice doesn't scare me like it should, and maybe that's half the problem here.

"I want to know about your past and why there is nothing to find?"

"I'm really not sure what you're asking about. I don't have anything to tell. I'm nobody special. Trust me." My response is so practiced that I don't even think about the words anymore. I spent my whole life hiding who I was, not telling anyone where I came from or who I was related to.

"I never said I thought you were anybody special." Could he sound more dismissive? "And I would never trust you in any way."

"But you can't stand not knowing all there is to know about me, can you? So which is it? Am I nobody special, or am I haunting your imagination?"

"Enough!" He slams his open palm against the table hard enough to make the plates jump. I flinch before I can stop myself, holding my breath, my teeth gritted.

When he hits me with a curious look, I lower my eyes and keep them that way. He's made his point. If there's one thing I know, it's not to push a man past this point if I can help it. All of this is bad enough without a swollen face to go along with it as a reminder.

Slowly, I continue eating. Somehow, the food tastes even worse than before, but that's not going to stop me from eating.

For the rest of the meal, the only sounds in the apartment come from his knife and fork, our chewing, and our drinking. He says nothing to me, and I know better than to breathe another word to him.

He's interested in me, though. In my past. *Why?* How is he going to use that against me? I'm so tired of trying to predict what yet another man has in mind.

Once we've finished eating, he gathers the plates and leaves them on a tray by the door. Now I observe a little more, finding the apartment comfortable but not exactly warm or inviting. It fits the guy who lives here. The clock over the stove reads eight-thirty. At least I have a sense of where we are in the day. Not that it matters much.

I would ask him what he does when he's in here alone. How he spends his free time and all that, but I'm afraid he'll start swinging if I say another word. Even now, it kind of irritates me that he's won, in a way. He's scared me into silence, and by shutting down, I'm giving him what he wants.

"I'm going to bed."

Okay, then. "I'll go to bed, too."

He looks me up and down like I'm either the stupidest or most pathetic person he's ever met. Maybe both. "That much should be obvious. Have I given you the wrong idea? Were you thinking you have any say over what you're doing here?"

"No."

"I hope not because you're going to be extremely disappointed." With a wave, he signals for me to get off the sofa. "Let's go. I don't like having my schedule fucked with."

It seems Lucas is in more need of a blowjob than I thought. I've never met anybody wound so tightly.

As usual, he pulls me to the bathroom off his bedroom. When I'm alone, I stare at myself in the mirror, breathing deeply in an attempt to make my pulse slow down. So far, so good. He hasn't given me any serious reason to be scared. If he wanted to hurt me, he could've done it by now.

Still, I jump when he knocks on the door.

"I forgot, I bought you a toothbrush." I open the door just wide enough for him to slide it through, then close it again. At least I have this.

It would be a bad idea to let it go to my head. I know that much for sure when I exit the bathroom and find him holding the same ropes he used on me last night. "Oh, no…"

"I thought we discussed you not having a say in this." He stands by the bed, a pillow on the floor just like before.

"Why can't I sleep in the guest room? You can lock me in the same way you did today. I won't be able to get out."

"Here. Now." There's something in the way he narrows his eyes and flares his nostrils that gets me moving—but my feet are heavy, thanks to my disappointment.

I'm not looking forward to another night on a hard floor. At least I took a nap in a bed earlier. I had a little slice of comfort today.

"What if I have to pee during the night?"

"Hold it or learn to love sleeping in piss." He finishes restraining me and barely bothers to check how the tight rope cuts into my skin before standing. "See you in the morning."

I get one last look at his hard, unfeeling expression before he flips off the lights. After a trip to the bathroom, he takes off his clothes—it's too dark for me to see anything, which is sort of a shame—as he gets into bed. I might as well not be here.

Though considering how much worse things could be, maybe that's a good thing.

12

LUCAS

*I*t's been three days since Delilah became my little captive. For the last two, she has been behaving extremely well, keeping her back talk and flirting to a minimum. Instead of complaining, she kneels in front of me, holding out her hands for me to tie them together. She has been eating the disgusting food I bring her like it's a gourmet meal and sleeping on the floor like it's a Sleep Number bed.

I know better than to trust her faked innocence. She is staying quiet, but that doesn't mean she isn't plotting. I'm on high alert when it comes to her, and I don't think that's going to change any time soon.

She still hasn't shared anything about her past, which has me trying a different technique today.

"Come sit on the couch. You can watch a movie while I work."

Her surprise is written all over her face. "Really?"

"Yes. Really." I point at the couch and watch her carefully step toward it. As if testing for booby traps, she pads the sofa cushion before finally sitting down awkwardly.

She relaxes slightly after I turn on some movie and sit down at the kitchen table. It takes her another fifteen minutes before she actually leans back and pulls up her legs to get comfortable.

She pretends to be interested in the movie, keeping her eyes glued to the screen, but I know she is faking it because her reactions to anything happening on the screen are basically zero. No laughter at a joke, no sadness when someone dies. She simply stares at the screen with the same facial expression throughout the film.

"Enjoying the movie?"

Her head snaps up, startled by my voice. "Beats sitting in my room and staring at the wall."

"So TV and movies are not your thing?"

"Not really, no."

"So what do you do for fun?" Getting her to talk is like pulling teeth, so I'm surprised when she actually answers.

"I grew up in a single-wide trailer with a chain smoker who didn't do much besides watching soap operas and talk shows during the day and movies at night. So fun for me means doing literally anything besides that."

"Like going to the mall?" Seems like something teenage girls would do.

"Didn't you hear the part about the trailer park? Where do you think I would get money from to go to any mall?"

"Your dad had lots of money."

"Well, he wasn't keen on sharing it with me," Delilah grits through her teeth. Her hatred for her father seems real, but that doesn't mean much. Valentine's blood still runs through her veins.

"If you say so." Getting up from my chair, I walk up to where she is sitting and reach for the remote next to her. "I'm leaving for a few hours. So get back to your room."

"Where are you going? It's Saturday, isn't it?"

"That's none of your business. Get up."

"No." She crosses her arms over her chest like a bratty teenager.

"No?" A smirk tugs on my lips. "I must have given you the wrong impression by letting you sit on my couch and watch a movie. That's my fault. I shouldn't have treated you this well."

Her vigor leaves her right away. She lets her arms fall beside her, and her shoulders slump. "I don't deserve to be locked up like an animal."

"That's where you're wrong. You deserve all of this and more."

"Why? What did I ever do to you or anyone?"

"You exist." That's the short answer. I don't have any proof she is guilty but having Valentine blood run through her veins is enough for me. She is part of that family. She is the only one left to punish. And I will be the one doing the punishing.

In one quick move, I grab a fistful of her hair. An ear-piercing shriek rips from her throat as I force her down on the couch. Her arms flail out, her short nails digging into my skin.

Her fight is short-lived when she catches sight of the knife I pull from my boot. The light catches the sharp blade, making it shine just like I want it. The panic in her eyes grows, and the strength in her arms diminishes.

I press the blade against her slender throat, not hard enough to pierce the skin but firm enough to scare her. She is only wearing one of my white shirts. Her chest rises and falls rapidly, pressing her tits against the thin fabric. I can see her rigid nipples through it, wondering if she is more than frightened.

Wedging my knee between her legs, I hover over her, reveling in the sight of my blade against her skin. I could hurt her so easily. Make her suffer until she begs for me to end her.

Replacing my knife with my hand, I wrap my fingers around her throat to hold her in place while I lower my knife to the collar of her shirt. Dipping the tip inside, I slice up and through the fabric until it gives away.

Delilah holds her breath and lifts up her chin in hopes of avoiding being cut. Lucky for her, I don't plan on cutting her just yet. Instead, I slice through the rest of the shirt until it's completely open and falling to the sides of her body.

She is completely naked underneath, and with my knee between her thighs, her legs are parted enough for me to see her pretty little pussy.

"I wonder how loud you would scream if I fucked you with my blade?" I let my favorite knife travel down her body, through the valley between her tits, down her belly button, until I reach the top of her mound.

"Please don't." Her bottom lip quivers. "I'm sorry. I'll go to the room."

"Are you sure? It seems like you wanted to play games with me. So let's play." I dip the knife lower, running the dull side of it through her folds. Her whole body is frozen now.

She is so still that I don't even see her blink.

"I'm sure. Please stop," she begs, tears forming in the corners of her eyes.

As soon as I pull away, she scrambles off the couch and runs to the guest room. She slams the door shut behind her without another word.

I guess that's what it takes to make her shut up.

Returning to my bedroom, I change into some workout clothes before leaving the apartment and making my way to the gym.

When I get there, Aspen and Quinton are already waiting.

"It's about time, old man," Quinton jokes. "Did you have to clean your dentures or something?"

"Watch it, boy. I'm not too old to kick your ass."

"Calm down. You need to watch your blood pressure at your age."

"You need to watch your mouth before you lose some teeth."

"Okay, okay. That's enough." Aspen waves her hands between us. "You go workout," she tells her husband before turning toward me. "And you need to show me some new ninja moves."

"All right, let's start with something easy." We square off on the mat, and I run through some simple techniques on how to unarm an assailant. She uses what I taught her before and defends herself with ease.

After that, I show her a few ways to take someone down. Aspen is quick on her feet, but I'm still quicker. She shoves at my arm and steps back, but I slide my foot behind her, making her trip.

Falling backward, she lands on her butt with a huff. Quinton glares at me from across the gym, yelling something about breaking my hip. I shake my head at him and hold my hand out to Aspen. She grabs it, and I pull her back to her feet.

"That wasn't bad. Just need a bit more practice."

"If you say so."

"I know so. It's in your blood…" The words hang in the air between us uncomfortably, and I regret saying them.

"It's okay. You don't have to avoid the topic. Just don't expect me to call you dad any time soon." She smirks.

I know she is trying to make a joke, but now I can't help wondering what it would feel like if she did call me dad one day. Do I even deserve to be called that? I've never done anything to earn that title.

"I wasn't planning on it." My throat is suddenly dry. "Let's get some water."

Aspen nods, and we each grab a water bottle and sit on the bench. I use the time it takes me to unscrew the cap and take a sip to think about what I could ask her without intruding too much or making her upset.

"You don't have to answer this if you don't feel like it. But I was wondering…"

Why is this so fucking hard to ask? "Did you have a happy childhood?"

"I did, yes." Aspen nods. Her eyes turn soft, and her lips curl up in a smile like she recalls the past with great contentment. "I guess I grew up pretty normally. My parents seemed normal. I had no idea my dad was into anything illegal until I was older. They kept me out of that part of their life."

"That's not a bad thing."

"It was just a shock. I always had a better relationship with my dad. I don't know who decided to adopt me, but looking back on it now, I think he wanted me more than she did. Especially when I got older, I noticed how she distanced herself from me. I never understood why."

"You still haven't heard anything from her, have you?"

"No, the last time I talked to her was months ago. Do you think something happened to her?"

"I don't know, Aspen. It's just as likely that she is hiding. I'll ask Nic to look for her if that's what you want."

"Thank you for offering. Xander made the same offer. I just don't know if I'm ready for that yet."

"I understand. If you ever change your mind, you know where I am."

"I do. Speaking of where people are... where is Delilah? I haven't seen her anywhere."

At the mention of her name, my mood goes from bad to worse. I don't want to lie to Aspen, but how the fuck am I going to tell her I have Delilah locked up in my apartment.

"She has been spending most of the time in her room. I check in with her a few times a day."

"Oh... that's nice of you. Where is her room? I haven't seen her in the dorms or the cafeteria."

"She is staying away from the dorms for now. I've been making sure she has food and everything she needs. In a few days, she'll be ready to start classes and move into the dorm." Just not sure if I'm going to be ready.

Of course, Aspen is not satisfied with my answer. Getting up from her seat, she props her hands on her hips and gives me a stern look. "Where is she? You didn't make her stay in that room I was in before, did you?"

"No." I glance past her at Quinton, who is offering no help at all. "She is in my apartment. My guest room, to be exact."

Aspen's eyes turn into slits, scanning my face like she is analyzing it. "Is she really?"

"Yes, she is. I'm not lying. I figured it would be best to keep an eye on her. She is somewhat of a risk, after all. I know you think she is innocent, but the fact remains, she is related to the Valentines. Quinton killed her entire family, then kidnapped and held her captive. Who is to say she isn't going to try to hurt you?"

Aspen wants to argue, but when she opens her mouth, not a single word comes out. She knows I'm right. There is hardly anything we know about Delilah's past.

"As long as she is not hurt."

"No one is hurting her. I swear. She is perfectly fine and ready to start classes in a few days."

"I believe you." Aspen sinks back down to the bench. "I don't know why I'm so worried about her."

"That is also in your blood." This time, talking about Charlotte feels more natural. It feels like something I should share with Aspen.

"Is it bad that right now I'm more interested in finding things out about the woman who gave birth to me but not the woman who actually raised me?"

"Not at all. It's natural to want to know where you came from and why things played out in the past the way they did."

Aspen wrings her hands nervously in her lap. "Do you remember the last time you saw her?"

I suck in a deep breath, sifting through my mind for the last memory of Charlotte. It's all hazy, not only because it was close to twenty years ago, but I was also extremely high that day.

"I think somebody knocked at the door," one of the guys tells me. I don't even know his name. I let him in because he brought the good shit, and I want more of it.

"Someone go open the fucking door," I slur, not even caring if it's the cops or the neighbors.

One of the other guys, Tommy, I think, gets up from the couch and unlocks the door. He steps aside and reveals a woman standing in front of my door. I have to squint my eyes to see her clearly. Her long blond hair is down today, she is wearing a sunflower dress that fits her body perfectly, and she's clutching onto her purse like she is worried someone is about to snatch It.

"Charlotte," I croak. My mouth is so fucking dry that I can barely talk without throwing myself into a coughing fit.

"Who do we have here?" The guy next to me coos.

"That's one fine piece of ass if you ask me," someone else says, and the rest of the guys start laughing.

"Lucas, I need to talk to you." Charlotte's eyes bore into me from across the room.

"I don't think Lucas is up for talking right now. But why don't we have a talk in the bedroom, sweet cheeks?" Thomas grabs Charlotte's arm and starts dragging her toward the back of my apartment.

Somewhere deep inside my mind, alarm bells go off, but my brain is so fogged up from my drug binge that the thought drowns within it.

"Lucas!" Charlotte's panicked voice pierces through once more before a wave of high washes it away again.

I'm catapulted back to reality with the most unsettling feeling in my gut. I haven't thought about that day in a very long time, and it's taken me this long to realize what was actually happening.

Did she come to tell me she was pregnant? Did I let my friends rape her while I got so high I don't even remember the rest of the night?

Fuck.

"Are you okay?" Aspen asks, concerned, her voice so similar to Charlotte's.

"I'm sorry, I've got to go." I jump up and jog out of the gym. I don't even know where I'm going. All I know is I have to get away from Aspen. I can't bear looking in her eyes right now, wondering if she can see the monster inside.

13

DELILAH

*H*e's back. I hear him moving around outside the guest room. Before this morning, I was actually going to ask for access to books or something to help pass the time, but now, all I want to do is stay out of his way.

When he held the blade to my skin, I wasn't sure which way it was going to go. It was a tie of him killing or fucking me. It wouldn't surprise me if he thought of both. He is unpredictable.

I glance at the shredded T-shirt in the corner of the room. Luckily, I had an extra one in here to change into, or I'd be sitting here wrapped in nothing but a sheet. A shiver runs down my spine, thinking about how he laid on top of me while I was spread out for him. I was scared, but when the cool blade touched my hot skin, I felt more than fear.

I hoped wherever he went would give him some time to calm down, but now that he's back, I feel like he's gotten worse. The sound of somebody being thoroughly pissed off comes through the door. I know what to listen for. It's been practically the soundtrack of my life. A slammed cabinet door. Heavy footfalls, almost like he's stomping. The sound of something being dropped on the floor and his muttered profanity.

I need him to feel better for my sake. I don't want him taking it out on me, whatever it is.

When I hear the shower turn on, I breathe a little easier. He's not coming straight for me. Maybe a shower will calm him down a little before we're face-to-face. Men are such babies. They can't handle the slightest thing, yet they want us to believe they deserve to be in charge. What a joke.

The water stops running way too soon for my comfort. How do I handle this? If he's pissy, it'll be better to stay out of his way and keep quiet. I've done a pretty good job of that the past couple of days.

I've had a lot of practice. I can handle one man having a hissy fit.

The key slides into the lock, and I sit up a little straighter.

"Hi," I murmur once he opens the door—and that's all I manage to get out because, hot damn, he didn't take the time to get dressed. He's barely even dried off; water droplets glisten on his chest and shoulders. There's nothing but a towel wrapped around his waist to hide the rest of him. But what I see in front of me is more than enough to make me forget all about being afraid.

It's not like I couldn't guess at the body under his clothes. His biceps and shoulders tend to make me wonder if the seams on his shirts are extra strong since there are times when it looks like he's about to pop out like the Hulk or something.

But this? The chiseled abs, the way the deep V cut at his hips leads down to what's barely hidden by the towel? The happy trail of dark blond hair peeking out from over the top...

And his tattoos. All they do is make him hotter and, somehow, more human. Like there's more to him than the cold, unfeeling tightass he's shown me so far. He has a past. How did he end up here?

And why can't I stop staring at him?

I'm no good at hiding it, either. He snickers, and I pull my attention from his impressive chest. "What?" he teases with a smirk. "Right, you've been away from men for a while."

"I don't know. Would you use that word to describe the two sacks of shit who were guarding me?"

He looks me up and down, still smirking. "You shouldn't be so obvious, is all I'm saying. I might start considering that offer you made the first night you were here."

Be calm. I dig my nails into my palms to center myself before I go and ruin everything. I don't need him seeing how eager I am. "What offer was that?"

"Right. Like you forgot this soon." He folds his arms, his biceps bulging, and I almost forget to breathe. He wasn't kidding. It's been too long since I've been around any man worth looking at. "Did they knock you around a little too hard back there? Is your memory faulty?"

I snap my fingers, pretending to come up with the memory. "Oh, right. When I offered to suck your dick." Is it just me, or does he twitch a little under that towel when I say it? At the end of the day, he's just a man. He can pretend all he wants to be something better, something bigger, but he's only kidding himself.

He shakes his head and lets out a little sigh. "Yes. That's the offer I was referring to."

"So you're feeling a little more open-minded, is that it?" I sit back down on the foot of the bed, lifting an eyebrow. "Listen, I get it.

You've probably got a really stressful job. Everybody needs to unwind somehow."

"Something like that." He twitches again, much more obvious this time.

And he's not backing away, either. Nor is he pulling that holier than thou act on me like he did before. Things are starting to go my way here, and it's time to see if he's bullshitting me or not.

When I get up, he doesn't move. He remains rooted in place even when I cross the room and come to stand in front of him, even when I slowly get on my knees.

Using both hands, I grab the edge of the towel and tug. It falls to his feet, revealing the rest of him—including his huge, semi-erect dick. I look up at him through thick lashes.

He still hasn't stopped me or vocalized that he wants me to stop. I swallow around the knot in my throat. This isn't exactly my favorite thing in the world to do.

Nash taught me everything he liked, and I got pretty good at it after a while. At least, that's what he told me.

He was never somebody who handed out compliments when they weren't earned. He wouldn't have told me I was good at something if I wasn't. I latch onto that thought, letting it give me the confidence I need to continue forward.

Just like he taught me, I wrap my fingers around Lucas's shaft and give him a few gentle strokes. I can hear Nash's voice in my ear.

"Don't squeeze too hard. Get it wet, so you don't rub it raw." I lick my palm before stroking him again. His deep groan tells me that was the right move. He's hard now. *Hard and thick.*

I lick my lips before taking a lick of his head, and he twitches. "Mmm." I grin up at him before licking the mushroom-shaped head once more. Like I like it.

Like this whole thing is fun for me and not boring at all. It's not boring for Lucas. I might as well be holding his life in my hand. He's staring down at me, completely still, except for the way his nostrils flare.

Instead of licking again, I let him slide between my lips. His sharp intake of breath is followed by a long sigh. "That's nice. Just like that. Go slow."

I do, taking him an inch at a time until he hits the back of my throat. *"Relax the muscles. Open it up."* Nash always did like it when I deep-throated him.

"Oh, shit." I glance up at Lucas, and his eyes are wide with shock. "You're good at this, aren't you?"

In my mind, I'm at Nash's place, in his room. There's music playing to drown out any noises we make, though it's not like anybody around his house cares. I'm on my knees while he lies back on his bed, hands in my hair while my head bobs up and down. *"I've finally found something you're good for."*

I pull back before taking him deep again, sucking only a little at first. I don't want this to end too soon. It's better when it builds up slowly, and I want this to be good. I want him to think about this when he's alone in his office. How much he wishes I was sucking his dick, hidden under his desk while a student hangs around.

Plus, this is the only way I know how to gain a little power.

Nash was always nicer to me right before I blew him and right after. I learned to use that power over him to get what I wanted.

Sometimes, that meant just a little bit of affection or attention. Sometimes, I wanted to go out to eat or see a movie. The sort of stuff I couldn't always afford to do for myself.

With my tongue, I flick the underside of his head right over the bundle of nerves Nash told me was like a guy's version of a clit. Lucas groans louder than before, then cups a hand around the back of my head. "Fuck. That's good."

I moan in response, and he groans again, louder this time as his fingers tangle in my hair. Picking up the pace, I suck a little harder, taking slow, deliberate strokes. His breathing picks up speed, and his hips start moving in shallow thrusts.

"Fuck, yes." He takes my head in both hands and holds it still, thrusting into my mouth.

All I can do is try not to gag now that he's taken over. "That's right," he grunts. "Take it. Let me fuck your face."

I brace myself and suck in as much air as I can when he pulls back far enough for me to breathe. When he plunges in again, he buries himself deep enough that my nose is pressed up against his base. Fuck, I'm pretty sure I'm going to throw up if he keeps doing that.

"You like choking on my cock?" He grinds even deeper, and I can't stop myself from gagging this time. Instead of grossing him out, it makes him laugh. At least he withdraws a little so I can breathe.

"Come on. You're the one who wanted it." He drives himself in deep, hard. Harder. "Take it. Take my cock. How much do you love it?"

I look up at him and moan while saliva drips from the corners of my mouth. I don't wipe it away. Let him do what he wants and get it over with. If I break into it, he'll only take longer.

Our eyes lock, and his lip curls in a snarl. "Oh, yes. You should always be this way. With your mouth full of my cock." His fingers dig into the side of my head. I can feel his anger stronger than ever, flowing into me like an electric current. His eyes fall closed, and he picks up his pace. I might as well not be here. He might as well be fucking a blow-up doll. Damn, it's worth it. I have to keep reminding myself of that.

Especially when he groans, "I'm going to come. Are you ready to swallow my load?" He pulls out and takes himself in his fist, pumping up and down in a blur.

I hold my mouth open, tongue out just in time to catch the first rope of cum. The taste makes me gag all over again, but he doesn't notice. He's too busy coating my tongue and lips with one spurt after another until he finally lets out a resounding sigh. He's satisfied, and thank god for that.

I swallow what he left on my tongue, then wipe my lips with the back of my hand. I guess I should be grateful he didn't get it in my eyes. At least he tried to aim. Such a gentleman.

"See?" I tease with a smile I don't feel. "I told you that would do the trick. Don't you feel better?"

The satisfied grin on his lips falters, and his gaze turns ruefully. "This stays between you and me." He wraps the towel around him again. Not that he needs to now. I've seen what it's covering. I've had it in my mouth and everything.

"Of course," I murmur as I climb to my feet. I can't wait to brush my teeth, but I don't want him to think I'm as disgusted as I feel. I need him to walk away from this thinking it was fun, not a bad idea.

"Not, of course." He lowers his brow. I'd swear his eyes get darker, too. "You're not going to tell anyone about this. Say it."

"I'm not going to tell anyone about sucking your dick." I lift a shoulder. "Who would I tell, anyway? It's not like I have any friends here." *Or anywhere.* "And you're the only person I've seen so far."

"Yes, but it can't always be this way. Eventually, you're going to have to start attending classes."

"I won't say a word then, either." I'd make a big X over my chest, but that might be overdoing it a little. Besides, it seems to be enough to convince him. He leaves the room, and a moment later, I hear him in his bedroom. It's almost a shame he can't walk around in that towel all day.

I need to get a hold of myself. He's not some hot guy. I can't even afford to think of him as a man. He's my captor.

Only now, I have something on him, and he'd better hope he never gives me a reason to use it.

14

LUCAS

Goddamnit. What the fuck is wrong with me? It was one thing to keep her here. I could say it was to keep her safe from rumors and accusations. That I'm doing it to punish her for her role in what was done to my daughter. My flesh and blood.

But this? My cock is soft now, but it wasn't a minute ago in Delilah's mouth. I should've left her kneeling there, feeling like an asshole.

Instead, I let all my old shit take over, and now the worst possible thing has happened.

I liked it, and I want more. Not even so much the blowjob, which was fine and everything. I want to use her the way I did back there. I poured all my anger and guilt over Aspen into her. I punished her because I couldn't punish myself enough.

Lauren would be so pleased with me if she knew I was connecting the dots like this. She might even say I'm growing. No, on the other hand, growth would mean stopping myself before making a pathetic mistake like letting a teenager suck my dick.

She's nothing. She's nobody. I shouldn't even bother asking myself questions like that. It's something that happened, and it'll never happen again. Besides, if I'm being honest with myself, I have to admit it felt damn good. It's been a long time since I've vented my anger that way. Now I remember why I liked it so much. Being in control. Making somebody else hurt the way I was hurting. Getting off on their discomfort or pain.

It seems like this girl brings out all the worst parts in me. But it's not like I can let her go. Obviously, I need to figure out a plan because the way things are going, I'll end up fucking my entire life.

We eat dinner in silence. Only once do I look at her and find her smirking down at her plate. I want to ask what the hell she's smirking about, but I know the answer. The snide little bitch thinks she has something to hold over my head. She can only do that if I make a big thing about it, so I can't let myself do it even when I want to climb over the table, take her throat in my hands, and demand she tell me what the fuck is so funny.

This is a problem. Now that I know how good it feels to use her, I'm going to need to do it again. She makes it so easy. And fuck, I want to. I didn't know how much shit I was bottling up in my gut until I vented some of it earlier.

"You'll sleep in the guest room tonight." It's the first time either of us has said anything, and I waited until gathering up the used dishes after we're finished eating to say it.

"Oh, really? What did I do to deserve that?"

Smart-mouthed little bitch. I count to five in my head before setting down the dishes. Otherwise, I might've thrown them on the floor. "Nothing," I grit out, my back to her. "I don't want you sleeping in my room anymore. That's all."

"Okay." She sounds meek again, which is how I like it. Eventually, she'll have to learn to stop fucking with me. What if I told her there's no way I'd be able to stop hurting her once I got started? That having her that close, prone, and at my command might be too much to resist? She'd drop that bullshit flirtatious tone real fast.

"Come on. Might as well settle in early and get it over with." I give her time to use the bathroom and wash up before taking her to the guest room. This is a good idea. Out of sight, out of mind. She looks worried when I turn to give her one last look before closing and locking the bedroom door. I like that look too much. It means I got through to her, and maybe she'll stop pushing me too far.

Though getting her out of my face hasn't helped. I'm restless and agitated, pacing the apartment like a caged tiger. I decide to call my brother and let him talk me off the edge before I do something stupid.

Sitting at the small desk in the corner of the bedroom, I flip open my laptop and video call Nic. He answers so quickly that I wonder if he has been waiting for me.

"Hey fuckface," I greet.

"Very mature." Nic shakes his head, giving me a disapproving stare.

"I have to be a full-blown adult all the time. If I can't call my brother fuckface every once in a while, what's there to live for?" I joke.

"Is that the only reason you called?"

"No, I wanted to see your ugly face too. It reminds me that I'm the better-looking brother."

"Good night, Lucas." He lifts his hand as if he is about to hang up on me, but I stop him.

"Okay, calm down. I'll cut it out."

He sits back in his chair, still frowning like he is judging everything I do. So typical of him. His demeanor doesn't stop me from needing his advice, though.

"Quinton found out Valentine had a daughter no one knew about."

That piques my brother's interest. He leans forward on his elbows, listening intently. "Go on."

"He was holding her for a while, questioning her, but couldn't get anything out of her. There is very little information on her past. Valentine went to great lengths to keep her secret."

"Where is she now?"

"Here... in my apartment."

Nic's eyebrows shoot up. "Is that so?"

I fill him in on the rest of the story, even telling him about the blowjob.

"It looks like you've got yourself a situation there."

"Tell me something I didn't already know. The point is to give me a clue how to get out of it."

He lifts an eyebrow the way I've seen so many times. "You really need me to tell you? You're sure you don't already know?"

For the second time tonight, it's either count to five or lose my shit. "I'm not in the mood for this. What do you think I should do?"

"I don't think. I know you need to get that girl out of your apartment. There's no reason for her to be there."

"Aside from making sure she stays away from Aspen?"

"Remind me again what she's ever done to Aspen. Last I heard, she didn't have anything to do with it. She was mixed up with the wrong people, that's for damn sure, but she wasn't there at the time. Kids are stupid."

"Not this one. She seems pretty sharp."

"I still go with stupid. Everybody's stupid in one way or another."

"So you're defending her?"

The sonofabitch has the nerve to roll his eyes. "No. I would never do that. Why would you even think it?"

"She might've put the whole thing together for all we know. I'm still not sure." And I'm no closer to finding out since she's damn good at dodging my attempts to know her better.

"Regardless. You need to get her out of there. What happens next? Fucking her? Maybe hurting her?"

It would be so easy, too. I didn't have to force her to suck me off today. She got on her knees and got to work. All it would take is her screwing around again, testing her boundaries and my patience, and I might lose control. "I don't like the idea," I insist anyway since letting her go means giving up control.

"What were you going to do otherwise? Keep her locked up with you forever? Because that's the alternative." He brings the phone closer to his face. "Get her moved into a dorm room. Send her to class. Pretend this is all normal."

That's going to take some pretending. Nothing about this is anywhere remotely normal.

"You know what else?" He pulls the phone back so I'm no longer staring up his nose. Now I see how concerned he looks. "You've got bigger issues."

"Such as?"

"Such as your kid. The one whose entire life you've missed up until now. You're putting all the effort you should be giving her into this girl locked in your guest room."

I want to tell him he's out of his mind, but that would be a lie. He doesn't get what it means to know he treated his own child the way I treated mine. The kind of guilt that carries. How it can stand in the way of building a relationship. "It's been complicated."

"I know. But it won't get any less complicated as time goes on unless you spend time on it." Again, he fills the frame. "Get your head out of your ass. Send the girl to the dorms. Spend time with your kid. You know it has to be done."

I do, which is why I'm starting in the morning.

"I know I don't say this a lot... but you're right."

"I'm right all the time."

"Sure, you are. Before you go, I wanted to ask you something else. I was trying to remember the last time I saw Charlotte. I think she came to my place, but I was high. Some other people were there. I think one of them was Tommy Perez or something like that."

"I know exactly what night you are talking about."

"You do?"

"Yes, because I was there." Dumbfounded, I stare at the screen, trying to recall my brother being there that night. "You were already passed out when I got there. I heard a scream coming from the bedroom. One of the guys was trying to rape her, but she hit him in the nuts with your lamp."

"Fuck... I think she came to tell me she was pregnant."

"Possible, yes. Which is why she never tried again."

And she had every reason not to.

"Wake up. I've set an appointment for you, and I don't want to be late."

Delilah blinks, rubbing her eyes. "Huh?"

I stand over her, beside the bed, and can't help but think about how helpless she is. "Up. You have things to do."

"Like what?"

"You're going to get a full checkup by the doctor. It's standard for all students, and since you're going to be one soon, there's no choice."

"A checkup?" She sits up, squinting at me. "Like, all over?"

"I imagine so. Get in the shower. Dr. Lauren has a schedule to keep, and we shouldn't make her wait."

She holds up a hand before I can walk out of the room and wait for her. "Um... I don't know how to say this..."

"What is it?" I snap, and it's almost too gratifying when she flinches. I did the right thing, having her sleep separate from me last night.

She folds her arms before lifting her chin defiantly. "I was wondering if I can shave while I'm in there. It's kind of embarrassing to walk into a checkup like that when you haven't touched a razor in forever."

The idea is ridiculous enough to make me laugh. "Right. Let me hand you a razor and see what happens."

"I doubt I could do much damage with a disposable razor."

"I don't use disposables. And don't get any ideas. I keep them locked up now that you're here." She groans when I shake my head. "Not going to happen."

"Fine. You feel that way about it? Maybe you could do it for me." Her lips twitch. She thinks she's being cute again. Like if she embarrasses me, she wins.

"You have a point. I'll unlock my razor. You get undressed and wait for me in the bathroom."

"Wait a second." Now she's in a big hurry to get out of bed, scrambling to her feet.

"No time. Let's go." While she's sputtering and probably wishing she hadn't suggested this, I go to my bedroom closet. Maybe she thinks I'm only kidding about the razors, but she couldn't be more wrong. I'm not taking a chance with her. I haven't needed to use this lock box for a long time. It sat at the back of the shelf, gathering dust until I brought her here. I pull out the handle along with a fresh blade, watching to make sure I'm not observed. She's still dragging her feet. Probably wondering if I'm bluffing. "Don't keep me waiting," I call out.

"This is uncomfortable. You don't have to do this."

"You're the one who made a big deal about it. Stop wasting my time." I prepare the razor, pull out the shaving cream, and set them on the edge of the tub. "Come on. Clothes off."

"Fine." With my back to her, she quickly strips. I have to remind myself not to let my imagination run away from me. This is about teaching her a lesson.

"I'm ready." I turn to find her sitting on the edge of the tub, wrapped in a towel. Without saying a word, I drop to one knee in front of her, then turn on the tap for the sake of rinsing between strokes.

"Just stay still." When I pick up the shaving cream, she stiffens, then flinches away. "What?" I snap.

"Can I at least do this part myself?" she holds out her hand, and since it doesn't seem like she could do too much damage with a can of cream, I give it to her. She makes quick work of lathering up her leg before propping her foot on the tub.

"Do you do this a lot?" she asks. There's a nervous edge to her voice.

"Oh, sure. My office has a sign-up sheet for anybody who needs a shave." I touch the razor to her skin, and she flinches. "Seriously?"

"You're holding a sharp razor to my skin. Sorry if it makes me nervous."

"All the more reason to stay still." She grumbles but offers no further argument while I swipe the blade over her shin. There's something satisfying about cutting a line through the layer of foam. Exposing her clean skin. I rinse and do it again. Again. She doesn't make a sound except to breathe—quick, shallow breaths. The way a person breathes when they're waiting for something terrible to happen.

"See? No catastrophes." I have to lean in closer and take special care with her knees. "This part is trickier than it looks," I admit.

"Imagine having to do it all the time." She cranes her neck, examining the razor while I guide it carefully over her knee. "So there's only one blade in there, huh?"

"Yes, a single blade."

"It looks like it does pretty good work. Go figure."

"People shaved this way for years before manufacturers convinced them it takes five blades at once to get a good, clean shave." I finish one leg, and she rinses off. This isn't so bad. So long as she quits with the teasing and smart-ass comments, being with her is almost bearable.

Until she shifts her position so I can take care of the other leg. It means spreading her legs, causing the towel to fall open at the bottom, giving me a look at what rests between her thighs.

Not now. For Christ's sake, get it together. It's a pussy like any other. But the sight of it takes my breath away, just the same.

"Everything okay?" Her question snaps me out of it. She's lathered up her leg while I knelt here, thinking way too much about the fact that she's not wearing underwear. And I am very close to that pretty little pink pussy of hers.

"Fine." I should work faster if only to get this over with, but for some reason, I move slower than before. Examining every curve of her leg, from ankle to kneecap to thigh. She's so young, so fresh.

Once I'm finished with the bottom half of her leg, I run a hand over her calf before holding it still. She can't suppress the soft gasp at my touch, the sound traveling straight to my cock and making it twitch. "Hold still," I mutter, my voice choked.

"I'm trying." From the corner of my eye, I see her chest rising and falling faster with every inch of skin I cover. The closer I get to her pussy, the sharper her breathing.

"Am I bothering you?" I ask, leaning over to rinse the blade. She's flushed, biting her lip. Somewhere in the back of my increasingly overheated brain, there's a sense of victory. Maybe she'll think twice the next time she wants to challenge me.

"No." But damned if her legs don't spread wider. Now nothing conceals her puffy lips, the tip of her clit protruding ever so slightly. Dark, pulsing need builds low in my body, thickening my cock, forcing me to remind myself of a line I shouldn't cross.

"Oh, I didn't realize you meant that, too." I hand her the can. "Go ahead. Unless you want me to prep you myself."

She looks down, then back up at me. Her legs snap shut. "Oh, no. No, you don't have to do that."

"It looks like you normally do it yourself unless my eyes deceived me."

Her cheeks color, eyes lowering. "I normally do."

"Then, by all means. We need to make sure you're ready for the doctor." I look her in the eye, fighting off a grin at her obviously flustered state.

She lets out a long, shuddering breath before spraying cream on her hand and spreading it over her mound. I realize I'm holding my breath as I watch, my mouth practically watering. How tight would she be? How sweet would she taste if I shoved my tongue up inside her?

"Lean back a little. Spread your legs wide." And she does, and now her glistening hole beckons me, promising pleasure, release. It occurs to me I might have played myself while trying to punish her.

Too late to back down now. She stiffens all over as I lower the razor. "Stay extra still," I murmur, one hand on her inner thigh to keep her steady. Goose bumps cover her skin, and the slight twitching of her muscles under my hand reveals her strain. She's wondering what I'm going to do. If I'll hurt her. If I'll lose control.

I'm damn close to it, but instead of sliding my fingers deep inside her, I drag the blade across her mound. Again. Again. Every swipe reveals clean, smooth skin. Skin I want more than anything to mark somehow. With my teeth, with my cum. I swear I can smell her, and the scent calls to me. It reminds me of all the reasons she shouldn't be here—can't be here. At my mercy. So ripe, juicy, begging to be taken and eaten.

I glance away from my work long enough to find her staring down, watching intently. She's hardly breathing, but then neither am I. It doesn't seem like there's enough air in this room.

Finally, I finish, leaving her bare. "There you go." I have to get out of here. This was a mistake. If I don't leave the room within the next five seconds, I can't be held responsible for what happens next. As it is, it takes a little maneuvering to keep my very obvious hard-on from announcing itself when I stand.

"Hurry up," I mutter on my way through the door. "I don't want to keep the doctor waiting." I close the door and lean against it, breathing heavily. The razor is still clutched tight in my trembling hand while my cock aches to be free from its prison.

Nic's right. I need to get her out of here before everything blows up in my face.

15

DELILAH

*T*hat just happened.

And now that I don't feel like I have to hold my breath, waiting for what comes next, I'm panting a little. Leaning against the cool shower wall while my overheated body tries to make sense of what it's feeling.

I know what it's feeling. It's just that I'm not sure I should be feeling it about him.

But facts are facts. He's a man, and that was maybe the hottest thing that's ever happened to me. He didn't even touch me, not where it aches the most right now, but my body is buzzing in a way it never has before. Even the times it was the best with Nash, I never felt like this.

Is this the way I was supposed to feel all along?

He was so careful, too. Like it actually mattered that he didn't cut me. I run a hand over my bald pussy, and it's totally smooth, not a single hair left. I don't want to know if he's done it before. If that's how he did such a good job. I don't want anything to ruin the memory of how deep he was in concentration, staring at my pussy while he dragged the razor over my skin.

The sound of him moving around outside the bathroom snaps me out of my hazy memories. I need to get moving before he comes in and makes me move, so I turn on the shower, but I'm still too distracted by the aching in my pussy to care much about washing up.

His face keeps flashing in my memory. God, he was so close to me. It would have been so easy for him to set the razor down and do other things. My nipples harden at the thought, and when I brush a hand over them, I have to grit my teeth to hold back a moan.

What if he had touched me? What if he made me come? I wish he had. I'm disappointed he didn't.

This is too dangerous. I can't think about him this way. He's my enemy. He has me locked up, for fuck's sake.

But the slickness now coating my smooth lips tells another story.

I slide a finger along the length of my slit and sigh, closing my eyes and spreading my legs a little, so I can touch more of myself. So my lips part, and my clit protrudes. The tiniest brush against it, and I gasp. The sound is loud in here, echoing off the tile.

I need to come, or I'll explode. I wish he was in here with me. Touching me with those thick fingers that were so gentle when he was holding the razor. I bet he could be rough with them, too. I bet he'd shove them deep inside and fuck me with them while he used his tongue on my clit.

My finger takes the place of his imaginary tongue. I move it in quick, light circles, breathing faster, bearing down on the pressure and rocking my hips while water runs over my skin, dripping off my nipples and down my crack. My whole body's on fire, my nerves tingling, my head thrown back while every ounce of my concentration narrows down to the inch or so of flesh I'm working faster and faster.

"Yes," I whisper while I hump my hand, imagining it's Lucas's face instead. What would he look like down there, head buried, eyes locked with mine? Holding me down while he forces me to take all the pleasure he's giving? "Fuck, yes... yes..."

Is he listening now? Standing outside the door with that huge cock twitching in his pants? Maybe he's touching himself, jerking himself off to the sound of me fantasizing about him. I let out a moan in case he is close enough to hear.

And something about that heightens the tension. The thought of him getting off to me. "Yes," I whimper as water splashes everywhere now that my touch is frantic. Needy. "Please, Lucas... make me come..."

I bear down harder, a scream building in my throat when the tension in my core becomes too much. It's driving me crazy and is going to kill me. "Please...!" I whisper, straining, images overlapping in my brain, the memory of his groans while I blew him mixing up with my imagination until it's too much. Until there's nothing to do but explode.

"Lucas!" I gasp a second before it happens. When the unbearable tension dissolves, the sweetest relief washes over me like the water still running down my body. I jerk my hips once, twice, lost in bliss.

Then it clears up, and I come back to reality. To the shower I haven't finished, and the doctor who is waiting for me. At least I won't walk into my exam all heated and dripping wet after Lucas left me hanging.

I wash up quickly, then waste no time drying off. The sooner I get this over with, the better. I hope nobody sees me walking around with him, even if I know it's inevitable. I'm going to run into Quinton and his little wife eventually. Just not today.

He's not waiting for me in the bedroom, but he left me something on the bed: clothes. Actual clothes made for actual girls, not whatever sweats he manages to find for me in his dresser. They aren't new— no tags or anything, and they smell like detergent—but I don't care. It's not like I've never worn castoffs, anyway.

I'm most thankful for the soft socks and comfortable sneakers. The cuts and bruises on my feet have mostly healed, but they still feel better protected while I move around.

"You almost ready?" he barks from out in the living room. I'm amazed he would even leave me alone like this. I wonder if he heard me after all. I wonder what he's thinking.

"Yeah, give me a minute." Then, as an afterthought, I add, "Thanks for the clothes."

"Thank me by putting them on so we can get this over with. I have other things to do today."

I roll my eyes but move faster, anyway. Now he's all growly and irritated again. At me, or himself? I can't help but like thinking I can throw him off his game this way. He's not in total control of the situation if he can't be in the same room with me after shaving my pussy. I bet he wishes he'd let me do it myself.

Unless he's not. Unless he's kicking himself for not doing more than shaving. He's just a man, after all. There's only so much clear thinking they can do when a pussy is around. Now he knows what mine looks like...

I need to stop thinking about this, or I'll go into this exam all worked up again.

He won't look me in the eye once I'm out of the bedroom, now wearing jeans and a sweater. "Everything fits?" he asks, heading for the door.

"Yeah, it's great." Once we're out of his apartment, my apprehension swells. I can't help but feel like there's a target painted on my back, even down here, away from the students, on the faculty floor.

This place is a maze. I want to memorize the layout so I know where to go if I have to run, but he's walking too fast. We take the elevator, and he practically runs me down a wide hallway where—thank god—we're the only two people walking. Is everybody in class? Maybe he chose this time specifically with that in mind.

There's a pair of doors at the end of the hall. He opens one and steps aside so I can enter the room, where a woman with brown hair and a friendly smile is waiting.

There's an exam table waiting, too, telling me what I have to look forward to.

"Dr. Lauren, this is Delilah." Lucas waves a hand between us. "She's here to get checked out, as we discussed."

He's a real charmer. The way her lips twist in a tiny grin suggests she's thinking along the same lines. "Hi, Delilah. I'll put you through your paces today, but it won't take long. We'll start with drawing blood."

I pull the sweater's sleeves over my fists without thinking about it. "Really?"

"It'll only take a minute. I'm a pro at finding a vein on the first try." She waves me over to where a syringe is waiting, along with a handful of vials. The woman wants to bleed me dry.

But there's something about her that makes it easy to be trusting. She seems kind, which I'm not used to always seeing from doctors.

So it's not so nerve-wracking, pushing my sleeve up so she can stick me with the needle.

"There. All done." She places gauze and tape over the prick from the needle before marking the vials. Once she's finished, she looks up at Lucas with a smile. He hasn't moved since we came in. "Thanks, Lucas. I think we can take it from here."

It's obvious from the way he hesitates that he doesn't want to leave me on my own in here. He's afraid of what I'll say. The doctor clears her throat. "Privacy, please," she murmurs, raising her eyebrows. They stare at each other for a long moment—then he sighs and turns on his heel, marching out of the room and closing the door with a loud click.

She shakes her head, snorting. "Men, right? Always thinking they know what's best."

"They do that," I agree in a soft voice.

"Why don't you get undressed for me," she suggests, though it's not a suggestion. I know I don't have a choice. "There's a gown on the table. Meanwhile, now that we're alone, I'll move on to the personal questions." She checks out her tablet, scrolling with the stylus. "Do you have a family history of any major diseases?"

"None that I know of." Unless she wants to count being a bunch of insufferable assholes as a disease. "Though I didn't have a close relationship with my family. I didn't know a lot of them very well." Though after the way my father treated me all my life, I wouldn't mind finding out he had ass cancer.

"Fair enough. What about your personal history?"

"I've never had any major diseases."

She gives me a gentle smile. "What about the not-so-major things?"

"I've been pretty healthy, really."

"Heavy periods? Migraines? What about anxiety or depression?"

"Why are you asking me these questions?" I turn to her, now wearing the paper gown she left for me. There's a chill in the air, and I shiver from the cold.

She lowers the tablet, frowning at me. "I'm sorry. I didn't mean to offend or overwhelm you. These are standard questions asked of all incoming students. It helps if I know what to expect—or whether students need medication, so I can have it on-hand."

Of course. I'm being an idiot, looking deeper into things than necessary. "Sorry. I've—"

"You don't have to apologize. We all have our reasons for keeping our privacy. But it would be helpful if you'd answer my questions."

So I do while climbing up onto the table. "My periods are pretty regular. I've been taking birth control since I was sixteen. The depo shot. Occasional headaches but nothing severe. No history of depression or anxiety." At least nothing that's ever been officially diagnosed. It's not like my aunt had the resources to take me to specialists, not that she needs to know that.

"Lucas filled me in on what happened to you, but he didn't give me a lot of details. Were you sexually assaulted while you were held captive?"

"No one fucked me against my will."

Dr. Lauren raises one eyebrow at me, and I immediately regret not simply saying no. "Did they do anything else to you?"

"I'm fine."

"That's not what I asked."

Ugh. Why didn't I just tell her no? I don't want to open this fucking can. Dr. Lauren doesn't look like she is letting it go.

"They made me get naked, so they could jerk off on my tits." Just saying it out loud makes me feel dirty, and I want to scrub my chest clean all over again. As if the soap will help get rid of that disgusting feeling in my gut.

"That's not something to take lightly. They might not have physically harmed you, but that doesn't make it any less of a sexual assault."

"Can we not talk about this anymore?" I just want to forget this ever happened.

"Of course, but I'm always here to talk if you need to."

She goes through the rest of the examination in silence, and I'm more than glad about it.

Once we're finished with the only minorly embarrassing part of the visit, it's time to get down to the truly humiliating stuff. She takes a look under the hood, checking out all my parts until I'm blushing while staring at the ceiling and waiting for it to be over.

"Okay. You're all set." She rolls her stool away from the table while peeling off her gloves. "The results from your blood work should be in within a few days. I'll let you know if I find any abnormalities, but if everything's okay, I won't bother you."

"Thanks." I wonder if I should warn her in advance about my Vitamin D levels. Something tells me it's going to be pretty damn low after not seeing the sun for weeks.

"You can get dressed now." She turns away and starts typing on her laptop. "Don't pay attention to me. I want to put in a few notes while our visit is still fresh in my mind."

I'm sure she's making a note of how suspicious I am, wondering what made me this way. I could tell her a few things since I'm sure there is no way she would know what's been done to me lately. If so, would she be obligated to go to the cops?

Who am I kidding? If there's any hope of living through this, I need to wise up. Nobody around here is going to the authorities for any reason, small or large. This school isn't for families who rely on the law. It's just the opposite. If I'm going to make it out of here, the only person I can rely on is myself.

The doctor is still pounding the keys when I finish putting my clothes back on. Rather than announce I'm finished, I glance around the room...looking for something, anything.

I'm on my own. I need to think defensively. I need to be able to protect myself. That's why a pair of scissors sitting with the medical equipment on a wheeled tray gets my attention. She still has her back to me, so I hold my breath while inching toward the tray.

"Are you all set?" Her question makes me jump.

"Just about." She's still not looking my way, but she will be soon. It's now or never.

My hand shoots out, and I take hold of the scissors, my clammy fingers slip against the metal, but I keep my hold on them and gently tuck them into the back of my jeans.

I'll hide them between the mattress and box spring in the guest room. Lucas won't ever think to look there, and who knows when I'll need them. It's better to have a weapon to protect yourself than to face the enemy empty-handed.

16

LUCAS

"What is this?" She looks over at me from her corner of the sofa. The way she sits with her feet drawn up under her, anyone would think this is her apartment. I have to swallow back a flare-up of irritation.

"An effort at giving you a little culture. It's a good movie."

"It's not in color."

"Nothing gets past you, does it?" She scowls at the TV when it's obvious I'm the one she wants to scowl at. "Just give it a chance. You might enjoy it."

"Okay." She shrugs, still looking skeptical. I turn my attention back to my laptop, though it isn't exactly holding my interest, with Nic's advice running through my memory on repeat.

I need to get her out of here. I need to separate myself from her and turn my energy toward Aspen.

Yet the more I've thought about it, the more evident something is: it's easy for him to say. I knew it during our call, but now it's clearer than ever. The girl is untrustworthy. I still know nothing about her connection to the Valentines beyond blood.

She is part of them. She is the last Valentine, the family who hurt Aspen. How can I let her walk around, free and clear until I'm sure she won't turn against Aspen? No matter how irresponsible it makes me to keep her here, it'd be ten times worse to let her go until I'm certain she's not a threat.

I can hardly live with everything I've done. How could I live with myself if my daughter is hurt again—and I had the power to stop it but did nothing?

Nic doesn't get it. I'm doing this for my kid. Not for me.

The sound of her soft chuckles lifts my gaze to the TV screen. "This is actually pretty funny," she murmurs once she notices me watching.

"It's a classic screwball comedy."

"I didn't think these old movies were actually funny. I figured they'd be all boring and dry and stuff."

"I still can't believe your aunt never introduced you to any of that. You said she watched movies."

Her mouth sets in a firm line. "I guess that's why I was never interested. Sitting with her to watch a movie meant breathing in her smoke. Have you ever been trapped in a room with a chain smoker, and the windows don't open?"

"I can't say I have." It sounds miserable, one more layer of unhappiness in what seems like a generally unhappy life.

That's what I still don't understand and can't help mulling over while she turns back to the movie. What am I missing here? She's a Valentine kid, yet she lived in a trailer. No money—she was fairly clear on that. The rest of the family lived like kings while she was trapped in a double-wide of smoke.

She has to be lying. Addicts will tell any lie they can fabricate if it means getting what they need. They'll steal anything they can get their hands on and make promises even a child could see through. I spent years with people like that, and I don't get that same feeling about her.

Delilah's anger comes through in every word she uses when she talks about her past.

"Do you know more movies like this?" she asks, wearing a smile when she turns to me. Like she's forgotten who she is, who I am, what this is.

"Of course," I mutter, diving into my work. "There's plenty of them. I'm sure you could find some online."

"Right. I'll use all the free time I have on the internet."

I grit my teeth against a sarcastic response since I get the feeling that's what she wants. Obviously, I know she has a point. But it isn't as if she'll be here forever.

"When you get the chance. That is what I meant." She swings her head back toward the TV, and I'm glad. The less we talk about her future, the better since I don't know what her future will look like.

Eventually, she'll have to move into the dorms. It's only a matter of when. I hate how uncomfortable it makes me feel, the thought of letting her go off on her own.

Though it's not as if she'll be alone, technically. Someone will always be watching—maybe I can install cameras in her room as an added precaution. And if I'm able to listen in on her conversations, I could learn more about her ties to her family. That brother of hers who's better off dead. She makes it sound like they didn't have any kind of relationship growing up, yet she was still tied to him somehow. I have to know how she fits into the puzzle.

The movie ends around dinnertime, so rather than start another, we wait for our meal to be delivered from the cafeteria.

"You don't like to cook, do you?" she asks curiously while we wait.

I don't look up from what I'm typing. "What was your first clue? Nobody wants to eat anything I've prepared, believe me. Nothing short of a peanut butter and jelly sandwich."

"There's an art to making a good PB&J. You have to get the balance just right."

"Good point." This might be a way to open a conversation about her family. "What about you? Do you like to cook?"

"Cooking was a way to make sure I had something to eat. It wasn't something I did for, like, *fun*." I've noticed she tends to pull her sleeves over her fists when feeling nervous or threatened. She's doing it now, wrapping her arms around herself.

"You didn't get any help at all from your family? Not even grocery money?"

"Why are you so obsessed with my family?" She's curled into a tight ball, wedged into the corner of the sofa.

This is obviously a sore subject for her. I suspected it all along, but until now, she's always been flippant about them. She's deliberately avoided going any deeper than the superficial facts. Now, when I push a little harder, she's on the verge of snapping.

That confirms that I'm getting closer to the answers I seek. "Let me help you understand a little something about Corium. We can't afford to have anyone here whose past is a mystery. Typically, I know the history of every family who sends one of their kids here. It's a matter of security, both for the school and for the students themselves."

"And...?"

"You're no exception. Do you need me to spell it out for you?"

"I never asked to be brought here. I don't want to be a student here. I want to go home."

I snap before I can stop myself. "Really? You miss that double-wide you keep complaining about?"

She winces but doesn't back down. "It's still better than being here."

"I find that hard to believe."

"Yeah, well, you can believe whatever you want to." She stares at the darkened TV, her jaw twitching while her nostrils flare.

"Did it ever occur to you that it might be dangerous for you to go home?"

Her head snaps back toward me, her eyes blazing, and something inside me lights up. I don't know what it is. Perhaps the challenge? In no way is my role here at this school boring or easy, and I know too well how different my life could have turned out if I didn't straighten my shit up, but I've missed this kind of thing. Crashing against someone whose will is almost as strong as mine and breaking them. Is that what I've been trying to do all along?

A knock on the door interrupts us, and I get up to answer, not sure if I'm glad for the interruption or not. Delilah looked like she might have been about to unload on me, and who's to say she wouldn't have told me something valuable?

We're both silent as the staff sets up the meal. It smells like basil, thyme, and oregano. Italian, most likely. My favorite. I thank them as always before closing the door and carrying the trays over to the table.

"Well? Do you need an engraved invitation?" I'm already sitting, napkin in lap, by the time she grumbles her way off the sofa and into her chair. I know I'm an asshole. No need to be told, so why not continue to pick at the scab? Now that she's stirred up, she might be more willing to talk. "Did I shock you with what I said? About you being safer here than at home?"

I notice she's very slow and deliberate about unwrapping her silver-ware, then lifting the lid from her plate. Up until this point, I didn't allow her silverware. The opportunity for her to hurt herself or me was too likely. "How many ways do I have to tell you I have nothing to do with that family before you actually believe me?"

"Even if I believed that—and I'm still not certain I do—there are plenty of people who haven't sat down and discussed it with you. As far as they're concerned, you could have been your father's golden child. And you just happened to get lucky enough to avoid the bloodshed that went on."

"Listen." She looks me straight in the eye with no bullshit or playful smirks. "We both know what happened. Let's not pretend it was all done by some shadowy figure without a name or a face—or a wife who goes to school here with him."

"I would think you'd rather be here, protected, than out there in the wild of the world. Unless you forgot how easy it was for him to pluck you off the street. It could easily happen again, maybe by someone worse than him."

"I didn't do anything," she grits out, sawing into a piece of chicken like she has a personal grudge against it. "As for my family, I hated them. I still do. I don't care who believes me. I'm tired of trying to convince people who aren't willing to listen."

"You can't pretend it doesn't sound unusual. Why did your father send you away?"

"You would have to ask him," she mutters before taking a mouthful of chicken.

"I can't ask him."

"Oh well." She lifts a shoulder, now twirling spaghetti around her fork. "I guess you'll have to take my word for it."

Fucking infuriating little smart-ass. Though that isn't enough reason to keep a close eye on her. This school is teeming with smart-ass kids—spoiled little shits who've never had to face the consequences of their actions. More than a few of them. Fuck, I used to be one of them.

It's still not a good enough reason to keep her with me.

"Did you know Aspen before she came to Corium? Like, did you ever meet her before that night?"

She shakes her head without hesitating. "No. I never set eyes on her before."

"You'd heard of her, though, right? That her father was rather infamous. Word spreads fast, especially in the underground."

"I don't know. People talk. I can't pay attention to everything." Now that seems evasive. Especially when she won't look me in the eye.

Still, I can't see the point in demanding she tells me more. Either she truly knows nothing, or she's skilled enough in the art of lying that even I can't crack her. It's sickening how much I want to. Not only for Aspen's sake. I need to know what makes this girl tick. How does she fit into any of this? She was involved, if only tangentially. *Why?*

The problem is, everyone else who would know why is dead, leaving her dangling like a loose thread. I hate loose threads. Especially when my daughter's life might still be hanging in the balance. In that case, how am I supposed to let her go?

"Tomorrow, you'll be starting classes."

That shakes her out of it, to the point I'm surprised the food she's chewing doesn't fall out of her mouth as she gapes at me. "Tomorrow?"

"What did you think that examination was all about? I told you, all students go through it."

"I didn't think it meant I'd be enrolled immediately and shoved into classes." I notice then that she's not so interested in eating and instead chooses to push the food around on her plate. It shouldn't give me a jolt of satisfaction to watch her tumble off her high horse, but then not much about the way my mind works makes sense.

"Don't look so glum. I'm sure you'll be fine." I lift my fork to my lips, trying to hide a smile.

"Yeah," she grunts, ending it with a snort. "I'm sure I will."

We both know that isn't true—and I'm hoping once she gets a sense of how dark and disturbing this jungle is, she'll be more willing to look at me as a protector. By then, she'll be more than willing to tell me everything I want to know... and if not, then we'll have to go to plan B.

17

DELILAH

*I*t's the first day of school; only everybody else already knows each other, and I have to catch up on what they've been studying all semester.

Oh, and everybody hates me.

Maybe I'm being too harsh, but that's very much how it feels. I'm sure word has gotten around—I wouldn't get so many suspicious looks otherwise. I wonder how much they know about me.

Like the unexpected, freezing vacation I spent thanks to the great Q, as they call him. They treat him like a king around here. I remember that much from hearing Nash talk about him.

That's why I'm getting all the nasty looks as I walk into math class. Everybody's heard about me, but they only know his side of the story. I'm the bad guy. They all treated Aspen like shit back when she first got here, but somehow, I'm the asshole.

"Hey. You're Delilah, right?"

I brace myself for an attack when a guy with dark hair and glasses takes the desk next to mine. I chose the back corner for a reason. I'm not trying to attract attention, and I certainly don't want to make friends with anyone.

"Hello." He waves a hand close to my face. "Nobody said you were hearing impaired."

"I'm not." I turn to him but don't bother trying to be nice. I don't have it in me to be nice when I'm too busy worrying about who will stick a knife in my back first.

"So why didn't you answer? That's rude."

"What do you want?" I whisper. "Just say something mean and get it over with." Class is going to start any minute now. Hopefully, once it does, there'll be fewer chances of this dude fucking with me.

"Who said I was trying to be mean?" He holds out his hand again, only this time, it looks like he wants to shake. "Sorry. We got off on the wrong foot. My name's Marcel. I was friends with Matteo and Nash."

My heart clenches at the sound of his name. How long will it be before that stops happening? "They never mentioned being friends with you."

"Let's be fair. I never heard of your existence, either. Not until recently." He has a point. I'm sure my brother never spoke of me. Why would he when I hardly existed in his world?

"Nice to meet you," I mumble while shaking his hand. And it is nice. At least somebody seems like they're on my side. He's not judging me like so many other people want to, with their knowing stares and the way they whisper things to each other loud enough for me to hear.

Especially the girls. "Traitor," one of them mutters as she takes a seat a few desks ahead of me. "Who lets that kind of shit happen to another girl?"

"It'd be a shame if it happened to her, huh?" another girl asks with a snicker. "She'd find out what it feels like."

Charming. I make a point of ignoring them, focusing my attention on Marcel. "I'm nobody's favorite person, and none of them have ever actually met me."

"People are stupid." He eyes the girls, shaking his head. "Especially the ones who believe everything they hear without using any critical thinking. But then, not everybody's capable of that, either." It's obvious from the disgust dripping from his voice that he doesn't like them. It gives me a little confidence.

Turning back to me, he lowers his voice and leans in a little. "How are you holding up?"

"Fine." It's an honest answer. I can't exactly complain. Sure, I have no freedom, but I'm comfortable, mostly fed and all that. It's a step up from the way things were not long ago. Still a captive, but one with better accommodations.

"Good. I'm glad I got the chance to talk with you. I've been wondering."

"I can't believe there's anybody around here who actually gives a shit about me," I admit with a tiny laugh.

"There is. There are people who care. Just keep your head down, and you'll be fine."

"That's what I'm trying to do."

"Is that why I haven't seen you around before now?" When I lift an eyebrow, he shrugs it off. "Word gets around pretty fast, you know. I heard days ago you were here. I was just waiting until you showed your face."

"Yeah, that wasn't exactly my choice." If I had my choice, I wouldn't be sitting here right now, even if it's nice to meet somebody who doesn't look at me like I'm some evil monster.

The instructor walks into the room, and most of the chatter fades to silence. Marcel, though, leans in a little closer. "I hate that mother-fucker for what he did."

I glance at him from the corner of my eye. "Q?" I mouth the single letter.

He nods. "He can't get away with it."

For the first time all day, I feel warm inside. Not so alone.

"I agree." And I'm not only talking about Matteo and Nash, either. There's a score to settle that's even more personal for me. I'll never get back the time he stole, locking me away like he did. I'll never forget the helplessness, pain, and fear.

It's those memories I can't help but go over in my head, even though I know I'm supposed to be paying attention to the lesson. I should have known this wouldn't be a typical math class.

It's more like a class on how to make illegal business revenue look legitimate. I don't think I'll ever need anything like that, anyway. I'm not here for the same reasons all of them are.

If Marcel is on my side, I wonder how many others might be. Until he approached me, I figured I was the only one who even missed Nash. Matteo? I still can't bring myself to care much. But at least somebody remembers him. At least somebody remembers why he's not around anymore. At least somebody wants to hold Quinton accountable.

Class is about to wrap up, judging by the way everybody starts getting their stuff together. Marcel nudges me when the instructor isn't looking. "Do you need anything?" he whispers and continues, "Is there anything I can do for you?"

It's been so long since anybody actually cared about me that I might cry. The only thing that stops me is knowing how stupid that will look, not to mention how other people might misinterpret it. I don't want word to get around that I broke down sobbing on my first day of class.

"You could do one thing," I whisper back. "Can you get word to Nash's brother, Preston?"

"Sure thing. What do you want me to tell him?"

"Just let him know I'm here, and I didn't talk. Otherwise... yeah, that will do it." I can't think of anybody else who would care or go out of their way to find me. But Preston was always all right. We got along well. And he's my last connection to his brother.

"No problem. I'll do that." The instructor dismisses the class, and we both stand, with Marcel winking at me as he gathers his things. "Don't worry. You have friends here, even if we can't come out and announce it. Just keep an eye out and hang in there."

"I will." After all, what choice do I have? At least now I don't feel so hopeless.

I wonder if more people like Marcel will introduce themselves and rally around me in support. I'm not asking for parties, parades, flowers, or any of that shit, but it would be nice to feel less alone.

"Bitch," someone sneers. I don't know who said it, but the word crashes into me and reminds me that even if I have a few allies, I have a lot more enemies. I can't let myself get lazy. Like Marcel said, I have to keep an eye out.

Unfortunately, the first people my eye lands on once I'm out of the classroom are the only two people here who know exactly what I went through when I was locked up.

It's like everybody parts to let them walk through the hallway. Like there's a special light shining on Quinton and Aspen. They walk hand in hand, Corium royalty.

I wouldn't be surprised if people bowed or curtsied or whatever people do to show their respect. Their appearance is enough to bring a sour taste to my mouth.

Do they even know who they're looking at? The guy is a murderer. I've seen firsthand what he's capable of. He's cruel, heartless, brutal. And he's worshiped. What hope does somebody like me have against that kind of bias?

Aspen spots me first. She nudges Quinton a little bit, bringing his attention to me, too. His dark gaze narrows to slits, an expression I remember well. It's like a total mindfuck, seeing him here when I spent so long dreading him showing up at my cell.

Now I have to pretend that didn't happen.

Why couldn't she keep walking without giving him the heads-up? Just another reason for me to hate her. This whole thing is her fault, even if her husband is the one who destroyed my world as a result of shit I had no hand in planning.

They come to a stop in front of me, blocking my way. Of course. I feel the curious stares of more than one student as they filter past us, not to mention a few giggles. I'm surprised they don't all whip out their phones to record this in case something interesting happens. Knowing my luck, it'd be used against me at a later date.

"They look nice on you," Aspen offers, and I realize she's looking at the sweater and skirt I'm wearing.

I look down at them. "Thanks," I mutter. Is that her idea of an opening line?

"I had a feeling they would fit you pretty well. Keep them as long as you need."

Oh, fuck me. "I didn't know they were yours." What kind of game is this? Was there nowhere else Lucas could find clothes for me? Jesus Christ, don't they get deliveries around here? He could have had some clothes overnighted, brand new. It wouldn't even cost that much.

But no, I guess he finds it funny, having me wear the clothes of the girl who's the reason all of this started in the first place. Just when I think I know how deeply twisted he is, he goes and shows me how much worse he can be.

Meanwhile, Little Miss Perfect is staring at me, smiling. I guess I'm supposed to say something. "Thanks for lending them to me. They do fit well."

"That's great." She chews on her lip before turning to look up at her husband. He hasn't breathed a word yet, and I don't think he's going to. Not that I'm complaining. I don't want to hear a single syllable come from his murderous mouth.

I guess he can't be bothered to say anything when he's so busy giving me a death glare. I know the last thing I need to do is antagonize him, but I've never exactly been good at ignoring this kind of thing. No matter how much I know I should. I don't want to come off as being weak, either. Not in front of him. Not in front of any of these assholes.

"Anyway, we better get going." Aspen offers a smile that I can't believe she actually means.

And I match her smile, just as fake as she is. "Thanks again. That's really generous of you, making sure I have what I need." I make it a point to stare at Quinton for a beat.

When he blinks first, a surge of satisfaction makes my smile widen. It's actually genuine now. "I better go. Don't want to be late for class."

I have to bite my tongue to keep from laughing as I hurry away. He didn't expect me to put on a friendly act. That much is obvious.

Then again, what would he have preferred? The sight of me weeping and begging for forgiveness? *Probably.* He's got a long time to wait if he wants that.

I realize this newfound confidence is all thanks to Marcel as I cut my way through the hall. There are still whispers, stares, and all that. But I feel less alone. Like there's a shell around me now.

If Quinton Rossi thinks I'm going to break that easily, he didn't learn anything about me while I was locked up. I will always find a way to get through, no matter what.

18

LUCAS

$\mathcal{I}$ can't remember ever waiting with so much anticipation. Not even when I was in the ring, waiting for the bell to ring so I could knock my next opponent out. I was pretty fucking insufferable about it, too.

But this? This tops anything. Why isn't she back yet? I know her entire schedule inside and out—considering I put it together, it only makes sense. She should have been here ten minutes ago, but she's not. I deliberately left my office and went to the apartment to wait for her, and she was not here.

It's incredible, really, how many scenarios can run through a person's head in the span of no time at all. Did she run away? No, somebody would have come to get me by now.

Did Quinton decide to finish the job? I would hope not since I don't feel like dealing with any of those ramifications. Though I doubt there would be any. If what she's told me is true, nobody wouldn't be asking after her. It'd be as if she simply vanished from the face of the earth. Essentially, that's what she's already done.

As far as I know, there hasn't been a mention of her in the outside world, almost like she never existed.

When the door to the apartment opens, I have to restrain myself from pouncing on her like a father waiting for his daughter to return home from a night out.

"What the fuck took you so long?" I bark.

She cringes away, eyes wide. "What? I came straight here after class."

"That's a fucking lie, and we both know it. You should have already been here if you'd come straight from class."

"What, have you timed it?" She puts her hands on her hips, snickering and even going so far as to look me up and down. "I mean, I already knew you were uptight, but this is way worse than I anticipated."

"Keep your fucking useless opinion to yourself. I asked you a straightforward question. Why did it take you ten minutes longer than it should have to get back here?"

"What are you expecting? For me to confess I was scheming?" She smirks, and I want to wipe the floor with her face. "Maybe I built a bomb and hid it somewhere."

"Quit with the fucking jokes. I want an answer."

"For one thing, I wasn't alone in the hallway. There were a ton of people all around, and they sort of slowed me down." She rolls her eyes. "And I got a little lost. Okay? Are you happy? I couldn't find my way."

"It's not that difficult."

"Maybe not for you. However, except for that visit with Doctor Lauren, today was the first time I've left this apartment. It's not like I had a map on me. I had to try to remember."

"You could have asked someone for help."

"Right." She taps her chin. "Excuse me. Instead of living in the dorms like everybody else, I'm staying with Lucas in his apartment. Can you direct me to it?"

I grit my teeth, my jaw tightening to the point of pain. She pushes my buttons, every single one of them. When I don't respond and continue to stare at her, she throws her hands into the air. "I'm sure that would have gone over really well and that it wouldn't paint an even bigger target on my back once everyone found out where I was living and with who."

"You believe there's a target on your back?"

"Give me a break, would you? We both know there is. Or was there some other reason for you to look so smug yesterday when you told me I had to start classes today?"

White-hot fury rolls through me, burning up my insides. How the fuck does she do that? It's like she reads my mind. "You don't know what you're talking about."

"Don't I?" A heartbeat passes. The air between us grows hotter, like the flames of a fire moving in. "Fine. Whatever." She stomps past me and to the guest room like a child throwing a tantrum.

"Where do you think you're going?" I demand, following her. "I wasn't finished talking to you."

"I'm getting changed."

"Not until I'm finished. I want to know how everything went today."

"It went fine." She tries to shut the door in my face, but she's not quick enough. Besides, I have a key—though even if I didn't, I'd kick the fucking thing down.

"Anybody give you any trouble?"

"No. In fact..." She spins on her heels, then has the audacity to jab a finger against my chest. Bolts of electricity span across my chest. It's like being electrocuted. "You could have told me who these clothes belonged to. You mean I have to wear her fucking clothes around school? Do you know how that made me feel when she told me they were hers?"

"Wait, she told you? You spoke to her?"

"Yes," she breathes, placing a hand over her heart, her lashes fluttering against her cheek. "I spoke to the great Aspen. Beautiful, shiny, madly in love with a certifiable psychopath. She had to make sure I knew it was her generosity that led to me wearing something other than your clothes around school."

"Don't talk about her that way." I barely bite back a growl.

"Is there any aspect of my life that belongs to me? I can't even say what's on my mind. I have to wear somebody else's clothes. I have to live in someone else's apartment and sleep behind a locked door. I have to take classes at this godforsaken school that I never wanted to go to or agreed to attend. And now I can't even talk about how embarrassing it is to know the girl everybody holds me responsible for hurting provided me with clothes." Her voice breaks. "I don't even deserve new clothes. How do you think that makes me feel?"

"I don't recall asking you how you feel," I growl and continue, "Do you know why that is? Because I don't fucking care. If you did the right thing and stayed away from the wrong people, there wouldn't have been any reason for Quinton to take you in the first place. You wouldn't have gone through that shit. And you wouldn't be here, whining like a baby about not getting brand new clothes."

Her eyelids flutter, crimson flooding her cheeks. "That's not how I meant it."

"That's sure as hell how it sounded."

"I'm telling you, it's humiliating. What, you think I never wore castoffs? You think I didn't shop at Goodwill? That's all I was ever able to afford. The problem isn't having *new* clothes. It's that these are her clothes."

"She happens to be the only girl around here I know well enough to ask for clothes."

"Well, here." She pulls the sweater off over her head, balls it up, and shoves it into my chest. "I don't want them."

"Because that's going to solve all your problems." I toss the sweater onto the bed, but she sweeps it off with her arm.

"No! Don't do me any favors, and I sure as hell don't want her doing them for me, either. She already thinks she's better than me."

"She is better than you."

She rocks back on her heels. Part of me knows that was the wrong thing to say, but the bigger part of me relishes the effect my words have on her. Her eyes glisten with what looks to be tears.

Her chin quivers. "Good. At least I know where we stand on that." With that comes the skirt, which she lets drop to the floor before kicking it away. My frustration toward her mounts. I don't have time to play childish games.

"Are you finished with your tantrum?"

"Fuck you," she spits.

I'm on her in a flash, even before I know what I'm doing. She gasps, but most of the sound is cut off with my hand circling her throat.

Fear floods her eyes and drains the color from her cheeks. "Is that what this is all about? You want me to fuck you? You've practically been begging for it since you got here. Is that what you want?"

She tries to shake her head but can't move much. "No," she chokes out.

"So it was some other Lucas you were thinking about in the shower the other day?" I lean in, so close our noses touch. Her shallow, panicked breath is hot against my face. I love it. I want her fear, her tears. "When you were fingering yourself? You mean to say it wasn't me you were thinking about?"

With my other hand, I cup her ass, blood surging to my cock and stiffening it almost instantly. "Fucking tease. Saying my name out loud like you did. Knowing I would hear you. And now, this little striptease?"

"Not a striptease," she chokes. She's gone stiff, frozen in fear, and that's good. I like that almost too much.

"Face it. It was an excuse to get naked in front of me, or as good as." I throw her onto the bed, where she bounces hard enough to almost knock her back off. She rolls over, trying to get away like wounded prey, but doesn't she know that when you run, you only make the predator want you more. I take hold of her legs, flip her onto her back, and wedge myself between her thighs.

"Here. Let me take care of the rest for you."

"Stop it!" she screams.

"No, you're right. You shouldn't have to wear anything you don't feel comfortable in." I tear off her panties, shredding the thin cotton with no effort. She lets out a choked sob that should stop me but instead reaches that dark place deep inside that I've tried so hard to suppress and ignore. It's like a drug, and it goes straight to my head.

"Isn't this better?" I ask, laughing at the way she tries to pull her ankles out of my grasp. "Fight all you want. We'll see who tires first. I promise it won't be me."

"You've made your point. Let me go!" Her face is red, her eyes wild with fear.

"No. Not until I say so."

She squeals when I land on top of her, smacking at my shoulders with both hands, bucking wildly like she wants to throw me off.

"That's right, keep fighting," I grunt, working at my belt and unzipping my fly. "You're only getting me harder. That's what you want, right? To tease me? To get me off?"

"Just stop," she pleads. When I get back up, she blinks in obvious disbelief—then tries again to run away from me, crab-walking her way across the bed. This game is one I enjoy far more than I should. I want her to think she's getting away, think that she's safe, and then I want to snatch that safety right out from under her.

I easily take her by the leg again and pull her back to me while she sobs out her dismay. "You know what. I like you better with your mouth full." She tries to turn her head away when I aim my cock at her lips but changes her mind once I take a handful of her hair and pull.

She's not so eager this time, not like before. Now she has no choice but to take what I'm feeding her, which is all of me, until she gags with her nose smashed against my base.

"This is what happens when you push me too far." I hold her there until her face goes bright red, then pull back just enough for her to suck a breath through her nose. "Eventually, you'll learn not to fuck with me."

I squeeze one of her tits, increasing the pressure until she sobs around my cock. Nice tits, too, full and firm with tiny pink nipples. "That's just how I like it."

Her distress makes me laugh as much as it makes me fuck her face. Harder than before. That was fun, a way to vent my anger. This? This is punishment, pure and simple. Nobody takes what I offer and throws it back at me.

For a few moments, there's nothing but the sound of her gagging and my heavy breathing. "Good girl," I mutter, my grip on her hair tightening. "Suck that cock. Suck it until I come. Where should I put it this time?"

I look over her body; so young, fresh, and ripe. "Maybe your ass? Or on your tits. Maybe I'll go old-fashioned and cum all over your face."

She's struggling to take me, struggling to breathe, saliva dribbling down her chin, dripping onto the bedspread. "Is that how you want it?" I ask with a laugh before slamming into her again. "All over your face? I'll see what I can do."

She whimpers, which makes me laugh again. It also brings me close to the edge. Her humiliation, her fear, it works on me like an aphrodisiac. I'm caught up in exhilaration, a sense of power that only heightens the pleasure.

"Oh, yes," I groan as my head falls back, and I jackhammer into her mouth. "I'm going to come. Oh, fuck."

I pull out in time to direct my cock, and I decide at the last second to coat her tits instead of her face. They're perfect for this like they were built for me.

"Fuck... yes, oh, fuck yes!" I paint her with it.

Ropes of cum splash onto her fair skin, rolling down the slopes of her tits and dripping over her nipples.

While she lies still. Taking it. Eyes closed, chest heaving, her chin and throat glistening with saliva. A tear rolls down the apple of her cheek and soaks into the hair fanned out under her head.

I'm spent, physically and otherwise. Wiped clean, unlike the cum-stained mess on the bed. "Next time somebody does something nice for you, don't throw it back in their face. Maybe they didn't teach you that in the trailer park, but you'll learn it real fast here. Consider this your lesson." I back away, tucking myself into my pants.

She takes a deep breath, letting it out slowly. "Can I clean myself up, please?" Her voice is shaky like she's holding in a sob. This is a far cry from the smart-mouthed brat she was just a few minutes ago.

"Go ahead but be quick about it." I follow her to the bathroom door and wait while she turns the water on.

I could've followed her in, and I doubt she would've tried to stop me, but it seems I've gotten my point across. Besides, I don't feel like seeing her cry, which I suspect she's doing. That kind of thing turns me on when I'm already aroused, but right now, it would only irritate me.

A few minutes later, she emerges from the bathroom. Her head hangs low, and I grab her by the wrist and pull her in the direction of the guest room. "Come on." We walk inside the guest room, and I release her as she sits on the edge of the bed. Confusion fills her features.

"Wait. What are you doing? We haven't even had dinner yet. Can we at least eat?"

The locking of the door serves as my response. I have nothing more to say to her tonight. I'll leave her with her thoughts and the reminder of the punishment inflicted.

19

DELILAH

The events from a couple of nights ago haunt me, reminding me that even if I feel safe, I'm not. It's all a game. A sick and twisted game and I'm caught in the middle. I think the worst of it is that even as terrified and fucked up as it was, a sliver of my demented soul loved it.

The feeling of being taken and used. It was different compared to those douchebags back in that cell. They wanted to hurt me, but I got the feeling Lucas didn't really want to cause me pain. He wanted to scare me, but more than that, he wanted to punish me, show me who was in charge.

Well, he succeeded.

For the first time in my whole life, I'm looking forward to math class. I spent all last night wishing time would move faster. If I had free run of the place, I would have tracked Marcel down rather than waited to see him again in class.

Then again, if I had free rein of the place, who knows how much harder life would be? I hate being locked up here, but that doesn't mean I don't understand why it's necessary. I don't have enough people on my side to protect me.

I make sure there are a few minutes to spare when I reach the classroom. I take the same desk as before, in the back corner, and hope Marcel isn't late or—God forbid—absent. I need to know if he got a hold of Preston. I don't know why it seems so important. Maybe because he's the last tie I have with my old life. I can't believe it already feels like a lifetime ago when Nash was alive. I'm a different person now.

Students start to filter into the room, and my heart leaps every time. Still, Marcel doesn't appear, and doubt starts to take root in my mind. What if everything that happened before was yet another way of torturing me? For all I know, Marcel is Quinton's best friend. Was he only pretending so he could get my guard down?

The thought doesn't remain in my mind long, not when he finally comes walking in. I barely stay seated in my chair. The only thing keeping me there is the fact that I have to pretend not to care. If anyone notices, they might say something to Quinton or Lucas. I need to fly under the radar as long as I can.

When he acts like he's never set eyes on me, I have to remind myself not to take it personally. He's only looking out for me. At least, I hope. Plus, I'm sure it wouldn't do him any favors, letting people know he's an ally. Just because nobody has come straight out and made a death threat doesn't mean I'm safe. Sometimes, it's not the enemy you should fear. It's the enemy disguised as a friend. A wolf in sheep's clothing.

It's only once he's sat down and settled in that he finally acknowledges me. "I have something for you," he mutters from the side of his mouth. His head's on a swivel, moving back and forth, surveying the room, so all I can do is wait until he thinks it's safe.

What could it be? A message, maybe? No, it's better than that. When nobody's looking, he pulls something from his pocket and reaches over, placing it in my lap. I catch a glimpse of silver and realize it's a cell phone. "Hide it!" he orders.

I could cry. I'm so happy right now. A cell phone. After being out of touch with the rest of the world for all this time, it's like he handed me the keys to everything. As soon as nobody's looking, I whisper back, "Thank you so much."

He nods slightly but doesn't offer any other response, either focusing on the instructor or pretending to.

Meanwhile, the phone is burning a hole in my pocket. The urge to escape this room, run into the bathroom, and make a phone call surges through me. I'll call anyone. I don't care who.

Except, I don't have any numbers memorized. It reminds me of my aunt complaining that back in the day, she had to have her friends' phone numbers committed to memory or written down somewhere. Nowadays, all we have to do is program it into our contacts once, and it's there forever.

In other words, I'm still kind of screwed.

But it gives me enough hope to get through class feeling a little more like myself. Like a normal person with a way to at least call for help if I ever need it. As class drags on, I find my mind wandering. If I ran away, how far would I need to go before reaching a town with an airport?

Once my excitement cools off, I realize he didn't answer the question that's been brewing in my mind since he first came in. Not that he gave me a chance to ask, either.

It isn't until class is ending that I take a moment to lean in, watching to make sure we aren't noticed. "Did you get a hold of him?"

"Just use the phone. You'll see what I'm talking about when you do."

"I don't understand—"

"Just do it and never let anybody see it." *Right.* Like I would ever do that. Some things I don't need to be told.

Instead of saying that, I bite my tongue and murmur, "Thanks so much."

The second we're able to go, I grab everything and jump out of my chair. There's no way I'll be able to wait until I get back to the apartment later to find out what he means by: *just use the phone. You'll see.*

It's not like I'll be able to concentrate on anything until I do.

Which is why instead of heading straight to my next class, I make a detour to the bathroom. I need to know what he couldn't tell me. My hands tremble, and excitement bubbles up inside me.

I search the bathroom, checking each stall to be sure there's no one else inside, which there isn't. For once, luck is on my side. I duck into the last one, ears trained for any sounds while I power up the phone.

Once the screen lights up, I navigate to contacts, hoping I'll find something there. Shocked, I discover a number stored, just one.

But it's the only one I need.

"Preston." I whisper his name.

I press my finger against his name and then the green call icon, chewing on my bottom lip nervously as the phone rings and rings.

"Hello?" A boyish voice fills the receiver.

"Preston?" I whisper.

"Yeah." He pauses. "Delilah?"

"Yes! Did Marcel tell you?" That's a dumb question. Of course he did, or else why would Preston have guessed me out of all other people in the world who could call him?

"He told me. I'm glad to know you're all right. Until I talked to him, I assumed Rossi's crew got you, too. Where the hell have you been until now?"

How much should I tell him? I'm not prepared for this. I wasn't sure if I would ever talk to anybody from my old life again.

"Delilah? Are you still there?"

"I'm still here. It's been... complicated."

"How? What's going on?"

Screw it. What do I have to lose? Okay, maybe that isn't the best thing to ask myself, considering everything else that's happened, but the idea's the same. "I was locked up for a while. Let's start there."

"Locked up? Where?"

"I don't know, and that's the truth. I'd assume not too far from Corium since it took a helicopter ride to get here." My throat tightens. "It was the same place where they took Matteo. Where they killed him."

A hiss fills the line. "Motherfucker."

"Then, one night, this guy came and took me away. He brought me to Corium. It hasn't been awful compared to where I was before. But I'm still not free, and even worse, I don't know what I did to deserve this." Now that I've started, it seems that I can't stop.

"Have you run into Rossi?"

"Sure. And of course, I had to pretend he didn't hold me captive in a frozen hellhole for God only knows how long."

"Face it. Even if you told people, they probably wouldn't care. He could kill someone right in front of the headmaster, and he'd let him walk away."

He's right. The way everyone treats me, the disgust and hate, they might act like he was some big hero for almost killing me.

"I swear, it makes me sick when I see them walking around together, all while I know what he did to so many people. My brother and the whole family. *Nash.*"

"Quinton didn't kill Nash."

"He didn't? I assumed."

"No. It was that bitch, Aspen."

I have to hold myself up against the wall. Aspen? How could a little thing like her overpower Nash? He got rough with me once or twice, and I couldn't overpower him. "That can't be true. She doesn't look like she could kill a cockroach."

"She stabbed the shit out of him. I thought you knew that." He pauses, and suddenly, my head feels like the inside of a fish bowl. Preston continues, "You mean nobody's talking about it at Corium?"

My gaze drags down my body. I think I'm going to be sick. I'm wearing her clothes. That little bitch killed Nash, and I have to wear her clothes around school. I wonder if she laughs at me in secret? I wouldn't doubt it. "She spared my life," I whisper over the bile rising in my throat.

"Yeah, well, don't go getting any ideas about her being a decent human. She'd put a knife in your back the second it was turned."

Yes, now that he mentions it, I get that feeling from her, too. She'll smile to my face, but I'll bet she's cold and just as brutal as her husband when nobody else is around. She has to be, or else why would she want to be married to somebody like him?

When I don't say anything, he sighs. "Are you okay? Actually, don't answer that question. I'm sure it can't be easy being there, especially after everything that happened."

"I'll be fine. You don't have to worry about me."

"Good. Because I'm going to need your help."

"With what? What can I do?"

"You can help us take care of her."

I'm sure my heartbeat can be heard throughout the room. "Take care of her. You don't mean..."

"Yes, I do. She needs to die. She murdered Nash in cold blood. She shouldn't even be breathing now, but it's not exactly easy getting to somebody in that place. Especially somebody who's married to that motherfucker, Q."

My stomach tightens, and a pain twists deep in my gut.

"So you want me to do it?" I ask in a squeaky voice that doesn't even sound like mine. I've never been asked to kill anyone. I've never even considered it. I'm not that type of person. At least, I don't think so. "I don't even know how I could."

"Just leave that part up to me. Now that I know you're there, we can come up with a plan that won't look too obvious."

I hate her. She killed Nash. The only person who cared about me, who ever gave a shit. She took him away from me.

And I agree, she deserves to die. If there was any justice, she'd already be dead. Preston is right about that. But me?

"I don't know if I have it in me to do it."

"Everybody thinks that until they actually have to do it. And don't think she wouldn't do the same thing to you. She probably only kept you alive so she could feel like a good person. Like it balances out what she did to my brother."

He has a point. And yes, between that and the whole sharing clothes thing, it's obvious she wants to be superior. Like *Gee, isn't Aspen amazing, even after everything that was done to her.*

But killing her? With my own two hands? "Listen, I've imagined a lot of really awful things. Like all the different ways I want to kill Rossi. But I still don't think I could actually go through with it. I'm not that type of person."

"I see."

I flinch, squeezing my eyes shut. He sounds so much like Nash. That's how he always sounded when he was disappointed in me. It hurts more than I want to admit. "I'm sorry."

"I guess you forgot what Nash did for you."

There it is. The one thing he knows will break me down.

"I didn't forget." *How could I?*

"Please stop!" I sob, but my pleas fall on deaf ears. Nathaniel pulls back the cane once more, bringing it down on my already raw skin. He forced me onto his lap and tore my panties off shortly after my father left me at his doorstep.

A scream rips from my throat as I try my best to shove off his lap. That only makes him hit me harder. "Three more strikes, and you'll get your reward. I'll fuck your tight little pussy while you call me daddy."

Bile rises in my throat. I don't want this. I don't want him.

Another strike with the cane has me gasping for air. Burning pain radiates from my cheek down my leg. I notice something wet drips down my naked thigh, letting me know he finally broke the skin.

"Yes, bleed for me whore." Another hit, just as painful as the last. My vision blurs. I don't know how much longer I can take this.

Please let this be over soon.

"Last one. Let's make it count." Before I can brace myself, he slams the cane down again, on the same spot he just hit.

The pain is unbearable and splinters across my backside. Black spots appear in my vision, and I'm sure I'm about to pass out any moment.

"There you go. Now, be a good girl, get on your knees and suck me off for a little before I shove my cock into your cunt. Unless you'd rather I do it without lube?" he taunts, shoving me off his legs.

I fall to the ground with a thud. My muscles ache from the exhaustion of fighting him. My eyes are heavy and swollen from crying, but I force myself to get up anyway. Not obeying only means more pain; I've learned this the hard way in the short time I've been here.

Still, if I don't get away now, he is going to hurt me beyond repair. I have to try, no matter what the outcome.

Getting on my knees, I pretend I'm getting ready to suck his dick, reaching for his zipper. Instead of opening his fly, I ball my hand into a fist and slam it into his crotch with all the strength I can muster up.

His pained scream echoes through the house as I jump up and dash away as fast as I can. I don't care about being half-naked and barefoot. All I want is to get away. There is no such thing as shame when you're trying to survive.

My feet pound against the pristine tiled floor in the hallway. My legs push me forward as I make it around the corner, where I know the front door is. Only I don't run into the foyer like I hoped. Instead, I run into another person.

"Shit!" He groans, his strong hands wrapping around my upper arms to steady me.

"Please help me!" I beg, gasping for air. My whole body is shaking, my knees weak, and the pain from the punishment that was momentarily numb returns with a vengeance. "Please, I'll do anything."

I blink back tears and get a good look at the guy in front of me. He seems to be my age, maybe a little older. His dark hair is messy, and his eyes look sleepy like he just woke.

"Did my father bring you here?" Only then do I realize the resemblance to the man who did this to me. This is his son. Oh, god. "What did you do?"

"He hurt me. I... I punched him... in the... you know."

"Dick?"

I only manage to nod. A grin spreads over the stranger's face. "He is going to make you pay for that." My shaking intensifies. "But I could help you. I could bring you to my room and keep you safe."

"You would?"

"Yup." He nods. He shifts his hold on me, wrapping his arms around my waist, so I can lean against his side. "I'll do something for you, and you'll do something for me."

I'm scared to ask what exactly he expects from me, but somehow, I doubt it will be worse than what his father was going to do to me.

"I guess if you don't have the balls to do it, you don't." Preston's demeaning voice drags me back to reality.

Feeling the deep need to resolve some of his disappointment, I say, "I'll help if I can. Like, if there's anything I can do to make it easier for you, I'll do it. I just don't think I could actually do the deed itself."

"Hmm. Now that you mention it, that's not a bad idea. Even if you can't kill her, you could make it possible for somebody else to do it. That would work."

"Great. Whatever you need, I'll get it done."

My hand tightens around the phone until it hurts. She took Nash away from me, and now she gets to walk around like she owns the place while I have to live locked in a guest room.

"Okay. Make sure you're careful with the phone. Don't let anybody see you with it. I'm not sure I could manage to get you another if you get caught with it."

"I won't." For now, it will live along with the scissors hidden under the mattress.

"And I'll have Marcel let you know if I need to talk to you."

"That works. I've got to go," I whisper into the phone.

Preston doesn't respond, and a moment later, the line goes dead. I do the same thing and end the call, which is good since the door opens and the shuffling of feet and laughter filter into the space.

I'll wait here until they leave. I don't trust myself to go out there right now, anyway. If I ran into Aspen, I might have to pull every hair out of her head and shove it down her throat until she choked on it.

The longer I think about it, the more convinced I become. I'll do whatever it is Preston needs.

Aspen must die. There is no other way.

20

LUCAS

"*I* know you think I'm devastatingly handsome, but you don't have to stare at me like that."

Lauren's lips twitch, but she won't give me an actual smile. She wouldn't let me gain that much ground, especially not when we're on her turf—in the middle of a session.

"I'm waiting for you to say something, which you know very well. As usual, you're using sarcasm and charm to disguise what's going on inside."

"So you think I'm charming."

Her brows draw together, and her mouth screws up until it's almost invisible. "Lucas. Are we always going to do this dance? You know how seriously I take my work, even when it comes to you. Maybe especially when it comes to you."

"Thank you."

"And I don't feel as if I'm doing my job when all we do is sit here and go back and forth. I'm not serving you as your doctor when we spend half our time bantering before you finally decide to get real."

"You want me to get real?"

"I'd appreciate it very much." She follows the direction my gaze travels in. "Maybe without the Scotch this time. I'd rather speak with a clear-headed version of you."

The clear-headed version of me isn't in the mood to speak. It looks like we're at an impasse.

"Let's go back to what we discussed in a previous session." She crosses one leg over the other, tapping her pen on that blank notepad. "How are you managing your relationship with Aspen? How are you two doing together?"

"Pretty well. Taking it slowly, but I believe we're headed in the right direction."

She nods slowly. "Can you tell me why you scowled when I mentioned her name?"

"I did?"

"Like you wanted to rip my head off."

I scoff, folding my arms. "You would know for sure if I wanted to do that."

"Come on. Out with it. Why does the mention of her name stir up that reaction?"

I wasn't aware I had that reaction. I'm still not sure she's being straight with me. "Why would Aspen make me feel that way?"

"I'm asking you, remember?" She leans forward, her brows pinched together like she's in pain. "I know you carry guilt over that night, but you couldn't have known what would happen. I'd like to go over a few exercises to help you release that guilt."

"Do I strike you as somebody who does emotional exercises?"

"No. You strike me as someone who allows emotional pain to fester until it eats away at them from the inside out."

I'd crack a joke, but I'm not in a joking mood anymore. I wasn't in the first place. She sees straight through me—I'll do anything to keep from talking about my feelings.

"Would it surprise you to know I've done a lot of thinking about this?" To hell with her wanting me sober. I at least need to get a buzz on to go through this. The Scotch is waiting for me. This time, I use a glass, though I fill it more than halfway before returning to the couch.

She's waiting, patient as ever. I almost wish she wouldn't be so damn calm at times like this. No matter how I try, I can't get a reaction out of her. Ever the professional.

She expects me to open now, so I drain half the glass before admitting what's weighing heaviest on my mind. She won't let it go until I do. "It's not only that night. I know I said it was, and I doubt I'll ever forgive myself for leaving her unprotected."

I take another sip, the liquor burning its way down my throat. The sensation is a welcome one. "It's everything that came before that. How can I live with myself, knowing what I put her through?"

Lauren frowns. "The way she was treated when she first arrived, you mean?"

"Of course, that's what I mean. I allowed her to be abused. Practically tortured."

"You did what you felt had to be done to make an example out of her."

"Don't tell me you think that was fair."

"I never said that." Now she's scowling, and her normally warm eyes have hardened. "I don't think it was fair at all. No matter what her adopted father did, none of it was Aspen's fault."

"You don't know the way it is. The code we have to keep. The way we treat rats and traitors."

"I know enough about it, and my point stands. But that's neither here nor there. You did what you felt had to be done." She lifts a shoulder, sighing. "If you didn't, it might have been considered tantamount to excusing her father's poor choices. That would only have created trouble among the students."

"That's a fair point." I sip more of the Scotch, mulling this over. "I'm sure it's what I told myself at the time. It helped me sleep at night when I thought of her at all."

"You didn't know who she was," Lauren reminds me in a softer voice than before. "You can't blame yourself for that."

"Say's who?"

"Says the medical professional you visit for treatment."

I can't help but wince. "Do you have to call it that? You make it sound like I'm in a padded room."

"An unfair stereotype which only serves to scare people off. It does a disservice to the profession and to so many people who might other-wise have gotten help."

I give her time to finish before shaking my head. "Maybe that works for some people. I'll never feel like there's anything normal about this."

"Even if it keeps your darker side at bay?"

I'm not so sure it does anymore. Not after the way I've used Delilah. "How do I get over this, Doc?" I ask, ignoring her question.

"The guilt?" When I nod, she pulls a concerned face. "You're not going to like hearing it."

"I thought that went without saying."

"You're going to have to talk to Aspen."

"You're right. I didn't like hearing that." I sit up straight, then throw back the rest of the Scotch in one smooth gulp. "No way."

"It's the only way you can start to get past the guilt."

"You mean there isn't a, you know, breathing exercise I can do instead? Could I meditate or something?"

"Now I know you're going through it if you'd rather meditate."

I don't crack a smile. "I won't talk to her about it."

"Why not? What's the worst that could happen?"

"Since it's not going to happen, there's no point in going all worst-case scenario."

"What are you afraid of?"

"You know I don't appreciate the use of that word. I'm not afraid. Of anything, or anyone."

"You have a daughter now. There's fear in you, the same as there is with any other parent. You're only human."

"I would rather we not talk about this anymore. Not today." She doesn't know what she's asking. How am I supposed to broach the subject? What would I say? What kind of asshole would I end up sounding like? Sorry, I knew exactly what was being done to you and did nothing to stop it—in fact, I added to it. But I didn't know you were my daughter. Whoops, sorry.

"Fair enough." She lets out a deep breath. "How's Delilah doing? Has she started classes yet?"

"Yes, this week."

"Is she getting along with everyone?" It's clear from the tightness in her voice that she already knows the answer. Didn't we just finish talking about traitors and what happens to them? Aspen is virtual royalty now that she's a member of the Rossi family, and Delilah might've participated in the worst night of her life. I'm sure, according to gossip, she did.

"She doesn't have any cuts or bruises when she gets back from class. That's the best I can say."

When Lauren stays silent, I clear my throat. "What is it? You went away for a second."

She offers a brief, sheepish smile. "You caught me in the middle of asking myself whether sharing a piece of information with you would be ethical. It was shared in confidence, but it might be something worth reporting."

"Is it Aspen? Did something happen to her?"

"No. Delilah."

Shared in confidence. During her exam? Immediately after our encounter in the bathroom? "What is it?"

"I'm telling you this because I think it affected her much more than she was willing to show." She snorts, eyeing me up. "Reminds me of somebody I know."

"What did she tell you?" Why is my heart pounding the way it is? Now, the Scotch sloshes in my stomach.

"I'm afraid she was sexually assaulted."

Fuck. She told her about the blowjob. I knew it was a terrible idea, leaving the two of them alone. I knew she'd find a way to fuck me over.

"It seems it happened when she was being held captive."

The dread that bloomed in my gut a moment ago is now hardening into something else. Something just as potent. "Those lying fucks. They told me they never laid a hand on her—not that way. Quinton forbade it."

"They didn't lay a hand on her. They were clever enough to find the loophole in the rule."

"I don't get it."

"They..." She shifts in the chair, grimacing. "They jerked off and came on her chest."

My stomach drops like I'm on a roller coaster. "The fuckers. Disgusting pieces of shit."

I'm the biggest hypocrite who ever drew breath. I came on her tits, too, right after forcing her to suck me off. Yeah, she offered the first time, but the second... that was all me.

They're a couple of filthy pigs. I hate the thought of them looking at her, much less jerking off in front of her. Anger burns through my veins, followed by confusion. Why am I so bothered by the thought? She doesn't mean shit to me, yet in a way, she does.

I can't quite pinpoint how or why, and I'm not in the mindset to try to dive deeper into these emotions, nor do I want to admit to myself that there might be something deeper because to do that would make me feel like I'm betraying Aspen, and I never want to feel like I've let her down in any way again.

"I'll bring it up with her," I decide.

"Take it easy. Don't barge in and stomp around like a bull in a China shop."

"What would ever give you the idea I'd be capable of that?"

She checks the time, then pretends to wipe sweat from her forehead. "Wouldn't you know it, our time is up? We'll have to come back to this topic during our next session."

Rather than head to my office after leaving Lauren's, I go straight to the apartment. I won't be able to concentrate until I know whether this story is true or not. Why didn't she mention it? I can see not saying anything while we were still there, but she's been here for days.

More likely, she told Lauren some made-up bullshit story to gain sympathy. That makes much more sense. But then again, my first instinct was to believe her, and usually, my instincts are on point.

She's in the guest room, where I left her, lying on her stomach with a book open in front of her. Her head snaps up at my barging in, the pencil in her hands drops and rolls off the bed in slow motion.

"Is it true? What you told Lauren during your exam?"

She doesn't look surprised. "I knew she wouldn't be able to keep her mouth shut about that. I should've told her nothing happened."

"Is it true?"

"What does it matter to you?" Her chin juts out like she's ready for a fight.

"I would hate to know you're taking advantage of a caring doctor by telling a story you knew would get back to me. A way of making everybody feel sorry for you."

She glares at me with what can only be cold hatred. "You saw those guys. Would you put it past them to do something like that? They couldn't fuck me, so they figured out a way around it. They got off. They had the added pleasure of making me want to scrub my skin until it shredded."

She goes back to reading her book while I stand here, speechless. Something toughened this girl up. I suspected she had plenty of grit, seeing as how she made it through captivity in one piece.

But this is a different level. She's been hurt before. So much so that she's built thick walls around her. She has ways of coping, even if she doesn't know it. At some point, she was forced to adapt. "Why didn't you say anything to anyone?"

"You mean to you since you're the only other person I really talk to?" She barely glances at me before turning the page. "You said I deserved everything they did to me back there, right? I didn't feel like wasting my time telling you if you were only going to shrug it off."

Whatever words I want to say evaporate into thin air.

Of course, then she lifts her head, staring at me with a questioning expression. "Why do you care anyway? You literally did the same to me."

I don't have an answer for her. Especially when I've done worse to her, and that's infuriating. I'm not any better than those fuckheads. Since there's nothing to say, I leave her to go back to her work—though I make a point of leaving the door open.

We'll see how long it takes for her to come out. If she is going to come out at all.

21

DELILAH

This is different. It's the first time he's gone against his normal routine. I have to lie here and pretend not to notice or care, but now my brain is buzzing. Why did he leave the door open? Normally, the first thing he does is lock me inside.

I can't help but wonder what type of game he's playing?

I'm so damn tired of having to ask myself that question. This whole thing where I always have to be on my toes, looking out for danger. It's exhausting. I wonder if I'll ever get back to a life where it's possible to just live without having to worry.

Who am I kidding? I've never had that kind of life. I've always been worried about something or another. Looking over my shoulder, listening for sounds of anger coming from elsewhere in the trailer. Doing everything I could to keep her from blowing up at me. When was the last time I was able to relax? Have I ever?

He's moving around out there. I've seen him walk past the door more than once from the corner of my eye. So it's not like he forgot to lock the door and corrected himself once he noticed his mistake.

That tells me it was a deliberate choice. Is he starting to trust me more?

Maybe Doctor Lauren got through to him. I'm not super thrilled knowing she told him about those pigs and what they did. Still, it might mean better treatment, and I can't be mad about that. Especially not after what he did to me. I didn't even care about the blow job. It was the way he came on my chest that was too similar to what they did to me.

Maybe things will start to settle down, and I'll earn some freedom. I might be able to learn to live with that.

One thing I know for sure: there's no hope of concentrating on this book. I've been staring at the same page since he interrupted me, and the words mean nothing. I'm too distracted now. I keep pretending, so he thinks I'm being a good girl and following the rules.

That's one drawback to having the door open. He'll be able to watch me. It's still better than being imprisoned. Now, when I have to pee, I can just get up and go. What a refreshing change.

Moving to a sitting position from my belly, I stare at the open door. I can't see him, but I hear him. He's making a lot of noise. Pots and pans bang against each other. A cabinet opens and closes.

The only reason the sounds stand out is because I've never heard him in the kitchen before. I can't help wondering what he's doing. The water turns on, almost as if he's filling a pan. A moment later, I hear him place said pan on the stove. The stove makes a clicking noise, igniting as he turns the knob on. No, I must be imagining things. He doesn't cook. But he is, and now I'm too intrigued to stay cooped up in the bedroom any longer.

Still, I'm careful, creeping up to the open doorway and poking my head out to catch a glimpse. His back is to me, his shirt stretching over his muscles as he moves around.

I tiptoe farther into the room until I can see what he is doing on the counter. His shirtsleeves rolled up. I'm going to have to try to pretend that it isn't insanely hot, the sight of his forearms as he opens a jar of sauce and pours it into a pot.

He finally notices me, acknowledging my presence with a mere glance. "Take a seat. Dinner will be ready in a few."

I almost want to rub my eyes. "Am I imagining this?"

He rolls his eyes at me before turning back to the stove. He means it. He's actually cooking dinner, and I'm pretty sure I'm dreaming.

Maybe I fell asleep while trying to read. That would make sense. It would explain why he didn't lock me inside the room. Because there's no way that actually happened.

I pause for a moment to gather my thoughts and come up with something to say since hanging around silently feels weird. "Is there anything I can help with?"

"No. I've got it all under control." He jerks his chin at the table. "Sit down." I do it not because I want to sit or even because I want to avoid angering him. Now, I'm invested and need to see how this plays out. A man in the kitchen is more likely to burn water than boil it.

Yeah, I'm not going to miss that. Lucas appears to know his way around the kitchen. Granted, there's nothing that challenging about boiling pasta, but still. Nate tried to cook macaroni and cheese from a box one time, and he ended up setting the kitchen on fire. I'm still not sure how he managed that one.

I'll never get to ask him. The thought makes a lump form in my throat. Eventually, I'm going to have to deal with losing him, and so suddenly. Maybe it would be easier if I'd had the chance to say goodbye.

But somebody stole that opportunity from me, didn't she?

"You okay over there?" I didn't know he was looking at me, and now I had to fight to get my facial expression under control.

"I'm fine. Just thinking."

"About what?"

About how much I want to watch Aspen die for what she did. Yeah, right, that would go well. "Life, I guess. I don't know."

"How are classes coming along? Do you think you can catch up?"

What a fucking joke. Like it matters. What's the endgame at a place like this? To graduate? I thought this was supposed to be a stopover, a way for him to control me for as long as he could. He's making it sound like this is permanent. "I can handle it."

"Good." He stirs the sauce before turning off the heat under that pot. He then bends over, rooting around in the cabinet. I shouldn't stare at his ass, but it's right there in front of me. And it looks so perfect, round and firm. I've never seen an ass like that on a man. Just one more example of how disciplined he is.

Then there's his ink; the intricate lines and color make me want to lean in and examine his skin. And he definitely has a temper—I've been on the receiving end of that. I can't help thinking there's another side to him. A side I might like to meet.

He pops up a second later with a strainer in hand and drains the pasta, then dumps it back into the pot before pouring the sauce over it.

The next thing I know, he turns around with a plate in each hand, piled high with spaghetti. "It's not gourmet, but I can boil a mean pasta dinner."

How bizarre is this? Like we're two normal people having a normal dinner. He's almost like a real person. I was just getting used to the way he is, and now he's changing things up.

"Thank you. This is unexpected." The smell makes my mouth water, and even though I know he had nothing to do with it—it's not like the sauce was homemade—I can't help but warm a little toward him. I even smile, and it's a genuine smile, not one I'm using to get something I want. I don't think I understood until now how much I do that.

"Don't get used to this. I'm still locking you up after dinner."

"Of course." I don't even care at this point.

"Sometimes I like to cook up something, sort of keep my hand in the game, you know?" He almost seems like he's in a decent mood, too. What was he doing earlier before he came back? Whatever it was, he should do more of it.

Then like a ton of bricks falling from the sky, directly onto my head, it hits me. Him leaving the door open and making me dinner, being a little less of an asshole while trying to appear as if he cares.

He feels guilty because he basically did the same thing to me that Rick and Bruno did. I guess hearing about it from the doctor made him take a better look at himself.

I deliberately keep my eyes on my plate, twirling noodles around my fork. "You know, you don't have to go to all this trouble because you feel bad or something."

"Why do you say that?" he asks with a little laugh.

"Because of what you talked about with the doctor. And, you know..." I can barely get the words out, and now I wish I hadn't said anything. I can feel the warmth in my cheeks growing. "Because of what you did."

"I don't feel bad about that. You've got the wrong idea."

All I can do is roll my eyes. We both know he's lying. "I'm just saying, I didn't feel the same way when you did it as when they did. When they came on me, it was disgusting. I kind of wanted to die. But it wasn't the same with you. I just figured you might want to know that."

And now I really wish I had never opened my mouth because my face is burning hotter than the sun, and my heart is pounding, and I don't quite understand why. I shouldn't be embarrassed, but in a way, I am because I didn't realize until after that I liked what he did and only freaked out at the moment when it was clearly meant to be a warning. But there's more because the only difference between those two experiences is the men who came on me.

When Rick and Bruno did it, I was just as helpless and under their control as I was with Lucas.

If anything, Lucas was rougher. At least those two never touched me —not sexually, anyway. They didn't force me to suck their cocks before coming on me. There wasn't any face fucking from them.

And I still didn't hate it nearly as much. Because he's... him. He's hot, commanding, gruff. He's not nasty, sloppy, and gross like they were. He knows that now. At least, he's looking at me like he does, eyeing me from across the table while we eat. I would break the silence, but I didn't know what to say. I'm too embarrassed to speak, not to mention worried I'll embarrass myself even more if I do.

Every time I glance his way, he's staring. I wish I didn't blush so easily, but I can't help it. I've seen that look before, from him, from other men. Only, unlike all those other men, he doesn't make my skin crawl. Unlike Nash, I don't feel like I have to act all sexy to keep him interested.

I want him to look at me. I want him to do more than that, even though I can hardly breathe, and my stomach's fluttering so much I don't know how much more I can eat. But I'm not uncomfortable. It's more exciting than disturbing. Like he's looking at my clothes but seeing the body underneath.

It's never been like this. I don't know what to do with the heat stirring up in my core. I'm getting wet, too. He hasn't touched me, and I'm getting wet.

What would happen if he touched me?

Our eyes meet, and I have to force myself to look away again when my breath catches. He clears his throat and shifts around in his chair. "Had enough?"

Oh, right. We were eating. "I think so." He holds out a hand, and I give him my plate. When our fingers brush together, there's an almost painful tingling response in my pussy. It's a relief when he turns his back and goes to the sink. I lean against the back of the chair, weak and way too out of breath.

He clears the table quickly, silently, wearing a grim expression. What's he thinking? I can't keep sitting here like an idiot. "I guess... I'll go back to my homework," I mumble, even if that's the last thing I want to do when there's a feeling of something hanging unfinished between us.

When he doesn't try to stop me, I get up, my heart sinking. It's better this way, obviously. But I don't have to like it.

I'm halfway to the guest room when suddenly, there's an arm around my waist. "What are you—" Surprise steals the rest of my question when Lucas steers me back to the table, pushing me up against it.

Then he keeps going, laying me back against the cool wood. "I don't understand." He doesn't say a word, running his hands up my legs instead. Oh, god, yes. My eyes close, and I sigh before I know what

I'm doing. Not like I could help it if I tried. Not when his touch is what I want the most.

Still, it can't be right. I have to at least figure out what he's trying to do. Why now? What does he want from me? My pussy, obviously, or my mouth. Both, probably.

I can't pretend it isn't hot, being on the table like this. The idea he couldn't even wait to get me into the bedroom. When I think of it that way, the heat brewing between my legs intensifies.

He pulls down my leggings in one quick motion, so abruptly, I squeal in surprise. A grin tugs at the corners of his mouth before he runs his hands over my bare calves, knees, and thighs. Pleasure closes my eyes again, and it only gets more intense the higher his hands slide. The closer they are to the place where I ache the most.

When he parts my legs, I spread them wider. I force my eyes open in time to watch him settle into a chair and pull it up to the table. He looks me in the eye before opening the top button of his shirt, then the one beneath it. Holy shit, it's hot.

My chest rises and falls with every sharp breath. I know better than to ask what he's going to do next. Besides, I would rather feel it instead of talk about it.

"Do you always get wet this easily?" His voice is tight, deeper, and something about it makes me want to beg him to fuck me. Is this the way it's supposed to be? I never honestly wanted to beg Nash to do it. I only did it because I thought he wanted me to.

"I don't know." That's an honest answer, too. I really don't know. I also don't think he cares, either way. He's too busy running his stubbled cheeks over my inner thighs until my sighs turn to moans.

His fingers dance along the waistband of my panties, and I squirm away from his touch even though I want more. No. I need more. I'll die without more.

"Yes...!" I whisper when he starts peeling the panties away, lowering them slowly. I raise my hips so he can pull them off, then spread my legs again. The air is cool on my hot, wet lips. When he blows across them, I can't help but moan louder than before. I don't know what to do with what I'm feeling. How I should act or sound or anything.

I don't think he cares. "You smell incredible." He parts my lips with his fingers, spreading them open, before touching his tongue to my sensitive folds.

"Oh, my god!" I have to grip the sides of the table with both hands when an explosion in my head makes me pretty sure I'm going to fall off. This is better than when I touch myself. I've never felt anything like this before. Like I'm dying and flying all at once.

"You taste even better," he groans. Like he enjoys this. Like he wants to do it. Nash never went down on me. He never even made me come.

Now here I am, close enough that I already feel the familiar tightness building in my core. With this man's head between my legs, his tongue sliding up and down the length of my slit. Dipping deeper, probing my cunt, before circling my clit and driving me out of my mind.

I need to touch him. I find his arms wrapped around my legs, holding them still, and I run my hands over them before gripping the back of his head. He moans, lapping at me, and I burn hotter than ever at the sweet vibrations running through my pussy.

"That's so good," I murmur, writhing against his face, pulling his head closer. I don't care if it's the right thing to do anymore. It's what I need more than anything. More pressure, more of his moans, more of everything.

I don't know what to do. I've faked it with Nash before, but now that it feels like the real thing is coming, I'm sort of scared. It's too intense. Too much.

But I can't stop it, and I don't want to. I want to see how far he'll take me. "Please... please, let me come," I beg, running my hands through his hair, tugging at it. It feels so good I wish it would never stop, but I know I'll die if the tension doesn't break.

"Mmm." That's the most I get from him, but it's enough. He's breathing almost as hard as I am, his fingers digging into my thighs, his stubble scratching my skin while his tongue flies over my clit until—

"Oh, god! Yes! I'm coming!" My entire body stiffens, freezing for one heart-stopping moment before release shatters me into a million pieces. I can't hold back my screams and don't want to. It feels too good, letting it all out.

So that's how it's supposed to be? Holy fuck. What else have I been missing? The thought makes me laugh, even now, all the emotions mixing together with the bliss spreading through me.

He pulls back, wearing a satisfied grin. Like he's proud of himself. Either that, or he knows it's his turn now. I push myself up until I'm sitting and reach for his belt.

He's gentle but firm, pushing my hands away. "No. That's all right."

All right? He's practically breaking out from behind the zipper. "But... I mean, you did it for me... Unless you would rather fuck?"

His brows draw together, eyes narrowing. "I'm good. I just wanted a taste." He sets my hands on my thighs before standing up.

What is this? I didn't know there were guys who'd get a girl off for the sake of getting her off. Even if I did know, I wouldn't have guessed Lucas was one of them. Have I been that wrong about him?

He's washing dishes by the time I get it together enough to pull my clothes on. The man is a mystery. I don't know exactly what inspired him to do that, but I know I want him to do it again. How can I make him?

Out of nowhere, he speaks, shattering the illusion. "By the way, you're moving to the dorms first thing in the morning."

22

LUCAS

There's nothing like a phone call in the middle of the night to get a man's heart racing. A hundred ugly thoughts race through my head in the time it takes to fumble for my phone, pick it up, and answer the call. "Nic?"

"Sorry I woke you, but I didn't think this could wait until morning." Unlike me, he sounds wide awake. I glance at the alarm clock. It's a few minutes past three.

My heart catches in my throat. "What are you doing up?" I push into a sitting position, my thoughts racing, headed for the worst-case scenario first. Things haven't always been great with my brother and me, but no one has been by my side like he has. "Is everything okay there?"

"We're fine." He sighs. "Sorry. I didn't mean to worry you. Everything is fine here."

Fuck me. I could've had a heart attack. "You should've led off with that." I sigh. "Now, what was worth waking me up at three in the morning?"

"I found information on Delilah."

That did it. I'm more alert than I'd be if I stepped into an ice-cold shower. "What did you find that couldn't wait until morning?"

"Technically, it is morning, and money."

My grip on the phone tightens. If I'm not careful, I'll crush the damn thing before he gets to finish what he has to say. Breathe. I need to rein it in. I need to hear this. But somehow, all I can think about is how I had the girl on a table, legs spread, her fingers slicing through my hair as I licked her pussy until she creamed against my face.

"Specifics?" I croak, ignoring my hardening cock.

"Specifically, a trust fund."

That lying little bitch.

The force of my reaction rocks me. Like a snake darting out from the shadows, fangs out, and ready to strike. That dark part of me, the part I've worked to suppress. All it needs is an excuse to show itself, and this might be exactly that.

"Details?" I choke out.

"Valentine's the one who set it up. I can send you the info right now if you want." His pause is unsettling. "I want you to see it for yourself."

I'm moving before I know what I'm doing, walking out into the living room, pulling out the laptop, setting it on the coffee table, and flipping it open.

"Give me a second," I mumble. It's never taken me so long to open my email.

"I have nowhere else to be."

I snicker, casting a look toward the guest room. She's behind that locked door. Sleeping like a baby. Like she deserves to. "Bed, maybe?"

"At this point, why bother? You know how it is. You get deep in your work, and you lose track of time."

Nic's email is at the top of my inbox. I pull it up, leaning close to read some of the finer print of the PDF. It's a bank statement, pretty standard looking—except for the fact that there are a shit ton of zeroes involved. "Goddamn it."

"Ten million dollars."

"That lying little—" I have to lower my voice to a whisper to keep from waking her. I won't give her time to prepare for what's coming. I'm not the type of man to give a warning. Plus, she didn't give me a warning about her little trust fund. "You wouldn't believe the sob story she's been feeding me all this time."

"What did she tell you?"

It makes me cringe to think of it. How easily she misled me. "That she had no money and lived in a trailer with her aunt. Dirt poor, by the sound of it. No help from her old man."

He grunts. "Well, that could still be true. It's not as if she could access the money yet. It has only existed for a few months."

I zoom in on that little detail on the next attachment, and my stomach drops. This is worse than I assumed. "This is a genuine document?" I whisper, hoping against hope.

"Of course it's a genuine document. I found it myself. Since when have I given you a reason to question my work?"

I ignore his question altogether and stare at the date the account was created. My stomach churning in a way that makes me feel like I've just gotten off a boat that was lost at sea for months.

"The date..." I say more to myself.

"I know." His voice is quieter now, too. "That's why I didn't think it could wait. That was the day—"

I don't need to be told. I already know. "I have to go. Thank you for this. I'll keep you in the loop on what happens." I end the call, toss the phone aside, and sink my head into my hands.

I can't believe it's true, even if the proof is right in front of my face. Nic's right. His recon work is impeccable. And he had to know how it would shake me up to see the connection between the existence of a huge trust and the date it was set up.

He wouldn't have brought me this information unless he was sure it was the real thing. No wonder he hasn't gone to bed. Forcing all the air in my lungs out, I take a few calming breaths.

I have to confront her. I have to, but I also have to get my thoughts in order. I can't kill her or hurt her. I'm bigger than this. I'm better than this. Even Lauren thinks I've gotten better at maintaining my cool in stressful situations. It's times like this I have to fall back on the shit she's taught me.

I wish I could control myself more than I do. That's the problem. I want to hurt her. I crave her pain. And I'm tired of denying myself what I want. She's going to learn what happens to people who lie to me. There is no room for a rat or liar in this school. Pushing off the couch, I march toward the guest room.

My first impulse is to throw the door open. In my mind, I can see her bolting upright in bed, gasping in surprise when I storm into the room. Maybe she would clutch the blankets to her chest, trying to get away before I could reach her. It wouldn't matter; nothing would stop me once I got started. That's how it used to be for me. I'd fight and kill the person standing in front of me until I got the answer I needed or until the job was done. I'm no longer that man, though, and as satisfying as that would be, there's another method that appeals to me even more.

That's why I open the door slowly and tiptoe inside. She's fast asleep, on her back, one hand on her stomach and the other up by her head. Her face is turned to the side, away from me, her auburn hair spilling over the pillow. If there was a window and moonlight coming through it, it might glow like fire.

As far as I'm concerned, this is the last peaceful moment of her life.

I stand over her, watching, quieting my own breath in favor of listening to hers. She stirs slightly, even whimpers softly, but she doesn't wake. Not until I throw back the blankets all at once.

It's then her eyes fly open, soft breathing replaced by a sharp gasp. "Get up," I growl.

"What is it?" She's rubbing her eyes and scratching her head. Pretending? I can't tell. I don't know anything about this girl, and that's half the problem. She's a fucking mystery to me, and I need to solve her.

"You and I need to have a little talk. No more comfort for you. Get out of bed, now." When she doesn't get up immediately, I take her by the arm and pull her from the bed before forcing her to stand on wobbly legs.

"Okay, I get it!" She shakes off my hands and even has the nerve to scowl. "What's wrong?"

"Remind me of something." Arms folded, I stand in front of her, ready to jump on her if she makes a move. It was a mistake. It was all a mistake; loosening my grip, giving her space, being kind, and considering her feelings. This is how I'm repaid. I feel as if I've been dubbed. I should've known better. She's no better than her brother... but more than anything, nobody takes advantage of me.

"What?" she snaps.

"No. That's not going to happen." In a flash, I have her by the hair, twisting the strands around my fist while yanking her head back. A strangled little yelp erupts from her throat. "Please, tell me it's not an attitude I hear in your voice?"

"No." Her voice trembles, but she doesn't break. *She will.*

"Remind me of all the things you said about your family."

"My family?" Her voice cracks.

"Do I need to put you in a cold shower to wake you up? I don't have time to wait for your brain to join us."

"I don't understand why you'd do this in the middle of the night. What do you want to know?"

"Tell me about how you *didn't* have a relationship with them."

"I didn't. I still don't." There's uncertainty in her voice, but I can't tell if it stems from lies or from fear of me.

"That's a fairly extreme situation, isn't it? In our world, nothing is more important than family. You're telling me your family cut all ties with you?"

"Yes. That is all true."

"Why is that?" I challenge, pulling a little harder. She sucks in a pained gasp through her clenched teeth. "What brought it on?"

"I don't know! What, you think he sat down and talked about his feelings with me?"

"There's that smart mouth again." With my free hand, I take her by the throat. The thin column feels good in my grip, and I can practically hear her thundering heartbeat pulsing against my hand. "Be careful how you use it."

"I swear... I'm being honest. I don't know why." The expression on her face is both pain and confusion.

"You didn't have a fight?" I continue to press on.

"I didn't even know him." *Lie.* She's lying. She has to be.

"That's bullshit, and you know it," I sneer, my grip on her throat tightening.

"It's not! Why are you doing this?" The words escape her lips on a wheeze, and I know if I don't release her soon, I might actually kill her.

Leaning into her face, I grit through my teeth, "Because a man who treats his daughter the way you described doesn't turn around and put ten million dollars in a trust fund for her."

She was trembling, but now she's not. Now her entire body is still in my arms. "That can't be true."

"But it is. I have the documentation from the account. I have proof."

I squeeze her throat. "Do you want to tell me why it was opened the same day Aspen was kidnapped?"

She gasps. I tighten my grip on her throat, squeezing until she starts to squirm in my grasp. Her eyes fill with panic, and I release my hold just a little. "I swear to God," she croaks. "I don't know."

At that moment, I have to remind myself that she's no good to me dead, even if a small part of me wants to be the man to deliver that blow.

"You're lying to me again."

"I'm not. I don't know anything about it."

"Bullshit!"

"But it isn't. What do I have to do to prove it to you? I didn't know about any money until now. Until right this very minute."

Our heavy breathing is the only sound coming from either of us for what feels like an eternity. Why should I believe her? Especially when this entire situation is convenient to the point of straining credibility.

"It just so happened the man gave you ten million the day your brother kidnapped Aspen? You mean to tell me it's all a coincidence? And you had nothing to do with it?"

"That's exactly what I'm trying to tell you. I know it sounds crazy, but I don't understand it any more than you do."

I can't tell if she's lying or not. One thing I've always been able to do is spot lies. Am I losing my touch? Or is it my grip? Is it that I've let her get too close to me?

"Please," she whispers with tears in her eyes. "You have to believe me."

I release her hair and shove her away from me. She hits the bed but remains upright, rubbing her tender scalp.

"There are a lot of things I have to do, but that's not one of them. What I have to do now is make sure you don't leave my sight."

She rubs her tender throat, still breathless. "Ever?"

"You're sure as fuck not going to the dorms now. There I was, about to let you go and have some freedom, and I find this out."

"So I have to stay here?"

"You're pretty sharp at three-thirty in the morning." I jerk a thumb toward the door. "Let's go."

"Where?" she whispers.

I lunge at her, thrilling at the way she cringes. How did I think I could get rid of the part of me that wants to make her do it again? "Where the fuck do you think?" I grunt in her face. "My room. You've lost guest room bed privileges."

"Oh, please. I didn't do anything."

For the first time, I don't hear defiance in her voice. There's no anger, no sharpness. The smart-ass is gone. Now she sounds tired. Weak. Genuinely helpless. I'll chalk it up to the time of night and the fact that she was sleeping soundly before this happened. "Let's go. You wouldn't want to see me when I don't get a good night's sleep."

Her soft whimper makes me laugh as I pull her from the room. It's better this way. I must be losing my touch—the old me would never have considered trusting her to sleep alone. This is how it should be. She needs to be reminded of who she is and who she's dealing with.

I throw her into my bedroom, where she hits the bed and lands awkwardly across it. She's wide-eyed, flushed, and completely at my mercy.

When I advance, she throws an arm over her face in an attempt to protect herself. "Please," she whimpers. "Don't hurt me."

23

DELILAH

"lease," I whisper again. He stops moving. I close my eyes and brace myself.

Until he lets out a deep, exasperated sigh. "I wasn't going to, but you had to lie..." He opens the bedside table, and I know what he's taking out. *Again.*

I thought we were past this point. I was sure. How did we go from him eating me like he was starved to this?

"Don't do this." I know it's a waste of my time, but I can't lie here and let him do this without at least saying something.

"Why? Because you don't deserve it?" He's back to being nasty again. The difference between this version of Lucas and the one from dinner is like night and day. *Which is the real one?*

I know better than to try to fight him off. When he flips me onto my stomach, I go with it. I'm too tired to fight. Might as well get it over with.

Dammit. I can't believe I let myself think things were getting better. How many times have I been burned? Don't I know better by now?

Even biting into my bottom lip doesn't hold in a pained cry when he pulls me to my feet. It feels like my shoulder is going to dislocate.

Just like the first night here, he leaves me on the floor. Unlike that first night, he looks like he wants to kill me.

"It's about punishing me, right?" I'm not going to let myself cry. I won't give him the satisfaction.

His jaw twitches. "Yes. That's right. Be grateful you aren't getting worse." He flips the light off, plunging the room into darkness. I hear his footfalls as he walks around to the side of the bed and climbs in.

While I lie here, knowing my arms are going to cramp up. The only thing that seems to ease some of the pain is the knowledge that the sun will rise in a few hours, and I'll be able to go to classes. But what about tomorrow and the next day? I'm not going to the dorms now.

I don't understand his hot and cold treatment of me. I wasn't lying. I've never heard about that money until now. I could almost die. Ten million dollars? All for me? Since when? My father never gave a shit about me. It has to be a mistake. Someone is lying, and it's not me.

Seconds tick by, which turn into minutes. It's painfully quiet, my own breathing the only thing I can hear. No way am I going back to sleep on this damn floor, especially when I'd bet Lucas will be awake the whole time. Watching over me. Listening for the slightest breath that might be out of place.

I shake my head in disappointment. He thinks I'm lying. I can't believe how much that hurts. *Stupid.* I'm so stupid. All this because he made me come, and I think his opinion matters?

In the end, it does. He decides what happens to me next.

Let him beat me up, use me as a fuck toy, whatever. I can deal with the physical stuff. It's the deeper stuff that gets to me. Being misunderstood has always been the hardest thing for me to deal with. When I try to explain myself, it's no use.

All that does is make the pain worse, like pouring alcohol into an open wound. I bring my knees to my chest, shivering under the throw blanket. At least he's letting me have some form of comfort.

"Are you awake?" I whisper. "Please, if you are, tell me so."

He's going to leave me hanging, the bastard. No way did he fall asleep that fast. Not while being as pissed off as he was. I'm sure his blood pressure is sky high, yet all I get is silence.

"Fine. I'll tell you this while you're asleep." Somehow, in the darkness, it's easier to talk. I can't see him, and he can't see me. The darkness is my protector, and I lean into it, letting it shield me from the pain I'm about to expel.

"When I told you I had no relationship with my family, I meant it. That doesn't mean it was my fault. It wasn't anything I did. I didn't choose to break contact with them."

Then I snicker. "On second thought, I lied. I did do something wrong. I was born a girl, and my asshole sperm donor didn't want a daughter. He wanted boys. Son's because they carry the namesake. I meant less to him than the damn dirt beneath his feet."

A sigh fills the room, and I won't lie, my heart starts to pick up a beat. He's listening.

"That's why I had to live with my aunt," I continue. "He didn't want me around. I was inconvenient. And my brothers? I was probably safer away from them because none of them liked me very much. Matteo complained about me so much..." I pause, remembering the one instance among many. "The one Christmas I actually spent with them, I wasn't allowed to eat with the family. I don't want to think about what he would've done to me or the pain I'd have endured if we lived together."

"What's she doing here?" He looks me up and down with a sneer of contempt twisting his mouth. "Is it some kind of charity thing?"

Disappointment makes me lower my arms, and with them, the gift I hold out to my brother. "Merry Christmas," I offer in a pathetic little whisper.

He snorts, then gives a pointed look at the box in my hands. "You think I want a gift from you? What the hell could you give me? You don't have any money. If you did, you wouldn't be dressed in that Goodwill getup you've got on."

I look down at myself, at the dress I was so proud of when I put it on. Anger starts to bubble toward the surface. "It's not from Goodwill."

He laughs. "It looks like it, and I don't want trash around me on Christmas. Why don't you go back to your trailer, trash? Nobody wants you here."

The memory fades... he wouldn't cry over me if our positions were reversed. He couldn't even share a dinner table with me that Christmas. I ate in the kitchen by myself because he told our father I depressed him. That was the first and last time I was ever invited.

"Prick," Lucas mutters.

"He was that and so much more." I clear my throat. "I know Quinton expected me to be upset over his death, but honestly, that was the last emotion I'd feel. I mean, I wasn't cheering or anything like that, but I wasn't sad either. It was only a matter of time before his asshole ways caught up with him. Truly, I'm shocked it didn't happen sooner."

"Valentine deserved to die." Lucas speaks more to himself than me, but I continue anyway.

"I never spent Christmas or any other holiday with them again. Honestly, I didn't care. I already knew nobody wanted me. I didn't need them getting in my face about it. They didn't even try to put their feelings aside for one day."

It might as well have happened to another person. It feels that long ago. "They sat around, drinking and making plans, while I sat in a corner and kept my mouth shut. One thing they made sure to drill into my head. I could never ever mention living with my aunt, the trailer, or any of that until after the wedding. They wanted it to look like I was an actual member of the family."

My heart hurts so much—and when Lucas doesn't say anything, the pain becomes a deep crater-sized ache in my chest.

Did he fall asleep? Does he not care?

"All because he didn't feel like raising a daughter." Lucas finally speaks, his words soothing some of the ache. I close my eyes and let out a sigh of relief before agreeing.

"I suppose it had to do with the fact that my brothers had potential in the family business. I was nothing but a burden. I spent my whole life feeling worthless and broken." I can't believe I'm saying this. I've never spoken these words out loud, not even to Nash. Especially not him. But I have Lucas's ear, so I need to take advantage. I need to convince him. I need him to trust me.

"Like, why couldn't he love me? What was so wrong with me that nobody wanted me around?"

"But he left you a massive trust fund." There's that edge in his voice again. I should've known it would return. "How does that work?"

"If you ever figure it out, let me know. I don't get it. He never told me there'd be a trust fund. The man probably went weeks or months without even thinking about me. Why would he leave me a single dime?"

"But it's there."

"Then there must be some kind of a mistake. Dick Valentine hated the fact that I was alive. He never checked in on me. He never even threw a few bucks my way—not for food, not to keep the lights on, nothing. He wouldn't have parted with his precious money for my sake."

He has to believe me. He just has to. The only thing I have on my side is the truth, so it has to be enough.

Lucas grunts. "I'll have to look further into it because all the paperwork I've seen looks very official and real."

"Even if he did it, maybe it means he had a change of heart. Maybe he was sick and started looking back on his life and realized he was a worthless piece of shit."

At first, I don't recognize the sound coming from the bed, and then it hits me. Choked laughter. He's laughing. That's a good sign.

"Listen. I get why this looks bad for me, but do I have to sleep on the floor? There's so much room up there."

"I don't think so."

"Please. I'll tell you anything you want to know."

"No need for that."

"What do I have to do? All I'm asking for is to sleep in a bed. The floor is the worst. I'll wake up in so much pain I won't be able to walk straight." It's not a lie. It takes me forever to get my sea legs after sleeping on the floor.

He groans—but sits up, the mattress creaking beneath his frame. Elation, shock? One of those emotions pulses with life inside me.

"The only reason I'm agreeing to this is that I know you won't let me sleep unless I do. But don't get too excited. You'll remain tied up."

"That's fine. In fact, it's great!" It's a small win. I think I got through to him. He's gruff, yes, but that cruelty from before is gone.

He's gentler this time when he helps me off the floor.

"Don't make me regret this, Delilah. You've seen only a sliver of my darkness, don't make me snuff out the last little bits of light that live inside you because I will, and I won't even blink an eye of guilt while I do it."

"I won't. I only want to get a little more sleep."

I can't see his face in the darkness, but I feel his hands on me. He works quickly untying my hands from behind my back, lifting my arms and retying them to the headboard efficiently without hurting me.

My pulse picks up once more as his fingers slide over my pulse. "Don't even think about telling me this isn't necessary," he warns like he senses my thoughts. "I'll meet you halfway on some things, but you have no say in this."

"It's okay." So long as I don't wake up in pain.

Not to mention how interesting it could be to share a bed with him. I wonder if he'll be able to keep his hands off me after a while.

Maybe I can push his buttons a little and make it tougher for him to behave. It might bring us closer, which can only work in my favor. I need to use every tool I have available to me.

Although I don't think the way my pussy tightens, my panties grow damp when he climbs into bed has much to do with using my tools. More like how much fun it might be to let him use me.

24

LUCAS

"*K*nock it the fuck off," I mutter, not for the first time since tying Delilah to the headboard.

"What?" she asks, all innocence.

"You know what. You keep moving closer."

"No, I'm not." If I could see her in the dark, I know I'd find her smiling. Even now, she can't help herself.

"You fucking are, and you need to stop." I turn my back to her so my erection isn't visible under the blanket. "Do it one more time, and you're back on the floor."

"I really didn't mean to."

Tease. I bite back the comment, knowing she'll only argue, and it will all be lies. I knew bringing her up here was a bad idea, but she would never have shut up.

Even the sound of her legs sliding along the sheet is enough to make me harder than before. Those legs were sliding over my back and shoulders earlier when I made her come. I lick my lips, but the taste of her is gone, even if the memory is fresh. Her moans. The way they turned to screams.

If I don't stop thinking about this, I'll never get to sleep. And I'll never be able to keep myself from mauling her. Even now, when I'm more suspicious of her than ever, her body calls to me. How much louder could I make her scream with my cock buried deep in that sweet pussy?

Even the thought of suffering from blue balls isn't enough to push thoughts of her out of my head—especially when she brushes against me again. "Sorry…"

She's not sorry. I want to make her that way, though. Teasing me, pushing me like this. I roll over and find her on her side, her ass angled my way. The nightshirt she's wearing has worked itself up close to her waist, revealing her lacy thong.

"You think it's fun to play games with a man?" I growl, taking her hip in my hand and thrusting against her firm globes.

"I wasn't—" I give another thrust, this time sliding between her cheeks. She moans out the rest of her statement.

"You want to learn what happens when you fuck around?" I whisper in her ear before biting the lobe. She hisses—but pushes against me, wiggling her ass.

I pull back and roll her over. The sight of her there, wrists tied together over her head, sets off that familiar feeling in me. Deeper than lust. That darker side, leaping eagerly to life at the sight of a helpless woman.

With the shirt pushed up over her head, I take her tits in both hands and squeeze until she gasps. "This is what happens." I lower my head, taking one of her tight nipples in my mouth and giving it the same treatment I gave her clit earlier.

And just like before, she writhes under me like a whore. Only she's not putting it on for show, not with her pussy gushing until her thong is plastered to her lips. I stroke her mound while sucking her nipple, and the sound of her moans makes me drip.

She's never had a man like me before. Who wouldn't feel like a king, making her come until she covered my face in her sweet pussy juice? And now, she spreads her legs, jerking her hips to meet my touch. Moaning, her head rolling from side to side, eyes closed. "So good."

I release her nipple, giving it one last flick. "Is it? I should stop, then." Just like that, my hand is gone.

Her eyes fly open. "What? No! Don't stop!"

"Why should I reward you for being a tease?" A light brush against her nipples makes her writhe and moan helplessly.

"Please... it's so good..." She sounds like she's on the verge of tears, which is where I want her. I want her to beg. I want her entire existence to depend on what happens next. Whether or not I grant her pleasure.

"Is it? But you've been a nasty little tease. Rubbing yourself against me. Making sure I couldn't forget you're here." I roll my hips and grind against her pussy.

"Yes! Oh, god!"

"You mean yes, you deliberately fucked with me?" I lap at her nipple until she whines.

"Yes! Yes, I did, I did, and I'm sorry."

That was too easy. I was hoping to drag it out a little more, even with my cock dripping the way it is. "And why did you do that?" I whisper.

"Because I... I mean, I wanted..."

"To screw with me?"

"To do this."

"I see." I move away from her, rolling onto my back at her side. "Thank you for being honest."

"What are you doing?" she asks. She tries to twist herself onto her side so she can face me, but all she manages is to flop around.

"I'm sorry to say you've gotten me hard to the point where I'll have blue balls for hours. I have to come to avoid that." I toss my shorts aside and take myself in hand.

"You're... doing it to yourself?"

"I don't have a choice. Believe me. You think I'm a bastard without blue balls? You haven't seen anything." I sigh while my hand slides up and down.

"But I'm..."

"You're?" I ask, grinning to myself at the whine still in her voice.

"I'm right here. And if there's such a thing as blue clit, I have it." She wiggles closer like she did before, her legs rubbing against mine. "Please."

Fuck, how am I supposed to resist that? I don't plan to, but I'll let her simmer a little longer. It'll be better for both of us that way. "Please, what?" I ask, gritting my teeth to hold on while my hand continues its slow journey over my shaft.

"Really?"

"I need to hear it."

"Please." She draws a hitching breath. "Please. Let me come. Make me come."

"That's not good enough. How should I make you come?"

"With your cock."

Fuck, yes. "More," I groan. "What do you want me to do with it?"

"Um... fuck me?"

"Aren't you sure?"

She sounds pathetic when she whimpers, "Yes. I'm sure." She runs her foot over my leg. I have to bite back a groan. "I want you to fuck me with your cock."

Precum drips onto my fist at the sound of that. She's desperate for it. Hungry for me. For my cock. A woman doesn't sound like that when she's acting.

I'm on her before she can react, rolling her onto her side, away from me. I yank the thong down to her knees while whispering, "Be careful what you wish for."

She's sopping wet, like a river between her swollen lips. Lips I drag my head through, picking up her slickness. The heat is mind-blowing. "Mm, yes. That's nice." She moves with me until I'm hitting her clit.

I let her do it, closing my eyes and grinding my teeth to keep from shooting my load here and now. There's something insanely erotic about the way she moves. She's uninhibited and single-minded. Focused on chasing the high.

Until she starts crashing into me, and I have to take her hip to hold her still. "Don't break it before I get it in you." I slide over her hip, down her thigh, and around to her clit.

She arches against me when I make contact and begin circling it with the tip of my finger. "Ohh..."

"You're going to come for me first," I say before sweeping my tongue over the curve of her ear. She shudders, a high-pitched whine building in her throat that turns to a moan when I sink my teeth into her shoulder.

She's unlocking me. All of me. The savage, the brute. I want to make her come. I need to make her hurt. "How does that sound? You want to come for me?"

"Yes!" she shouts, moving her hips. Grinding against my finger, which means she's grinding against my cock at the same time.

"Show me how much you want it. Be a good girl and show me." I lift her leg and drape it over mine before returning to her needy clit. My strokes are light, rapid, and soon, she's humping my hand for all she's worth. "That's right. Come for me, and you get my cock."

"Yes... yes. I want... I want to come... Oh, god!" She shudders against me, sobbing out her release while her hips keep moving. I keep playing with her, teasing her orgasm out, keeping her on the plateau.

"How long do you think you can go?" I laugh at her broken sob. "Too much?"

"Please, I can't. I can't!" Her body is telling another story, hips still moving, juices coating my fingers.

"Sure, you can. You can come for me again."

"I can't!"

"Then you don't get fucked."

"No!" she sobs, making me laugh again.

"Then come for me, Delilah. Come for me." I bite her again, harder this time, and her back arches before she goes completely still—collapsing against me with a hoarse cry.

I can't wait anymore. She's still coming when I plunge inside her, her muscles rippling, pulling me deeper. "Fuck!" I shout into the darkness. She's tight, even tighter, thanks to her orgasm. And so wet.

"Oh, my god, Lucas!" She bends her knee to spread her legs wider, letting me go even deeper. "Feels so good."

It does. She does. She feels even better when I slide an arm between the pillow and her neck, closing it around her, holding her tight against my shoulder. I tighten it, and she groans but doesn't stop moving with me.

I dig my fingers into her hip, holding her still so I can hammer into her. Her moans turn into one long, hoarse cry cut off by my tightening forearm.

"Yes, that's right," I gasp, pumping faster, breathing heavily in her ear. She barely has enough room to breathe, and her pussy's getting tighter, and my balls tighten with it. "You wanted to get fucked, didn't you?"

Her tits bounce in time with my thrusts, faster and faster. Sweat begins rolling over my forehead, but I take her harder still, slamming into her, and now her pussy begins to tighten again. Her breathless cries turn to squeals before I tighten my grip on her neck, cutting off her air.

And she comes explosively, jerking hard despite my hold on her hip. I release her, letting her gulp in air while I pull out and fist my cock feverishly until I spray cum across her ass.

"Fuck, yes." She's still quivering and moaning while I empty my balls, my cum running over the curves of her cheeks. "Yes, Delilah."

She groans softly in response, limp, probably exhausted after coming so hard and so many times. If she thought my performance in the kitchen was good, what must she think now?

I don't say a word before rolling off the bed and heading for the bathroom. It's easier to see her once I flip on the light in there. She's still flushed, making the cum stand out in contrast. I wet a wash-cloth and take it to her.

She flinches at my touch. "Relax," I whisper while I wash her clean.

Her voice is small. "That was..."

"Intense?" I offer. She nods, her face still turned away from me. "It seemed that way."

"But it was good, too."

"I figured that out, as well." Once I've finished, I toss the cloth into the hamper and kill the bathroom light. By the time I climb into bed, she's on her back again. "Get some sleep."

"Can you untie my wrists now?"

"No. Just go to sleep." After the fucking I gave her, I'm surprised she's still conscious. Eventually, she's going to learn there are only so many requests I can handle before I blow up.

She sighs heavily but gives up the fight. For a long time, there's nothing but the sound of our breathing and the ceiling above me, barely visible in the light from the alarm clock at my side. I don't know why it feels important to stay awake until she's asleep. I only know I can't close my eyes until she's out.

Finally, her breathing evens, slowing down. Once she begins softly snoring—I wonder if she knows she does it—I can relax.

If it were only that easy.

She was trouble for me before this. Now I know what it feels like inside her. How eager she is to be used. How she likes it when I get rough. How tight her pussy is when she's coming on my cock. And I don't know if I can go back to a life where fucking her isn't an option.

What am I supposed to do now?

25

DELILAH

Something wakes me up. A noise. Nothing scary or loud enough to startle me, but loud enough to stir me out of a deep sleep.

My first thought: How long was I asleep?

My second thought: Holy shit, he untied my wrists while I was asleep.

Here they are, my hands tucked under my pillow, the way I usually sleep. I can't remember him doing it. I usually don't sleep deep enough that somebody would be able to mess with me without my knowing.

But then, I've never come like I did last night. I didn't even know it was possible to come like that. Not alone, not with somebody else. I thought I was dying for a minute there. It felt so good that it hurt, especially when he kept me going after I would normally have stopped. Once I'm finished, I'm finished, but he wasn't hearing any of that.

I'm glad.

I wonder what else I don't know. I never thought sex could be good for both my partner and me. I just figured it was a way to keep a guy happy. Not like I was grossed out by it. I just didn't really see any other point.

Now I know what it was that woke me: Lucas typing on his laptop. Once I open my eyes, I see him sitting at his desk, and for a second, all I can do is watch him. The light from the computer reveals his serious expression, like whatever he's working on is important. I don't want to make too much noise and distract him.

Really, what I don't want is the awkwardness of talking over what we did. It's funny how what seems totally normal and logical when you're in the moment can turn embarrassing. I don't know how to act. I don't want to make a big deal about it, especially if he doesn't want to. I guess I should hold back and let him lead the way.

"You're awake."

The suddenness of his announcement startles me. It doesn't seem like he's so much as glanced over here, yet he knows I'm awake. "Barely," I murmur, snuggling with the blankets and pillow. "You untied me."

"Mm-hmm." He still won't look at me. That's not a good sign. Is he regretting it? How could he not be? That's a stupid question. I don't know how to convince him he has nothing to worry about. It's not so much that I care about his feelings. In fact, I couldn't care less about them. Not for his sake.

For mine, though? I need him in a good mood. He's always nicer to me when he's horny, but I guess that doesn't make him different from any other man. That's how I need him. Horny, generally happy.

So instead of sitting up right away, I let my bare leg hang out from under the blankets. That earns me a quick sideways glance, but he turns his attention right back to the laptop. "What time is it?" I ask in a soft voice.

It takes him a second to answer. "Just past seven." So I didn't sleep all that long, but it was enough. I feel rested, wide awake. All it took was a few orgasms. I have to struggle against a smile that wants to creep over my face when I think about it. I still can't believe it happened.

"Do you always work this early?"

"Sometimes. It depends."

"I mean, there are other things you could do with the time..." I add a soft laugh to the end of that.

"Such as what?" His eyes are still trained on the screen, but he doesn't sound as distant. His hands aren't moving so swiftly over the keyboard. He's paying attention now.

"You know what I mean. Why don't you come back over here?" I scoot back on the bed, giving him room.

He doesn't so much as glance my way. "That's not happening."

"Why not?"

"Are we seriously going to do this today?" Now there's an edge in his voice. I need to be careful. It's impossible to tell where his line is from one day to the next.

"I'm sorry. I figured since you enjoyed it so much earlier, you might want to do it again."

"You figured wrong."

Dammit. There has to be a way to get him back to where we were. I can't rub myself against him while he's sitting in his chair and pretend I didn't mean to. That option is off the table. What else can I do? I never exactly had to seduce Nash, and he's the extent of my experience with things like this.

I sit up, making a big deal of stretching. He never did pull the nightshirt back down over my body last night, leaving it up around my wrists. He must have taken it off when he untied me, so now I'm totally naked. I pull the blanket up over my chest, but not too far. More than enough is visible to get his imagination going.

"I figured you'd be in a better mood once you woke up." One of my legs hangs over the edge of the bed. I swing it a little to catch his eye. It works.

Only it doesn't have the intended effect. He scowls and mutters something under his breath. "You can stop doing this. I don't feel like playing games today."

"Come on," I murmur with a smile. "Don't be that way."

"We need to talk about last night." He pushes away from the desk, swiveling his chair to face me. There's nothing about his body language or his pinched expression when he gets a full look at my near-nakedness to tell me he's thinking anything sexy. That is not a good sign.

"Did I do something wrong?" Maybe if we get talking about it, he'll soften up a little. Or harden up. Whatever keeps him in a good mood.

"What? No. That's not what I meant."

"I mean, I'm not super experienced. I guess you figured that out already."

"I told you, that isn't what I meant. We don't have to talk about it."

"What did you want to talk about, then?" I'm stalling. It's pathetically obvious. But I know what's coming, and I'm trying to avoid that.

"It can't happen again. That was a one-time thing."

Dammit. I can't believe how disappointing it is to hear that. "But I thought it was good."

He pinches the bridge of his nose, eyes squeezed shut. "That's not the problem. And you know it. Drop the innocent act, would you?"

"But it was good. Don't pretend it wasn't."

"What is your point?"

"I just want to be sure I didn't do anything wrong. I mean, it's sort of insulting. Hey, we fucked, and it's never happening again. No explanation."

"What do I need to explain? You have to know it was a bad idea. Just because it felt good doesn't make it any less of a terrible idea."

"I'm not going to tell anybody."

He shoots me a filthy look. "You'd better fucking know you're not going to tell anybody."

"I won't." I fold my arms and possibly pout a little. "I didn't tell anybody about the other times, did I?"

"We're finished talking about this." He turns back to his laptop. "You should go to your room and get dressed."

I can't do that unless I know something. "I'm really not moving to the dorms?"

"I already said you aren't, didn't I?" he fires back while typing something, his attention on his work. This probably isn't the time to remind him he doesn't always stick to his word.

I'll put up with a lot, but I don't stick around where I'm not wanted. I still have a little pride left, even if it doesn't always look that way.

I drop the blankets and get out of bed, wasting no time leaving the room. It's a little too cold in here for me, and I'm not wearing clothes. He doesn't acknowledge me again.

The asshole. I should've known better. He used me and had fun, but now that his dick's soft, I'm back to being garbage. Someone for him to push around, threaten, all that. He's still pissed about the money. It's his stupid pride. He thinks I lied about it, and he can't bring himself to believe me.

I flop down on the bed, which is as messy as I left it earlier this morning when he pulled me out of it. I should be mad at him for that and for so many other things—and I am. But right now, disappointment is winning out.

My shoulder stings where he bit me. I give the area a gentle touch and wince. What's wrong with me for liking it as much as I did? It was like I came even harder because of it. I think he did, too. It felt dirty and wrong and even hurt, but it was the same kind of hurt that's now throbbing between my legs. The kind that also makes me smile to myself.

What the hell is wrong with me? I'm lying here like I have a crush or something. He's brutal and disgusting, and the only reason he matters is he's sort of holding my life in his hands. He'll come back around once he gets an itch in his pants again. It's only a matter of time, especially when I'm staying here instead of moving to a dorm room.

I'm glad of that, even though it means risking his temper flare-ups. I'd rather deal with him than Quinton. Or, maybe worse, a surprise visit from Aspen.

Shit.

The memory of her makes me remember the phone. It's still safely tucked away under the mattress when I check for it. The door's closed—I don't hear Lucas in the living area, so he's probably still at his desk. I should be safe to check it.

I power it up while pulling clothes on, and by the time I'm finished, the home screen pops up. I have a text. My heart jumps into my throat before I glance toward the door again, just in case.

Preston: Thinking about it. You need to be friends with her. Get closer. Make her trust you.

That's all. He sent it early last night and didn't follow up with anything else. For instance, the slightest clue how I'm supposed to do the impossible.

A million red flags wave like crazy in my brain as I stare at the text like it's going to miraculously change. How the hell am I supposed to be her friend, even by pretending? And it would definitely have to be pretend since there's no fucking way I'd ever be her real friend. Not after what she's done.

I'm sure her husband would stand in the way. What about that? He's probably wedged so far up her ass that she doesn't make a move without him. He won't let me within ten feet of her. So that's sort of a wall I'm going to have to get over.

Then there's the whole part where I have nothing in common with the girl. I couldn't possibly. Little Miss Golden-haired Angel. It doesn't matter that bad things happened to her. She didn't grow up like I did.

I don't even know how to make friends. I never had any, no real ones. Other people seemed to make friends so easily, like it was nothing. I was always on the outside, looking in. What do I do? Walk up to her and announce we should be besties? Yeah, that would work. She would only make sure to avoid me from then on.

Me: No way.

My thumb hovers over the button to send the message, but I can't bring myself to do it. I don't want him to be mad at me. I did say I'd do everything I could, too. But this is something I can't do.

He's not going to want to hear that. Nash deserves justice, and Preston wants to make sure Aspen suffers for every stab wound.

I have to at least try. For Nash.

I delete the first message and type another one instead. I don't know how I'll make it happen, but I see the point. If she trusts me, she'll let me get closer to her. And that's when she'll be vulnerable.

Me: Okay. I'll keep you posted.

I send the text before turning off the phone and returning it to its hiding place. Did I promise more than I can deliver? I sure as hell hope not.

26

LUCAS

"We need a session. Now."

Lauren looks up at me from the thick text balanced on her legs. She's sitting at her desk with her ankles crossed on top, leaning back in her chair. "Excuse me?" she asks, arching an eyebrow.

"I said I need a session immediately."

"You do realize you could have just barged in here while I was seeing a student, right?"

"And?"

"And there's still such a thing as doctor-patient confidentiality. I owe my patients privacy and peace of mind. I can't promise either with a clear conscience if there's a risk of you charging into my office like you're ready to set the desk on fire."

"Are you finished?" I drop to the couch before rolling up my sleeves.

"This is unprofessional and, frankly, unacceptable. I'm sorry, but I have to set boundaries."

"Dick Valentine set up a ten-million-dollar trust fund for Delilah the day Aspen was kidnapped."

Her silence speaks volumes. I have the grim satisfaction of watching her process this while I make myself comfortable. "You ready now?" I ask once her mouth finally snaps shut.

"That's a big piece of information. I assume it's been verified."

"Nic was offended when I asked."

"I'm sure." She purses her lips before blowing out a heavy sigh. "And how do you feel about this?"

I can only sit and stare at first. "You're joking."

"One thing it's crucial to guard against in this line of work is making assumptions. I can only help if I know your feelings, in your words."

"I want to kill somebody."

"And?"

"And it's been hours since I found out, but the feeling hasn't subsided."

"I know I said I have to avoid assumptions, but I assume you haven't fallen back on any of the exercises I've described."

"Fuck the exercises!"

Her head snaps back. "All right, then."

"What do you want me to say?"

She's firm and calm in her response. "I want you to think twice before screaming at me. Please."

"Fine. I'll think twice." After taking a few deep breaths, I try again. "I'm beyond enraged."

"Why?"

"For fuck's sake."

"We have to get to the bottom of why you feel the way you do. It might not be the reason you think it is."

"Give me a break."

She's stone-faced when she points at the door. "Why are you here if you're not going to take my offers to help seriously? If you want somebody to nod and tell you how right you are, you're in the wrong office."

"So you think I'm wrong?"

"I think you need to work through your reaction. Remember? We've talked about this. You tend to jump at the first, strongest reaction. Anger. Violence."

"It's instinct."

"The nice thing about being human rather than an animal is the ability to think beyond our instincts. You have a mind. You have intelligence." When all I do is groan, she groans along with me. "It's what you said you wanted to learn, isn't it? Getting over the habit of lashing out before thinking?"

"I'm not in the mood to learn."

"Who's surprised?" She cracks a grin. "Now that we've calmed down a little, I need you to explain something to me. What difference does this discovery make? What connection have you drawn?"

"The obvious connection. Dick paid her off somehow."

"She wasn't present during the attack."

"So she says."

"What about everything she's told you before now?"

"Lies, obviously. She's been covering her ass."

"Do you honestly believe that?"

Dammit. She had to use the word *honestly*. "Yes."

"No, you don't. You hesitated."

I shouldn't have bothered coming here. "If I didn't know better, I'd think you were getting off on challenging me."

"Who, me?" She shakes her head. "I'm truly not. But I do believe you have doubts about your theory."

I can't help but recall Delilah's story. It doesn't take much to imagine Dick Valentine being that cruel, and I already know how he raised his monster of a son. Blazing heat rolls through me at the thought of what my daughter suffered, thanks to that family.

"She's too bitter when she talks about them to be faking it," I admit. "I can't make myself forget that."

"For what it's worth, I've examined enough students to know what it sounds like when they're lying for sympathy. She strikes me as the real deal."

"So what does it mean?"

"I don't know. What do you think it means?"

"I think it means I shouldn't have bothered with this."

"Okay, fine." She holds up her hands when I stand. "Hold it. I can take off my doctor hat for a minute or two since it's clear you're in no shape to get to the bottom of your feelings on your own. Have a seat and hear me out before you charge out."

I lower myself to the couch slowly, staring hard at her. "This had better be good."

"Even if you don't like hearing it?" I can't help groaning because who likes hearing shit they don't want to know about themselves? Especially me. I admit I have faults, but that doesn't leave me longing to shine a flashlight on them.

With her elbows propped on the table, she rests her chin on the tips of her fingers. "Are you sure you're not looking for a reason to be outraged? Because there's no proof she had anything to do with the trust being set up. The man owed her at least that much after years of ignoring and hurting her."

The comment goes unaddressed. "Do you think it's possible you're looking for reasons to hate Delilah?"

I can almost taste her skin, even now. My cock wakes up at the memory of her screams. Reasons to hate her? Yes. To hate her and to hurt her. "It's more than that," I murmur, willing my cock to behave.

"What else is there?"

"Aspen, obviously. I can't trust this girl until I know for sure she's innocent."

"And if she is? Are you willing to accept that and move on? Or will you continue looking for excuses to let that brutal side of yourself out to play?"

I'D NORMALLY RETURN to my office at this time of day, but I wouldn't get a moment's work done with Delilah on my mind. Lauren's little speech did nothing to ease the knot I'd carried in my gut all day.

I have to stop things with her. I have no idea how.

And I don't want to.

When I enter the apartment, the pair of women who normally clean during the day are still wrapping up their work. They jump like they've been electrocuted at my sudden entrance. "We're almost finished," one of them babbles, and the other nods.

"I'll stay out of your way." They're in the kitchen. I'll go to my room. I'm waiting for Delilah's return. I need to see her. I need to know she's here, locked up, away from anyone she might be able to hurt. If she's capable of it, anyway.

On my way past the kitchen table, a pair of scissors catches my eye. They're the only thing lying there, shining against the polished wood.

One of the cleaners notices me studying them. "I found them under the mattress in the guest room while I was changing the linens." It comes out sounding like an apology, delivered with eyes downcast.

Son of a bitch.

"Thank you for setting them aside," I offer, with what little calm I still possess, while inside my skull, there's nothing but a raging fire. My hands close around the back of the nearest chair. "Did you say you're almost finished?"

"Just about."

"Why don't we call it done for today? I'm sure everything's fine."

She looks at the chair, or rather at the way my hands squeeze the back of it. "Okay. Thank you." It comes out as little more than a squeak, and within moments, I'm alone.

The chair splinters when I pick it up and throw it to the floor. "Fuck!" I scream at the empty apartment.

Scissors. I don't know where she got them. I only know she was hiding them. For what? To use on whom? Not on me—she has to know better than to try it, even while I'm asleep. I haven't had a night of deep sleep in as long as I can remember. She could try, but she'd end up with those fuckers buried in her instead.

On Aspen?

And they were here, in my apartment, for who knows how long. I completely missed it. She could've carried them with her in the halls and stabbed Aspen.

Lauren's voice rings out in my head, barely rising over the chaos. *Are you making this up to be angry with her? How do you know they weren't meant for self-defense?*

I'm sure if I were to ask, that would be the excuse she'd give. That's why I'm not going to bother asking. I'm going to show them to her before...

What? What am I going to do?

I can see myself holding them to her throat. Watching up close as her eyes bulge, then fill with tears. As the color drains from her face. As she struggles to stop trembling for fear of driving the blades into her own flesh by mistake.

Is this what Lauren meant about using her as an excuse to let my darker side out to play? Why am I bothering to ask myself? Of course, it is. And it's damn tempting. Making her hurt. Feeling her tears hit my skin. The look in her eye when she understands her life belongs to me.

I don't want to be that man anymore. Right? I'm not sure now. Not when the evidence of her lies and schemes is in front of me.

She'll be back any minute. I have to make a decision. Do I confront her? I can't avoid it, nor do I want to. It would be irresponsible to let her go on thinking she's got me fooled. I have to put an end to this.

I close my hand around the cool metal. How will she react when she sees me holding them? I want to savor her fear, the moment of realization when she knows she's been bested.

She's here. My heart thunders in my chest, adrenaline racing through my veins.

I clutch the metal handle tighter.

The knob turns.

I raise the scissors, so they'll catch her eye immediately.

The door begins to open slowly, and it feels like I'm a child waiting for Christmas morning. One second passes, then another. I expect the metal gleam of the scissors to catch her eye first, but it doesn't.

"What happened?" Delilah's eyes are wide as she takes in the sight of the broken chair. She closes the door slowly while staring at what's left of the chair on the floor.

Somehow, I manage to keep my voice even. "I knocked it over. Walking around while reading something on my phone."

Her gaze finally lifts from the floor, and I can see the moment that she realizes she's been caught.

Fear trickles into her features, her hazel eyes are glued on the scissors, and I can imagine the thoughts circling her mind. Her cheeks grow flush, and her pupils dilate.

She's probably trying to come up with an excuse, but there isn't one. At least not one that she would want to admit to, especially not to me. I know I'm not that man anymore, or at least part of me isn't him, but I just can't help myself. The desire to give in to the game of cat and mouse is too much for me.

"I'll give you one opportunity to explain why these were stuffed between the mattresses in the guest bedroom, and it better be a worthy one."

Her lips tremble, they fucking tremble, but no words spill from them. I can't tell if I'm more pissed to find the scissors or that she won't admit why she took them in the first place.

Before I can think my next step through, she rushes toward the hallway as if she can really escape me. With minimal effort, I meet her at the mouth of the hall and cut her off.

I don't think I simply react and reach out; my fingers sink deep into her hair as I grab a handful of the locks and pull her into my face. She struggles like a mouse caught in a trap.

Inhaling through my nose to try to calm myself so I don't snap her neck right this second, I catch a whiff of her scent. Fear, but there's something else. *Man.* She smells manly like spice and citrus... like me.

The thought makes me pause for half a moment, and our gazes collide. Her teeth sink into her bottom lip to stop it from trembling.

I tighten my hold on her hair, but she doesn't so much as whimper.

"Tell me, did you plan to use these on me in the middle of the night? Or were you saving them for a special occasion?"

She tries to shake her head, but I want her words.

"Speak!" I yell into her face.

I need to terrify her, to remind her that I'm in charge and that no matter what we've done together, nothing will ever change that.

"No." Her voice cracks. "I... I took them to protect myself."

My lip curls. "From what? Have I hurt you? Have I tried to use a weapon on you?"

"No...but..."

Before she can continue, I bring the blade of the scissors to her throat. I watch with delight as her throat bobs, and I press the blade harder, watching as a thin line of crimson appears on the blade and her creamy white flesh.

I can see her pulse pick up, but she doesn't dare move. It wouldn't take much pressure for me to slit her throat and watch her bleed out on the floor, but I don't want to kill her. I want to terrify her. I want her afraid, worried that if I ever find her with a weapon again, she might die at my hands.

"I hope my intention is clear, Delilah." I speak the words into the shell of her ear. "Because I know yours were. You planned to use these scissors, if need be, against me. That's very brave of you, but also incredibly stupid." I ease the pressure on the blade a smidge and watch the relief fill her features before I do it all over again and press the blade into her skin a little harder. "If I ever find you with another weapon or the knowledge that you might try to kill me, your ending will be far worse than this. Do you understand me?"

The warmth of her body against mine, and the way she's trembling, makes my cock rock hard. It wouldn't take much to have her on her hands and knees, myself pounding into her from behind, but that's not what this is about. It's deeper than that.

"I understand." The words come out as a whisper, and I pull the scissors away and release her like she is on fire. She stumbles, and her knees knock together as she tries to regain her balance.

My eyes move to her throat and the tiny rivulet of blood that mars her skin. This strange urge to smear her blood across her skin overtakes me, but I clench my hand into a fist and ignore the ache.

"Get out of my sight before I do something that you'll regret."

Like a wounded animal, she scampers away, a hand to her throat as if I've gutted her, and she is bleeding out. I walk in the opposite direction and go into the kitchen to make myself a drink.

I could've killed her, I think to myself, but you didn't.

27

DELILAH

"*B*itch."

I don't even bother pretending to care anymore. That's the thing about hearing people calling you names every day. Eventually, it stops mattering. So long as they keep it this way and don't start getting physical, I can take it.

Aside from that, things haven't been too bad the past few days. After the scissor incident, Lucas is up my ass most of the time. I can't make a move without his approval. He won't let me sleep alone, but he hasn't touched me since that night in his bed. That part, I'm trying not to take it personally.

Besides, it's not like he won't eventually break down and give in to what he wants. I feel the way he looks at me. I bet he can't stop thinking about that night. I know I can't. I'm actually a little sad that the bite marks are fading. I wonder what Doctor Lauren would think about that. It must mean I'm a complete freak.

"Hey."

I was so busy fantasizing that I didn't notice Marcel falling in step beside me on the way down the hall. He's not so much walking with me as he's walking nearby. I get it. He doesn't want anybody connecting us.

"Hey," I murmur, looking at the floor. "Where were you this morning?" He doesn't understand how my life revolves around our meetings in class. Not that we talk about much, but I need the reminder that I'm not alone.

"I overslept."

"I was worried."

He only grunts. "How's it going with her?"

I don't answer until we're past a cluster of girls, all of whom shoot me dirty looks. It gives me a second to come up with an excuse, at least. "I haven't had a lot of time to do anything. I don't get a lot of freedom."

"You haven't even tried yet?"

My heart sinks in desperation. What does he want from me? I'm not a miracle worker. "It's not like there's any chance of us running into each other. We have nothing in common."

"You'll have to think of something. Don't you have any classes together?"

"No," I whisper, and now I'm looking at the floor to hide the frustrated tears that want to fill my eyes. I manage to blink them back. Once again, I'm trying to explain myself, but the idiot I'm talking to doesn't want to hear it.

"She likes books," he mutters as we turn a corner. Nobody seems to be paying attention.

"How do you know?"

"I've seen her outside the library a lot. You should pretend you like books, too. You could meet her there."

Pretend to like books? *Um, I like books, too.* I want to say but don't. "Okay. I'll see what I can do."

"You'd better. We've been waiting long enough to get to her. We have one chance at it. Don't screw it up for us." That's not exactly my fault, but it's not like I'd say it out loud even if Marcel didn't haul ass without warning.

I have a free period, meaning I could go to the library now. I don't know if she'll be there, but it might look more legit if I set up a habit of hanging out there. She could still be watching her back for all I know.

It isn't Aspen I have to worry about.

It's her asshole husband.

I barely realize it's him rushing at me until I'm already crashing against the wall.

"What the fuck do you think you're doing?" he snarls in my face.

"What did I do?" I whisper, and I hate myself for whispering because it makes me look scared.

"Don't fuck around with me. I saw you talking to him."

"To who?"

"Enough!" He pulls his fist back, and I cringe away from the pain I expect to explode across my face. When he hits the wall beside my head, it doesn't make me feel much better.

"You were talking with that piece of shit, Marcel, and don't pretend otherwise." He leans in close, blocking out almost everything around us. "I saw you."

I should've known. It doesn't matter how hard I try to watch out. Somebody's always paying attention. "He's in my math class. He was absent today and was asking me about what he missed."

"You're full of shit."

"It's the truth. What, I'm being forced to take classes here, but I can't talk to anybody about anything?"

"You have a habit of talking to the wrong people."

"How would I know, either way? I don't know who's who."

"Right." The snide smile he wears tells me what he thinks of that. It's not even completely a lie. If Marcel hadn't told me who he is, I would've figured he hates me as much as everybody else around here.

"If I didn't know better, I would think you miss your friends. Remember them? Rick and Bruno?" I can't pretend the idea doesn't chill me, which only makes his smile widen. Like he's genuinely happy to see me shiver. "I can send you right back there and bring them in to watch you again. Only this time, the rules won't be so stringent."

"What's going on?"

It's like magic. The sound of Aspen's voice changes him. He's still scowling openly, but he's not blocking me anymore.

She works magic on me, too, but in the opposite direction. My heart was already pounding, but now it's thanks to the rush of being so close to her. The murdering piece of shit.

But now she's here, in front of me, and I can't waste time imagining how I wish I had the guts to kill her. Quinton might've done me a favor in the end.

One thing I know how to do is fake a smile. "Hi. We were just chatting."

The skeptical look she gives him makes me wonder if she's already warned him against messing with me. It gives me hope, as much as I don't want to ever be grateful to her for anything.

I have work to do, though. I've got to focus on that. "I better get going. I wanted to check out the library, and I still keep getting lost in this place."

Aspen's eyes light up. God, I hate her. "I can show you! I could find it with my eyes closed."

"Could you? I was afraid I'd end up missing half my free period just trying to find it."

"It's not that difficult," Quinton mutters.

He's not even going to bother pretending this doesn't piss him off, is he? It's not easy to act like I don't notice.

"So how is everything going?" Aspen asks as we walk. I catch a few curious looks from others as we pass them by. I'm sure they're asking themselves what the hell we're doing together.

"It's going okay, I think." Is she for real? I can't figure out if she's asking because she genuinely wants to know or because she's pretending. Then again, when I remember what she's done, it's easier to go with pretending. Nothing about her is real. She's just putting on an act.

"Good. I know you'll love the library. It's where I spend a lot of my time. And Brittney is the best. She's really cool."

I wonder if her idea of cool and mine are even remotely the same. "Is she the librarian?"

"That's only a small part of what she's capable of. Believe me." Yeah, I guess I'll have to. Why does she sound so excited? I've never been able to stand people like her. She's so fake.

It's all worth it, though. And not only because this means I'm one step closer to living up to my promise. I can feel Quinton burning holes in the back of my head. He's absolutely furious his little wifey is even speaking to me, much less acting so friendly.

So even though having her this close to me and forcing myself to have a conversation feels a lot like I'm getting my teeth pulled one at a time, I can put on a happy face without much effort. It seems like the better we get along with each other, the more pissed he gets. It's sort of a bonus, in a way. I almost want to thank him for making my job easier.

When we enter the library, I have to take a second and look around. I can admit it's striking, and I feel very small under its high ceiling. "Wow," I whisper. "This is really nice."

"You don't need to whisper, you know," Quinton mutters.

From the corner of my eye, I see Aspen look at him over her shoulder and roll her eyes. I have to pretend I don't see, though, and again, I need to hide a smile.

"Aren't you supposed to whisper in a library?" I ask.

"Yes," Aspen assures me with a firm nod. "I always feel like I need to, as well." Oh, goody. Something we have in common.

I'm ready to assume the place is empty until somebody pops up from behind the reference desk. Somebody with blue hair. Somebody whose smile falters a little when she catches sight of me. I'm guessing she knows who I am. I never had a chance here. Nobody is ever going to see me for me.

"Brittney, this is Delilah. She needed a little help finding her way here." Something about the way Aspen speaks—slowly, clearly, deliberately—tells me there's another conversation going on here. Be cool. Don't make a big deal about it.

And Brittney picks up on the message, judging by the way her confusion seems to clear up. "Good to meet you, Delilah. It'll be nice having somebody else around here every once in a while. Especially someone who likes books, which I'm assuming you do if you're here?"

"It seems kind of empty in here," I observe with a wince.

"Some people just don't want to be exposed to literature." It doesn't seem to bother her too much. She shrugs it off. "Anyway, I'd love to show you around."

"That would be great. Thanks." I glance at Aspen, lifting my eyebrows. Brittney does the same.

"You know what? I think I'll come with you guys." And obviously, wherever she goes, Quinton goes. I wonder what that's like. He must be obsessed with her. Nobody could say I have experience with healthy relationships, but even I see the red flags here. It's like she can't make a move without him.

Though I'm sure my presence has a lot to do with that. "Do you come here a lot?" I ask her while he glowers at me. I'm surprised he hasn't dragged a finger across his throat yet.

"All the time," Aspen says. "This place has been my refuge." Right, because she was tormented way worse than I've been when she first came here. I remember hearing stuff about that. I guess this would make the perfect refuge, with no other students bothering to come in. It's almost like nobody is actually here to learn. What a shock.

"Besides," she adds, nudging Brittney. "It gave me the chance to make a good friend."

"That's good to know. Maybe I will, too," I suggest with a shrug. Brittney winks at me, which seems like a pretty good sign. I guess she's willing to take Aspen's word for it, like if she thinks I'm okay, it's good enough for her. She definitely can't be paying any attention to Quinton, who is now almost audibly growling behind me. I can't wait until I'm away from them, so I can laugh myself sick over it.

He needs to learn how to control his reactions rather than being so obvious—unless this is all an attempt at intimidating me, which is probably exactly what he's trying to do. He has no idea who he's dealing with if he thinks a little growling and a shove against the wall is going to make me break down. If everything that happened to me in that filthy, cold, lonely room wasn't enough to do it, how could he break me down?

I have absolutely no doubt he'd send me back there if he could. But I doubt he can, not anymore. Not with Aspen trying to make friends, and not without Lucas getting involved. I still don't think he likes me very much as a person, but he's not thinking about me as a person when he's inside me. The thought makes me blush a little while Brittney shows me the different sections of the library.

The more I think about it, the easier it is to see how perfect this is. If Lucas wonders where I am, I can tell him I'm going to the library. He can't possibly have a problem with that—and if he does, maybe I can get Brittney to talk to him. She does seem pretty cool, as much as I hate to agree with anything Aspen says.

The next time I talk to Marcel, I'll have good news for him.

28

LUCAS

"*I promise. I won't ever do it again.*"

I press the tip of the blade against her creamy flesh, my cock surging as I work it in and out of her tight cunt. Fear tightens her muscles, squeezing me until it's almost a challenge to move. Greedy slut, trying to milk the cum from me.

"*How do I know for sure?*" *I push a little harder, savoring the sharp gasp immediately followed by a thin trickle of blood tracing a path down her chest.*

"*I swear!*" *She's weeping, yet the fresh, hot juice coating my cock tells another story.* "*Please, stop hurting me!*"

The sharp knock on my office door brings reality crashing down around me. I was roughly three seconds from pulling my aching cock through my open fly and jerking off to the fantasy of what I want to do with those fucking scissors and the girl who thinks she can hide shit from me. It's been impossible to think of anything else, even while I'm in my office.

Whoever it is, I hope they don't expect me to stand while I greet them. "Come in," I bark after adjusting myself.

Quinton barrels into the room, red-faced, eyes blazing. "We have a problem."

My pulse picks up speed. "What is it? Is Aspen—"

"She's fine," he grunts. "For now. Unless she and Delilah get even friendlier."

"They're becoming friends?"

He drives one fist into the other palm. "I swear to God. What is it with her? She's determined to have everything her way."

"Slow down. Start from the beginning." One of us has to keep a calm head, and it's not going to be Quinton when he's practically breathing fire. "What's happened?"

"She wanted to go to the library. Made a point of mentioning it to Aspen out in the hall. Don't tell me that was a coincidence." He barks out a sharp laugh.

"Why were they together at all?"

He lowers his gaze to the floor. "We ran into her."

"Look at me." He lifts his eyes slowly, begrudgingly. "What are you doing to Delilah out there? Have you been following her around? Fucking with her?"

"And if I did? Who would try to stop me?"

"I'm not trying to stop you. I wish you would've let me know you were, though. People see what you do and follow your example. If there's going to be trouble, I need to know in advance."

"I wasn't doing anything much," he admits before sinking into a chair and scrubbing a hand over his head. "Most of the time, I try to avoid that bitch. I don't want to see her—and I'd rather Aspen not have to see her, either. The fewer reminders, the better."

"I would do the same."

"But I saw her in the hallway, talking with that piece of shit, Marcel. I couldn't help myself."

Marcel. His face flashes across my mind's eye. "They were talking? Were you close enough to hear?"

"No," he grunts. "She said they were talking about homework."

"Did it seem like they were?"

"Not even slightly. I've seen enough people trying to make it look like they're not acting suspicious. They might as well have worn signs advertising it."

"What do you know about him?"

"He always wanted to be better friends with Matteo and Rico than he actually was. One of those losers who kisses ass constantly, hoping to become closer with the group."

"Nobody important, though."

"No—but I don't trust him."

Neither do I. Talking with her out in the hallway. I can almost see them together. What game is she playing now? Trying to get her allies together? Did she know him before coming here?

What were they really talking about?

Did he touch her?

"So I got in her face a little. Reminded her she's not here to make friends. Then out of nowhere, she tells Aspen she was on her way to the library."

Since when is she interested in the library? "I see."

"You know Aspen. She jumped at the idea. She doesn't get it."

"No. She wouldn't." It isn't easy to be fond of her kindness at a time like this. After everything she's been through, she's the last person who should be kind. That's one thing she certainly didn't inherit from me.

"I'm not about to let Aspen spend a minute alone with her."

"Follow your instincts on this. I know you'll keep her safe." I tent my fingers under my chin, staring over his head at the wall but seeing Delilah. Flirting with Marcel, touching his arm, making the same suggestive comments to him as she's made to me so many times.

"That bitch needs to stay away from my wife."

"Leave that to me."

"You'll keep her away?"

"I'll do what I can. Including talking to her and Marcel. They have class together, you say?" He nods. "Not for much longer. Get to class or wherever you need to be now. I'll take care of things."

Marcel will be lucky to have a face by the time I'm finished with him. Nobody touches what belongs to me—and as long as she's staying with me, under my watch, Delilah is mine.

Within fifteen minutes of my sending for him, Marcel steps into my office. The sight of his face turns my stomach while my fists clench under the desk. "You wanted to see me?" he asks nonchalantly.

A moment later, Delilah knocks at the partially open door. The apprehension written on her face turns to understanding once she sets eyes on Marcel. "Sorry," she mumbles. "I can wait until you're finished."

She thinks she's clever. "I wanted to see both of you at once, as a matter of fact. Come in. Close the door behind you."

Marcel is still clueless, his gaze bouncing back and forth between Delilah and me. "What's this about?"

"I understand the two of you have a class together."

"Yeah. We have math together." Marcel glances at her again. "So?"

"Not anymore." I pull up his schedule on my laptop. "You'll be taking math Tuesday and Thursday afternoons for the rest of the semester."

His eyes go wide. "Why?"

It's not his reaction I'm watching. It's hers. She's staring at the floor, chewing her lip. Unwilling to look at me. She's hiding something.

"Because I said so. I'm sure you won't have trouble making the change." I forward the information to his school email address. "And now you have the time and room number in your email account."

"I don't understand why this is happening." His gaze turns hostile as he places his clenched fist on my desk.

"Are you forgetting whose office you're standing in?" I shoot a pointed look toward his hands, which he shoves into his pockets with a grunt. "It's happening because I say it is. Now, the two of you have no reason to meet up in the halls and chat."

I turn my full attention to her and relish the way she squirms. "Right?" I prompt.

"Right," she whispers before sliding a glance toward Marcel.

I look at him, smiling, though I know the expression doesn't reach my eyes. Nor do I intend it to. He's lucky he'll live beyond this moment. "Do you have anything else to say?" I ask.

He blows out a heavy sigh but isn't stupid enough to argue. "No. Message received."

"You can go." The sooner he's out of my sight, the better for him.

Delilah, however, thinks I'm speaking to both of them. She starts to follow him to the door, freezing when I clear my throat. "No. Not you. We have more to discuss." Marcel leaves without a backward glance. What a fucking surprise. He doesn't give a shit about the fact that he might've gotten her in trouble. Too busy thinking about himself.

The moment he's out of the room, she whirls around. "You can't blame me for this."

"Excuse me?" Standing, I glare at her until she shrinks back. "Who the fuck do you think you're talking to? I can see that asshole getting an attitude. He's not as intimately acquainted with me as you are."

She begins to back away as I advance, and that's good. It satisfies me. When she's afraid and under my control.

"You should know better," I murmur. "Just as you should know better than to make friends around here. Let me spare you the trouble. Nobody around here wants to be your friend, nor do you deserve any."

She reaches the door, her back pressed to it. For one brief second, her hand grazes the knob like she's considering making a run for it. I almost wish she'd try. All the more reason for me to make her beg for mercy.

"I was only talking with him about class," she whispers, her chin quivering. "What did Quinton tell you?"

"You assume this has anything to do with him?" I take one slow step after another, eliminating the distance between us. Her breathing picks up speed, as does mine.

But she holds her head high, just the same. "I'm not as stupid as everybody thinks. I know it has to do with him. He's the one who made a big deal about it."

"Did you ever stop to think he has a good reason?"

"I had nothing to do with what happened to his wife," she spits. "And he ought to know it by now. What else do I have to do to prove that?"

She stiffens when I reach out and brush my fingers over her throat, where her pulse flutters like mad. "You're all worked up. Why is that? Because you know you're lying?"

"No."

"From what I heard, that Marcel kid wanted to be an insider with the Valentines."

"Did he?" She raises an eyebrow. "How would I know anything about that?"

"You can't imagine him ingratiating himself with you as a result?"

"Considering everybody's dead, how would that make any difference?"

Always an answer for everything. I'm going to break her. If it's the last thing I ever do, I will make her wish she had never challenged me.

My hand closes around her throat. She doesn't flinch or tremble—if anything, it seems she was waiting for it. Her body relaxes. Obviously, I haven't gotten my point across.

Tightening my grip, I cut off the blood flow to her brain and watch with glee as the panic finally reaches her eyes. Her fingers wrap around my wrist, trying to pull me away, but that only makes me hold on tighter.

Using my hold on her neck, I spin her around and start walking her to my desk. Only when her face turns a hue of blue do I release the pressure on her jugular vein.

"What are you—"

"Shut up. No talking from you. Just nod or shake your head when you are asked a question."

Her whole body jolts when her ass bumps into the edge of my desk. I guide her body to lay flat on the surface, never releasing her throat.

"Are you flirting with other guys to make me jealous?"

Confusion flashes over her face before she slightly shakes her head no. Lucky for her, I actually believe her.

"Either way, I think you need a reminder of who this pussy belongs to."

Using my other hand, I make quick work of unbuttoning my pants and freeing my hard cock.

"Pull down your leggings and panties," I order while stroking myself.

She wets her lips, letting the tip of her tongue run over her bottom lip seductively while she fumbles to follow my command. Lifting her ass slightly, she pulls down her leggings and panties in one move.

"Good girl. Now turn around and let me fuck you like the little slut you are." I release her throat, and she immediately turns around, bending over my desk with her bare ass up. "Reach back and spread your cheeks."

"W-what?"

My palm connects with her right ass cheek with a loud slap that only slightly masks her pained yelp.

"I said no talking. Now do it before I fuck your ass without lube," I growl, staring at the red handprint on her creamy white cheek.

Groaning, she reaches back and spreads herself open. Her pussy lips part, and her glistening cunt is on full display.

"Of course you are already wet. You want this cock so bad, you can't help it. But you know what? I can't help it either."

Without warning, I bring the tip of my dick to her hole and shove myself inside of her until my balls slap against her skin. Her tight channel squeezes me until precum leaks from the tip of my cock.

"Fuuuuck." I don't give her time to adjust. I simply grab her hips and start fucking her like a madman, slamming inside of her over and over again, trying to get deeper every time.

Her moans mingle with my grunts, echoing through my office like they are meant to be heard. My desk shakes, pencils roll off the side, and the lamp is almost at the corner, about to fall off, but I couldn't care less.

I keep fucking her like an animal until my lungs burn and sweat drips down my forehead. The lamp finally makes it over the edge, falling to the ground and shattering on the floor into a million pieces.

My fingers dig into Delilah's hips when she lets go of her cheeks. "I didn't tell you to let go. Spread yourself. I want to be as deep as I can."

My demand still hangs in the air when my office door flies open, and a shocked yelp comes from the hallway.

Turning my head, I look at the door to find my secretary standing there, mouth gaping open and eyes as wide as saucers.

"I-I heard something break... I..." she stumbles over her words while I keep fucking Delilah as if we don't have an audience.

"Out!" I yell before turning my head to look at Delilah's puckered little hole.

I don't know if it's me fantasizing about fucking her in the ass or the fact that my secretary is watching us fuck, but my orgasm slams into me so unexpectedly I can't even think about pulling out. I hold myself inside of her as I shoot my entire load into her tight channel until my balls are painfully empty and stars have formed around my vision.

Collapsing on top of Delilah, I'm vaguely aware of the door slamming shut. It takes me a moment before I catch my breath, and as soon as I do, I bring my lips to her ear.

"You will not talk to him anymore. Do you hear me? You won't talk to any other man unless I approve."

Delilah is still panting herself, and I know her heart must be beating out of control like mine when her soft voice meets my ear.

"I understand."

I'm not sure why exactly I suddenly feel so possessive of her. I just hope she does understand. Because next time I see her with someone, I might kill him.

29

DELILAH

"What kinds of books do you like to read?" Aspen leads the way through the stacks, running her fingers over the spines of countless books that don't look like anybody's ever cracked them open. Considering we're the only people here, it makes sense.

Not the only people, though. Not quite. I have to correct myself when, turning the corner at the end of a row, I spot Quinton sitting at a table. His hands are folded on top, his posture rigid. He's staring daggers at me, obviously.

But he's not getting in the way. He hasn't said a word since accompanying Aspen to the library, where we agreed to meet up today during our free time. I guess I should be grateful for that much.

Still, I get the feeling we have to stay close to where he's sitting. I can just imagine the conversation they had before this. You can hang out with her, but make sure to stay close to me so I can hear everything you say. He needs to get a life.

She asked me a question, didn't she? I need to pay attention. "Oh, whatever I can get my hands on. We didn't have a ton of money for new books, and the library was pretty far away. I was never sure if I'd be able to get back there in time to return the books."

"That's tough."

"Yeah, it was. But when we'd go to thrift stores, I'd always hit up the book donations and grab everything that looked interesting."

"Favorite genre?"

She's such a goddamn nerd. I like reading, but I don't get all starry-eyed over it like she does. "I don't know. I liked romances, mysteries, and thrillers. When I was younger, I read all the Nancy Drew books."

"Me, too!" Oh, goody, we have something else in common. "Brittney has the complete set here. Hardy Boys, too. I didn't think anybody else read them since they're so old."

"I think my aunt had an old copy lying around from years ago, and that's what got me into them. I'm pretty sure I was the only kid I knew who read them."

"Same here." She pulls out a thick, heavy book. "I like history, too. But only if it's not too dry and boring. Some authors know how to make it interesting."

"True." God, this is painful. Watching her walk around, browsing for her next read. Like she doesn't have a care in the world. Why does she deserve to live but not Nash? Why does she deserve to be happy and in love and secure? She's a Rossi now, on top of the world.

"This is a good one if you're interested." She hands me a book about the Gilded Age, but that's all I know since I don't bother flipping past the cover. All my attention is trained on her. How to start talking about things that matter.

"What else do you like to do?" I ask. I'm throwing darts at a board right now, flailing around, but she doesn't seem to notice. Either that or she doesn't have a lot of actual friends. Only people who are afraid of her husband.

She seems to give it actual thought, even frowning a little. "I used to like going to movies. My mom and I would keep track of all the best movies that came out every year, and we'd root for our favorites during the Oscars. I miss that a little."

"My aunt used to love watching that," I offer. "Even if we didn't get out to see the movies that were up for awards. She still had her favorite actors and actresses based on what she heard on the talk shows she watched."

She still looks a little sad. Maybe this is worth digging into. "I guess there's not much of a chance of getting out to the movies around here, huh?"

"Not really." She shrugs it off with a little smile. "It doesn't matter. I know I'm lucky to be here. Things could've gone much worse. But..."

My heart's in my throat. From where we're standing, I can see Quinton watching from his chair. I can't get too personal or push too hard without him knowing it. "But what?" I ask in a softer voice. "You okay?"

She offers a soft chuckle. "I was thinking about my mom. It's been a long time since I've spoken to her. I don't even know if she's okay or not."

"I'm sorry." I'm not. I'm glad. She needs to suffer.

We move to the end of the row, then round the end of the shelves. "Lucas has been a big help," she murmurs while wiggling her fingers at Quinton. I wonder how he'd react if I gave him the same little wave. I can just see him launching himself over the table to get to me.

"Lucas?" A big help? I'm finding that hard to believe.

"Sure. He's been great."

Are we thinking of the same person? "How so?" I ask, trailing behind her. This isn't what I'm supposed to be interested in, but now that she's started talking about him, I can't help wanting to hear more.

"He's taken a lot of time to teach me self-defense. I've gotten a lot better at it." She grins at me over her shoulder. "I've even knocked him on his ass."

Right. Like she could do that. Then again, she killed Nash. Maybe she gets, like, serial killer strength when she's upset. "That must've been satisfying."

"It was. He's not a small guy at all, but I knocked him flat. It made me feel strong. Not physically, but, you know. Inside."

"Sure." And I feel strong inside when I remember how weak he is for my pussy. Yeah, she and I are not the same at all. "So you spend a lot of time together?"

"Whenever he can manage it. He's pretty busy."

No shit. She starts flipping through a mystery book like she's thinking about checking it out, while I can't stop staring and wondering why the two of them are spending all this time together. Has he been trying to get in her pants, too?

Part of me loves the idea of Quinton going nuts, knowing the school's headmaster has a hard-on for precious little Aspen. It must drive him out of his skull. Is that why he won't let her out of his sight? I mean, she's not in any danger around here anymore. Why is he up her ass all the time?

Is it because he hates all this time she's spending with Lucas? Maybe he doesn't trust him. I wouldn't, either, but then I know he has nothing against fucking the girls around here. Does Quinton know that, too?

"He's not as bad as he seems. Lucas, I mean." She's still going on and on, lost in her own world where she's the star and everybody revolves around her. "At first, I figured he was a total monster, but things are different now."

She giggles to herself. "And now that I've met the rest of his family, it's easy to see where he gets that edge from."

He even introduced her to his family? I figured maybe he has a thing for her, but now I'm thinking it's bigger than that. What is so special about this girl?

Why can't I be the special one for once?

Jesus, get it together. Preston would hate it if he knew I was letting myself get distracted. Nash deserves better than this. I can let myself obsess over Lucas later.

I lean a little closer to her but make it look like I'm reaching for a book. "I'm surprised Quinton doesn't mind you spending all that time away from him," I whisper.

I can't help it. He's still glaring at me. I'm not even sure if he's blinking.

She snickers. "His bark is worse than his bite. Most of the time."

Something tells me I don't count. Is she this naïve? Or just stupid and self-centered enough to think everybody is as lucky as she is?

"But seriously," I continue, still whispering, "how does he handle you spending time with Lucas and not with him?"

She lifts a shoulder. "Sometimes he's there with us. He does like to follow me around most of the time. We have to compromise."

How fucked up are these two? I only thought I knew before now. "I see."

"Don't let him get to you," she murmurs while flipping pages of her book. "Time will change things. It always does. Once he sees you're just a normal person, he'll get over it. I keep telling him life is too short."

Like Nash's life. I want to take this book I'm holding and smash it against her head until there's nothing left of her but blood and hair and bits of skull. She took Nash away and has the nerve to stand here and talk about time healing everything.

"Thanks," I mutter. "I mean, that's good to know."

The sound of Quinton clearing his throat cuts through the otherwise quiet space. I guess we're being too secretive for him. Now that I know she's basically cheating on him with Lucas, I can understand a little better why he always acts so jealous. If he feels helpless because his slutty wife can't keep away from Lucas, he'll want to take it out on people like me who haven't done anything wrong.

I can't believe he would fuck her. What's wrong with him? She's not even all that pretty. Does he stick his dick in all the girls around here? I bet I'm not even the first one he's fucked on his desk.

"I'd better go." Otherwise, I'll never get out of this without hitting her. I've been pretending long enough for now.

"Oh, okay. Thanks for hanging out with me." She's insufferable. Unimaginable. Smiling at me with those wide eyes like she's being genuine. I remember a time when she wasn't smiling. Only that memory is enough to keep me from screaming now.

Brittney lets me check out the book Aspen recommended, which I care about even less than I did before. "Good to see you," she says with a smile. "See you soon, I hope."

"I'll bring this back on time," I promise, though I'm not really paying attention. What the fuck is so special about that girl? Why is everybody so into her?

It's easy to forget there was a time I felt sorry for what she went through. It's not like I asked Nash to see the video. Who would want to watch that?

"Come on. You'll love it. It's rough and hot. Just pretend that's not your brother fucking her." He laughs a little too loud, a little too hard, and the sound makes me shiver with disgust. I can't tell if he is kidding or not—his sense of humor has always been a little dark, but this?

"I don't think so. Can't I take your word for it?" I rub his arm and give him the sort of smile he likes—flirtatious while biting my lip. "I thought we were hanging out tonight so we could spend time together." Not to watch a video of some poor girl getting tortured and raped and whatever else.

He only hinted at it, telling me he didn't want to ruin the surprise.

"We will." He wraps an arm around my waist and pulls me in close enough that his erect dick is pressing against my stomach. "It'll be like foreplay."

Foreplay. Sure, and he's already horny enough. It won't take him any time to come. Me? He doesn't care whether I do or not. It looks like I'll have to pretend harder than usual this time since the thought of a girl being brutalized doesn't turn me on in the least.

"Come on," he whines, even sticking his lip out in a big pout. "I really want you to watch it. You'll see how serious we are about traitors and what they deserve."

His eyes darken, and his grip on me tightens. "And it'll be a warning, too. Just in case you ever get any ideas."

My blood runs cold at the obvious meaning undertone in his words. "It's just I don't have a strong stomach for stuff like that," I murmur.

"Think of it as a movie. That's it. Just a movie." His dick twitches against me, and it starts to sink in that he's not going to let this go.

My heart sinks, but I nod yes anyway. "Okay. Let's watch it."

I never had a choice, did I?

His eyes light up as a smile begins to spread across his face. It's the look of a kid who just got the gift of his dreams. "And after, you can wear this." He reaches into the paper bag sitting on his bed and pulls out what I quickly discover is a blond wig.

I wasn't good enough then when I had to wear a wig to look more like Aspen while we fucked. And I'm not good enough now.

I never will be.

30

LUCAS

I'm on my laptop when she comes in—and immediately, the sense of her being in a hell of a mood envelopes the apartment. It isn't that she says anything to give me that impression. It's that she doesn't. Not a word comes out of her between the time she enters and the time she closes the door to the guest room.

Right away, I call out, "No closed doors. Not unless I'm the one who closed them." And locked them.

The door swings open, but Delilah makes a point of not showing herself. Things have been tense since I fucked her on my desk. Not because I did it, but because I didn't make her come after. I'm pretty sure she is mad. Either that, or she's still pouting because I wouldn't let her and her little friend stay in class together. Who the fuck knows with girls this age? It could be hormones, for that matter. I don't have the first clue how to manage that, so I won't bother.

I'm satisfied with going back to my work. She doesn't feel like talking and would rather do her studying in there? So much the better. Sometimes the sound of her voice grates on my last nerve. Still, I keep one ear tuned to whatever's going on.

For a long time, there's nothing but silence punctuated by the occasional turning of a page. I need to stop thinking about her so much. She's a distraction from the things that truly matter, such as reviewing student evaluations. It's easy to forget at times that I have an actual job to perform around here when I'm consumed with every move that girl makes.

It's not until we sit down to dinner—pasta again, since my range of specialties isn't very broad—that I know this mood of hers isn't some passing fluke. I watch, torn between amusement and irritation, as she stabs a noodle like it insulted her mother. I suppose she'd have to first have a relationship with the woman to care very much, but then she's never spoken of her. I can only assume there's no love lost.

"What's on your mind?" It's the first thing either of us has said to the other outside the heads-up that dinner was ready.

She attempts a half-hearted shrug. "Nothing."

Is this tonight's game? Running around in circles? "You sure about that? Because it's seemed since you came in that there's something wrong. You've been very quiet."

"So I don't always want to talk. Is that a crime now?"

"Last I checked? No."

"Then what's the problem?" She still hasn't looked at me.

"I don't appreciate the silent hostility."

"Who's being hostile?" Finally, she pries her gaze from the plate, and there's a world of accusations in her green eyes. The girl isn't hostile. She's hateful.

"You look like you'd enjoy sinking the bread knife into my chest."

She snorts. "But what else is new?"

I watch her from the corner of my eye while continuing to eat. Could it be Quinton? If it is, he's gone over and above his usual treatment. She doesn't normally bring her frustration with him back to the apartment. I'm sure I would never have known he was rough with her the other day if it hadn't been for him coming to my office. She's a pro when it comes to concealing that sort of thing.

"Did somebody give you shit today?" I offer.

"Besides you? What would it matter if they did?" Now she laughs briefly, bitterly. "What, would you stop them? I'm sure."

"Where is this coming from?"

"Oh, stop trying to gaslight me. You know, that's really fucked up. After the way you and everybody else have treated me, now you're going to sit here and act like I owe you something? Like I have no reason to ever be angry or upset. I'm surprised you even let me go to the library."

Funny she should mention that since that's what I wanted to ask her about. "Did something happen there?"

She rolls her eyes and makes a sour face. "Please. Like Brittney didn't give you a full report."

She did, naturally. How could I not use every pair of eyes at my disposal? "You know that's part of the deal."

"The deal where I can't ever have even a minute of freedom."

"The deal where I'll allow you to use the facilities so long as someone is watching at all times."

"Very generous," she mutters.

"Is that what this is about? You don't like feeling observed? I hate to tell you, but that's not changing anytime soon."

"You don't hate to tell me that."

"You know what? You're right. I don't. But unlike you, I'm trying to be polite this evening. You could maybe take a lesson, you know?" As it is, her backtalk has my temper on simmer. Much more of this, and I doubt I'll be able to maintain a hint of civility.

"So long as you drop the fake niceness."

"You don't like it when I'm nice? No problem. I won't be."

"Good. It's a lot more authentic than when you pretend to be concerned or whatever."

I'm the one eyeing the bread knife now. It might be better to get it off the table before one of us makes a move for it. "Did something happen today? If so, it might be better for me to know about it."

"What? You mean your buddy Q didn't come running to you again?"

The disdain in her voice when she uses his nickname would be funny if the circumstances were different. She can't be bothered to conceal her hatred. I suppose I can't blame her for that. Even if she deserved everything she got.

"Should he have?" I ask. How easy would it be to reach across the table and shake it out of her? I have to remember what Lauren said about using her as an excuse to vent my ever-present rage. It's like the girl was built to test and torment me.

"I'm sure he could have come up with something I did wrong. Like, God forbid, I was talking to his wife. Oh, no." She rolls her eyes and pretends to gag.

"So there wasn't any big blowup?"

"Do you make it a habit? Hooking up with the girls around school?"

The question hits me like a fastball to the head. "What?" It's all I can manage through my surprise.

"I'm just saying. Am I one of many? Do you make your way through the entire student body? No judgment or anything like that. I'm only wondering if maybe I'm getting in the way by being around."

"Where is this coming from? What gave you the idea I sleep with the students?"

"You mean aside from what we've done?"

I have to grit my teeth before answering. "Obviously. And I'm not in the mood to play games, so you might want to come out with it already."

She drums her fingers on the table, glaring at her plate. "She was talking a lot about you. Aspen. All this time you spend together and how great it is. It doesn't take a genius to put two and two together. Her whole face, like, lights up when she talks about you."

Was that supposed to clear any of this up? I'm more confused than ever. "I don't understand what you're driving at."

"How long have you been fucking her? Jesus Christ, it's like pulling teeth. Do you deliberately pretend you can't follow along?"

That's it? That's the problem? Maybe I shouldn't laugh, but how am I supposed to help it? "You are way off base," I manage before laughing again.

"Right. I'm sure it's just a really deep, beautiful friendship. And listen," she insists when my laughter only gets louder, "I don't care, I really don't. I just think it's kind of shitty. Unethical. She's an actual student here."

"You care so much about ethics all of a sudden?" I needed that laugh. I really did. And now that it's out of my system, there's room in my awareness for understanding. Is she jealous? Is that what this is about?

For a second, the evil bastard inside me considers dragging this out. Letting her suffer a little. However, she'll only make me suffer in the end. I don't know how, but she'll find a way.

"I don't think it's funny." She folds her arms, having given up the pretext of being interested in dinner.

"Neither do I. I don't think it's funny at all."

"So why are you laughing at me?"

"Because you couldn't be further from the truth if you tried." I push my plate to the side, folding my arms on the table and facing her head-on. "Do you really not know? I assumed you did. It's not a secret."

Color blazes on her cheeks. "So you do have a relationship with her?"

"I do, but it's not the kind of relationship you're assuming it is." I can't help but grin at her confusion. "Aspen isn't my girlfriend or even my fuck buddy. She's my daughter."

It's worth it, telling her if only to watch her jaw drop. Her face goes blank, almost like her brain shuts down for a moment so it can catch up. I'm unable to hide my amusement, though she doesn't seem to notice.

"Wait a minute. I thought she was some other guy's kid. The one who—"

"She was adopted. To tell you the truth, I didn't know I had a daughter until well after she came here. It was only after her adopted father was in prison that he told her the truth. It was his way of protecting her. Distancing himself from her. And I'm sure he thought she deserved to know where she came from."

"Did he know who her real parents were?"

"He knew who her mother was." It's still so fresh. A sense of shame grips me when my thoughts turn in this direction. My own child was hidden from me for her protection. I was that far gone, that twisted. "The father was never announced, but I put everything together once I heard the mother's name. Aspen's blood was drawn when she first came here, just like yours was. I had Lauren run a paternity test."

"And she knows you're her father?"

"Yes. That's why I've been spending time with her. I'm no one's idea of father of the year, but now that we know about each other, I want to do my best to be there for her."

She stares at the table, frowning, and I can't help but wish she'd tell me what's on her mind. What is she thinking? Trying to imagine me as a dad? She wouldn't believe it if I told her how many times I've done the same thing and with next to no success.

Or is she thinking about her own father and their lack of a relationship? I wonder if that's it. That's exactly where my head would go if I were in her position. Mather might have been a rat, but he was nothing less than a devoted father. And now, Aspen has another father just as devoted to her. Even if I don't quite know how to show it.

Delilah, on the other hand? She's never had anyone. No wonder she took it personally when she thought my relationship with Aspen was sexual. That would put them in competition.

Have I been spending too much time with Lauren? I'm turning into a shrink.

"Have I shocked you?" I can't help asking before going back to my food. It's a little colder now, but at least there's no hostility in the air.

"Yeah, obviously." She shakes her head a little. "No wonder you took it so personally. I mean, what happened to her."

"I don't want to talk about it."

"Of course." She notices I'm eating and is quick to pick up her silver-ware to join me. Now that the truth is out, she's back to her old self. "Anyway, I think it makes her happy to have somebody to talk books with. I doubt Quinton is much of a reader."

There's one more thing I feel needs to be said, even though it's insulting that I should have to point it out. "I've never fucked any of the other students around here. In case you were wondering."

"I wasn't."

"That isn't how it sounded earlier when you accused me of that very thing."

"I didn't think you actually did it, though."

"Right." I should've known better than to think I'd get a straight answer. I don't know why it matters. It shouldn't. She is the last person whose opinion I should give two shits about.

31

DELILAH

*P*reston: I'll call you at noon. Have the phone on.

It's three minutes to twelve, and I'm in the girls' bathroom closest to the library, pacing tight circles inside one of the stalls. I'm glad I thought to power the phone up this morning, or else I might have missed Preston's text. Now that I can't see Marcel in class, there's nobody to warn me that he wants to talk.

What could he want? Probably to get on my ass about the total lack of progress with Aspen. I mean, she's slowly but surely warming up to me. That's not difficult. It's not easy to get time alone with her, is all.

How am I supposed to get her to trust me if we can only talk about things Quinton approves of? What am I even supposed to be looking for? I wish somebody would tell me. The sooner I can stop pretending to like this girl, the better my life will be.

By the time twelve o'clock rolls around, my stomach is in knots, and my hands are shaking so badly I almost drop the phone when it rings. I answer immediately, lowering the lid on the toilet so I won't accidentally drop the phone in there. "Hi," I whisper.

"Can you get her alone today to set up a meeting?" So much for a greeting.

It's like he's reading my mind, only not in any helpful kind of way. "I was just thinking about that. I honestly have no idea how I'm going to do it." I'm chewing my lip hard enough to hurt, twirling hair around my finger, bouncing up and down on the balls of my feet. Please don't let him hate me for this.

"Yeah, Marcel told me he keeps her on a short leash." Preston snickers. "Pussy whipped. But that's okay. He'll be busy tonight."

"How do you know that?" How many spies do they have? I wish they'd get one of them to go through with this because I'm regretting ever agreeing to help.

"Marcel is taking care of it. Let's just say he'll be distracted once he starts digesting his dinner."

"So it's definitely happening tonight?" Jesus, Marcel is going to poison him? Not that I'd mind seeing Q drop dead, but this all seems to be happening so fast. I can't catch up.

"Yes, which means you need to figure something out, fast. Don't worry, though. We did the thinking for you. You only have to get her alone long enough to float the idea."

While I'm glad of that, I still feel like shit, thanks to the way he says it. He's disappointed and upset with me.

"What did you have in mind?" I ask, ignoring the lump in my throat.

"There's a sunroom there. Are you familiar with it?"

"I've never been there, but I've heard it exists."

"Well, that's another one of her favorite spots. Fucking nerd," he mutters. "You need to get her up there tonight."

"After the sun goes down?"

"Christ, you're fucking dense, aren't you? Yes, after the sun goes down. There's some big meteor shower tonight. Make up an excuse, like you want to watch it, but you're nervous about being alone. She's so hard up for friends, I'm sure she'll jump at the opportunity."

"What if she doesn't?"

"That's your problem, isn't it? The point is, get her there. Marcel will be waiting. He'll take care of everything else."

"What time?"

"Have her there at eleven o'clock."

This means I have to sneak out of the apartment. Lucas is usually in bed before eleven, though. With my luck, he'll decide to be a night owl tonight. What do I do then?

"Got it?" Preston barks.

"Yeah, I've got it." I don't. Not even close. But I doubt he'll take pity on me.

"Don't let us down." He pauses. "Don't let Nash down."

The words land with a thud in my head. He would have to go and say that, wouldn't he? "I won't. I promise."

A beeping noise tells me he's already ended the call. I don't even know if he heard me.

I need to find a way to convince her. And I have to pray Lucas doesn't change up his routine tonight of all nights.

Lucas. The thought of him leaves me leaning against the wall, breathless and guilty. It was different before I knew about him being her father. This is going to crush him. And I'm going to have to pretend to know nothing about it.

But I made a promise.

And she killed Nash.

I don't have a choice but to go through with this.

I push away from the wall, hiding the phone before exiting the stall. I can do this. I have to. She needs to pay, and this is the only way.

It isn't easy, faking a happy expression when I set eyes on her in the library. Not that it's ever been easy, but today it's extra challenging. I make it a point to ignore Quinton, sitting in the corner, his eyes following my every move as I walk through the cavernous space.

"Hey. How's it going?" Preston was right about one thing: this girl is hard up. I can't imagine anybody being so genuinely excited just to see me. She's practically beaming when I reach her, where she's chatting with Brittney at the desk.

"Pretty good." I slide my returned book across the counter.

Brittney's eyes bulge. "You read it already?"

"I don't have much else to do but read," I explain with a shrug. "And it was really gripping, too."

"We have the author's entire collection here."

"I'll have to check out the rest of it." I can't believe I'm standing here having this conversation like everything is normal. Like I give a crap about reading right now while cold sweat runs down the back of my neck.

"Come on. Let's take a look." Aspen leads the way, and I follow without thinking. My thoughts are churning, my heart racing. What happens if she turns me down? How could I convince her?

Oh, shit. What happens if she mentions it to her stupid, murdering husband? I'm sure he could be shitting his brains out, and it wouldn't matter. No way would he let her leave his side if he knew it was me she was meeting up with. I wonder what know-it-all Preston would say if I posed these questions to him. He'd probably tell me to figure it out before hanging up on me.

Now that we're out of Quinton's line of vision, I have to get this over with. If I don't do it now, I'll lose my nerve. "Hey, do you know if the sunroom is left unlocked at night?" I ask as I follow her.

"Sure. It's open all the time. I love hanging out there." She throws a curious look over her shoulder. "How come?"

"You're going to think it's totally dorky. I shouldn't have said anything." I even tuck my hair behind my ear like I'm shy or whatever.

"No, come on. What's up?"

"There's a meteor shower tonight. I thought it would be pretty cool to watch from there."

Goddamnit. He was right. "Oh, wow! What a cool idea. You could take a blanket, lie on your back, and watch the stars. That sounds really neat."

"That's what I thought. I just didn't know if I would be able to get in tonight."

"You shouldn't have any trouble." She comes to a stop, turning to me. "Were you planning to go by yourself?"

"I didn't think anybody else would be interested—not like I know a bunch of people, anyway."

"Would you mind some company?" She smacks her open palm against her forehead, sighing. "Sorry. I keep telling myself not to be too much, but it's like I can't help it."

"It's okay." It's too easy. That's what it is. The girl is determined to walk headfirst into her own destruction. Far be it from me to stop her. "And for what it's worth, I would love company. Honestly, it might be kind of creepy, being there all by myself. I don't really have any friends around here."

"Yeah. I know how that feels." Right, which is why she bends over backward to be nice to me. I need to keep reminding myself of that. She's not acting this way because of me, but rather because of her. What she's been through. Not like it matters since it works in my favor either way.

"Can I ask you something, though?" I look over my shoulder to make sure Quinton didn't slip out of his chair and follow us. "Do you think you could come alone? No offense, but he's kind of intimidating. I understand he hates me, but…"

"I get it. Like I said, I know how it feels." She looks over my shoulder like she's making sure we aren't being followed or listened in on. "What time did you want to go?"

"I was thinking around eleven? I heard that's the time the meteors will be most visible." A total lie, but what's she going to do? Look it up here and now to make sure I'm not tricking her?

"Sounds good. Don't worry. I'll be able to get out by myself."

I have no doubt about that. So long as Marcel does what he's supposed to do, she'll be free and clear. Unless Quinton gets so sick, she's afraid to leave him alone—but that wouldn't be my fault, would it? That would fall on Marcel's shoulders for giving him too much of whatever it is he's going to dose him with.

"Cool. It'll be nice to hang out one-on-one. You want to meet here, in front of the library?"

Her head bobs up and down. "That sounds great. I think it'll be fun."

Sure, it will. Just not for her.

～

FOR ONCE, something is going my way. In a strange turn of events, Lucas turned in earlier than usual, closing his bedroom door before the clock struck ten thirty, leaving me in the guest room.

It gave me plenty of time to prepare myself for this. I was so nervous, I almost forgot to bring a blanket. Not that I'm going to need it. As soon as Marcel deals with her, I intend to head straight back to the apartment as quickly and quietly as possible. But I have to keep up appearances until we reach the sunroom.

This is it. The homestretch. All I have to do is follow the plan.

Still, my heart pounds the entire way to the library as I trot down empty halls. What if Quinton was so sick that she couldn't leave him? What if she's only going to meet me long enough to tell me before she heads back to nurse him? That wouldn't be my fault. I have to keep that in mind. And if we need to come up with a new plan, that's not my fault, either.

I never thought the sight of her would bring me relief, but that's what I feel when I catch sight of her waiting for me in front of the closed library doors. "I didn't think I would be able to get away," she confesses in a whisper before we head for the sunroom. "Quinton isn't feeling very well. He just went to bed before I left."

"What's wrong with him?" I ask since that's what people do at times like this.

"Some kind of stomach thing. I'm sure he'll be fine by tomorrow." Well, gee, isn't that a relief? As if I care. "Anyway, it made it easier for me to get away. Does that make me a bad wife? It feels like it does."

"The way I used to overhear my aunt and her friends talking about their men, that's nothing." She actually giggles at that, and I can't help but laugh, too. Poor, delusional thing.

I have to admit, the sunroom is pretty impressive, but that's the case with most of this place. Everything is done on a big scale, and this room is no exception. "Wow, there are actual trees and stuff," I say in a whisper as we enter.

"I know, right? I really love coming here and sitting in the sunshine when I get a chance. You should join me sometime. We can just hang out and read." The happiness in her voice almost makes me feel guilty. I have to remind myself why I'm doing this, and that guilt dissolves. She's getting what she deserves.

"Sure. That sounds good." I raise my voice enough that anybody waiting in the shadows or behind a tree can hear me. Is he here? It's a couple of minutes past eleven. He'd better be if there's any hope of this working.

She starts to spread out her blanket, and I guess I should, too. I don't know what Marcel is planning or how he's going to surprise her, but I need to play along until it happens or else risk her running away.

He doesn't keep me waiting long. I'm straightening out my blanket when I catch sight of movement from the corner of my eye. I have to pretend I don't notice so she won't have a clue. She's too busy talking, anyway.

Meanwhile, Marcel is sneaking out from behind a tree, creeping toward us. This is it. It's finally happening.

I glance toward him. He's carrying a syringe in one hand, moonlight glinting off the needle as he moves silently. Every muscle in my body is tense, my senses on high alert. I can practically hear my hair growing. It's happening, and it's out of my hands. This is what she deserves.

She finally gets her blanket situated, then plops down next to me—before her jaw drops. "Quinton?" she blurts out, scrambling to her knees again.

At first, I think she must be confused until the sound of two bodies colliding grabs my attention. They're moving too fast for me to understand right away what's happening, but soon it becomes clear.

He followed her. The son of a bitch followed her anyway.

And now he's got Marcel in a headlock, cutting off his oxygen. "I'll kill you, motherfucker," Quinton grunts while they struggle. Aspen and I both cry out, but for different reasons, as he pulls the syringe from Marcel's hand before plunging it into his neck. Marcel gasps, grunts, then goes limp.

It's over. It was never going to work in the first place.

A gray-faced, sweating Quinton glares at me, Marcel's unconscious body at his feet. "Now," he pants, "let's talk about your part in all this."

32

LUCAS

For the second time in a week, a phone call awakens me. I fumble for the phone, bleary-eyed, having just fallen into a deep sleep. "Yes?" I mumble on answering.

"Sir, we have a problem."

"What kind of problem?" I ask, sitting up, rubbing my fists over my eyes.

"A situation in the sunroom. We need you right away." I vaguely recognize the voice of one of the guards. My alarm clock tells me it's just past eleven. What could be going on up there at this time of night?

"And you need me, why exactly? Couldn't this wait until morning?"

"Sir, it has to do with your daughter."

I'm out of bed in an instant. "Why didn't you say that to begin with? What happened? Is she all right?"

"She's safe, sir, but you're needed."

"I'll be there in a minute." Fuck my life. When is this going to end? When will she be safe? I throw on sweats before heading out of my room. The door to the guest room is closed, as usual at this time of night. I wonder if I ought to let Delilah know I'm going out, but she might be asleep already. So long as I lock the door, it won't matter.

Besides, I don't want to lose a moment's time. I take off for the elevator at a run, then nearly run down the hall when the doors open again. A pair of guards wait outside the sunroom, both of them nodding in acknowledgment before stepping aside so I can enter.

The first thing I see is the last thing I expect: Delilah, sitting cross-legged on a blanket I recognize as the one from the guest room, her hands cuffed behind her.

"What the fuck happened here?" Glancing around, I spot Quinton leaning against a nearby tree, a trembling Aspen in his arms.

Quinton jerks his chin, and I follow the direction of his gaze. "Marcel," I grunt. He's unconscious, his chest rising and falling evenly, his mouth hanging open. He's sprawled out on the floor like he was already out before he hit it.

"I got here just in time," Quinton says. There's murder in his voice, though he sounds weak and looks like hell.

"What happened?" I go to Aspen, touching her shoulder. "Are you all right?"

"I'm fine," she mumbles against Quinton's shoulder, her face still hidden from me.

"It seems Marcel here had plans to inject Aspen with whatever he's now under the influence of," Quinton explains with a nasty smile. "I'm guessing that motherfucker has something to do with the fact that I've been sick as a dog since dinner, too. My theory is he wanted to get her away from me long enough to put that syringe in her."

"But why?" Then, on top of everything else, the question I don't dare give voice to. What did Delilah have to do with this?

"That's a good question. Considering this one's taking a nap, only one person can explain it." He glares at Delilah, his lip lifting in a snarl. "But she's not talking. Are you?" he asks her, raising his voice.

There's roaring in my head. Heat spreads through my chest, tightening it and making it difficult to breathe. "Are you sure you're okay?" I manage to ask my daughter, who nods without lifting her head. So long as I know that, I can turn my attention to other things.

"What do you want us to do with him?" one of the men asks, nudging Marcel's limp body with one foot. I know what I would like to tell them to do. I know what I would like to do myself, and it involves sticking a red-hot fireplace poker up his ass—for starters.

But dammit, I have to think about the school as a whole. This isn't only about my kid. It's about Corium, and while there aren't many rules around here, the ones that exist are firm. "I want him off-premises by the time he wakes up," I announce. "He's suspended indefinitely. And if he knows what's good for him, he'll never show his face to me."

"I knew he was up to something," Quinton growls. I can only grunt in agreement and wish I had done more than separate him and Delilah. I didn't exactly have a reason to kick him out, but I could have come up with something. Anything, so long as this could be avoided.

Once again, I failed my daughter.

And I have the little bitch on the floor to thank for it. She's still staring at the blanket under her, unmoving, barely breathing. "Well?" I bark, but she doesn't flinch. "Are you going to speak up for yourself? What was the plan, Delilah? What were you doing here?"

How could she lie to me? What the hell is wrong with me that you were able to so easily get past me?

She doesn't say a word. I can't say I'm surprised. If there's one thing I've learned about her, it's how fucking stubborn she is. But I also know how to break her—and how much fun it is when she gives me a reason to make her sorry for what she's done.

If she thought she was sorry before, she's in for a big surprise now. She hasn't begun to learn the meaning of the word.

"Get her on her feet." I back away from her, sick at the sight of her. All the freedom I've tried to give her. Every little smart-ass comment I've taken pains to overlook. I stopped locking the guest room door and look what happened. This is how she repaid me.

Aspen finally speaks up, lifting her head and looking over her shoulder to where Delilah now stands between the two guards. "What are you going to do to her?" she whispers.

"She'll be taken down to one of the holding cells," I assure her in as gentle a voice as I can manage, considering I want to burn the fucking school to the ground with Delilah still inside. "Don't worry. I won't kill hee."

"We'll go back to our room." Quinton chimes in, pulling Aspen closer to his side. I would thank him for taking care of her, but even in my half-crazed state, I know how condescending it would sound. She's my daughter, but she's his wife. He has just as much of a stake in her life as I do, if not more so.

Quinton shoots one more murderous look toward Delilah before leading Aspen away. I notice she doesn't look at the prisoner, and a blade pierces my heart. I allowed this to happen. I told myself it would be all right for her and Delilah to spend time together so long as they were supervised. The fucking lies I tell myself. When will I ever learn?

"Let's go down to the cells." Delilah only twitches slightly at that, probably surprised I'm going with them. If she is, she's forgetting who she's dealing with. As if I would let this be the end of it. Oh, no. Especially when the cells are soundproofed. Nobody will be able to hear her scream.

Except for me, of course, and I intend to savor every moment.

I follow a few steps behind, watching the men drag her down the hall. How could she? Is she that deeply broken? How much of what she's told me is a lie? Was there ever a single grain of truth?

My daughter. There's not a doubt in my mind about what Marcel intended to do once she was unconscious. Who's he working with? There has to be somebody on the outside if he was able to get his hands on drugs strong enough to knock a grown man unconscious.

Am I kidding myself, thinking she'll tell me? I saw what she went through when Quinton had her locked away, and she didn't admit to a single thing then. What makes now any different? I won't flatter myself into thinking I'll make a difference since I haven't up to now. Even knowing Aspen is my daughter, she still did this.

How much of this is anger over Aspen, and how much is anger for my own sake? Lauren would have a field day with this shit.

The guards shove her into the first room we come to. I have the sick satisfaction of watching her stumble and fall against the metal sink. "Thank you," I tell them both as she struggles to get to her feet, her hands still cuffed behind her. "Now, leave us alone." She gasps softly, and I have to wonder why she's surprised. Doesn't she know me by now?

I wait until the door closes before sighing. "I'm going to give you a chance," I grit out through clenched teeth. "You have this one single chance to explain yourself. Tell me why you were there, who told you to do it, and you might make it out of this in one piece."

When she doesn't say a word, I can't help but growl as all the old instincts rage within me. I'm barely holding them back now, hanging on by a thread. "Or you can pretend not to know a thing," I continue, "and then I can't promise you'll live to see tomorrow. So which is it? Are you going to be upfront with me for once, or are you going to force me to hurt you?"

Not even that gets a response. She doesn't even remind me it would be my choice if I hurt her. "Did you lose your voice?" I demand, my fists clenched. "Fucking answer me. Why did you do this? What was the purpose? What did you think was going to happen?"

Our eyes meet for one instant, but she looks away.

For some reason, that's what does it. The fact that I know damn well she hears me and understands but is still too fucking obstinate to give me what I want.

My hand shoots out, taking her by the hair. I yank her head back, staring into her now fear-filled eyes. "This is how you want it?" I hiss in her face. "Is this how you like it? When I fucking hurt you? Then you're going to love this, you lying little bitch."

She yelps in pain when I pull her across the room by the hair before throwing her onto the cot. That yelp moves through me, lighting up all my darkest corners. It reminds me of who I am. Who I've always been. Who I get to be now while she's helpless to stop me.

My hands are already at my waistband, pulling the sweats down low enough to let my cock spring free. "You don't want to use your mouth for explaining?" I mutter, stroking myself as I lower myself to one knee on the cot's edge. She tries to push herself as close to the wall as possible as if that's going to help. The sound of her quiet little whimpers is music to my ears.

"Remember, you could've avoided this." When she tries to turn her face away, I take her jaw in one hand and force her mouth open before slamming my cock inside. She gags hard enough that her body convulses. "Don't like that, do you?" I slam into the back of her throat again and hold her there, nose smashed against my base as she groans and gags around me.

"It didn't have to be like this," I remind her while she struggles for air. "You could've stayed in bed tonight. You could've minded your business. Instead, you tried to kill my daughter. My fucking daughter!" I roar as tears roll down her cheeks.

I pull back, and she wheezes before I plunge in again, cutting off her air. "So far, I've been nice enough to let you breathe before you pass out. I'm not feeling so nice tonight. I might lose track of time."

She sobs in response, urging me on, making it impossible for me to stop now. No, instead, I grind myself deeper, savoring her frantic attempts at sucking in a single breath.

She used me. Lied to me. Even now, she won't be honest. She deserves this.

"You feel like talking now?" I ask, pulling back so she can breathe. The sight of her red, tearstained face is an aphrodisiac. "Sorry. I can't quite hear you." When she moans in dismay, I laugh, plunging deeper.

"That's right," I grunt, fucking her face while she weeps. "Get it nice and hard. Nice and wet, too. Trust me. You're going to want it to be very wet when I put it in your ass."

She squeals like the fucking pig she is, making me laugh again.

"What?" I taunt, thrusting in and out, using her the way she needs to be used. This is all she's good for, anyway. "Don't like that idea? Nobody ever fucked your ass before? That's good. It'll be nice and tight for me." She tries to shake her head and scream out her refusal, but all it does is make me take her harder.

"Maybe now you'll learn I'm not the guy you fuck with. Maybe now, you'll finally remember." God, it's almost too much, the joy of giving in to the brutality still living in me. I know she'll have bruises by the time we're finished—that will be the least of her problems. And it thrills me. It makes me want to hurt her more.

"Please!" she gasps when I pull free, dripping with saliva. "Please, don't!"

"Now, now." I laugh at her attempts to fight me off as I roll her onto her stomach, her useless hands trapped behind her. "It's too late for that. I gave you a chance, remember?"

"Please, I'll do whatever you want!" She lets out a high-pitched shriek when I respond by yanking the yoga pants she's wearing down to her thighs, along with her thong.

"Damn right, you will," I grunt, parting her ass cheeks to reveal her puckered little hole. It's clenched tight, but then it would be. It'll be that much more fun to force my way inside. "It just so happens I want to come. You're going to squeal for me, aren't you? You're going to squeal while I tear your ass open. You did this to yourself. I want you to remember that."

She's still trying to fight me off, but all it does is make her ass bounce up and down. I watch for a moment, mesmerized, before spitting on her asshole. She recoils, her hole clenching tighter. "Trust me, you want to relax." I laugh.

"Lucas. Don't do this."

"Don't you dare." I take her by the hips, digging my fingers into her firm flesh until she sucks in a pained gasp. "Don't you act like you have the right to talk to me like we're equals. We've never been equals. And all you've done is spit on the trust I tried to give you."

She sobs at the pressure from my head against her back door. But I notice she's not fighting as hard anymore. Like she knows there's nothing she can do to stop me.

I roll my hips, pushing forward, and her body tenses in time with a broken scream tearing itself from her throat. I close my eyes, lost in sensation. Her muscles grip me so tight, like a vise, but still, I push my way deeper.

"Oh, fuck, yes," I groan, pulling her by the hips while I force my way in.

There's no going slow. No holding back. I need to punish her, and I do, taking her hard, relishing the way she softly weeps into the pillow. I place a hand on the back of her head and hold it down, my balls tightening and lifting at the sound of her muffled sobs.

And every time my balls hit the backs of her thighs, I remember what I could have lost tonight. All thanks to her. Nothing I could do would be too harsh after what she's done.

"I'm going to come," I announce, and I think she sobs in relief this time. "Where do you want it? Should I fill your asshole with my cum? So you can feel it dripping out?"

I slam myself deep again, close to the edge. "And when you lie here..." I grunt before thrusting again, "and you feel it... you'll remember why it's there."

The rush comes over me all at once, and I give in to it, roaring out my release, pumping cum into her until it spills out around my shaft and runs down her thighs. "Not so tight anymore," I observe with a chuckle after I pull out and survey my handiwork. She only weeps in response, a broken, haunting sound that satisfies me deeper than any orgasm ever could.

"Remember," I mutter as I stand and tuck myself into my pants. "This is all your doing. I did everything I could to help you avoid this." All she does is lie there, trembling. I pull her pants up for her, but that's the extent of the dignity she deserves—and that's only because I know the guards will check on her, and I don't need their fucking questions.

The last thing I see before closing the door and leaving her alone is the heaving of her body as she breaks down, sobbing harder than before. It gives me something to smile about on my way back to the apartment.

33

DELILAH

*H*ow many days has it been? I don't have the first idea. Time has ceased to mean anything all over again. Just like before. No clock, no windows, no way to tell whether it's day or night in this always bright room.

For maybe the millionth time, my eyes sweep the walls, the corners, the ceiling. There has to be a camera somewhere. I just haven't found it yet. Every time I close my eyes for more than a second, somebody pounds on the door. I haven't slept yet.

How long can a person live without sleep? I feel like I read that once, but now I can't remember. Not that it really matters since I have no way to tell how much time has passed. I could lie here and count the seconds, but that would only drive me crazier than I'm already going.

I can't believe I'm doing this again. I should be used to it by now, though this feels worse than before. Maybe that's because now, I have something else to add to the torment... guilt. I fucked up. I should have known Quinton would find a way to ruin everything.

Marcel doesn't know him like I do. I know how far he's willing to go for Aspen—not only cold-blooded murder but weeks and months of torturing somebody before killing them.

I should have said something to Preston on the phone. I should have warned him. But most of all, I shouldn't have betrayed Lucas. Logically I know there wasn't any other way. It's not like he would ever choose me above his daughter. He probably wouldn't choose me over anyone.

I don't even owe him anything, so why does it feel like I do? Why do I feel guilty for betraying him? And why do I want him to forgive me?

I guess I'll die asking myself all these questions. Once I'm on the brink of death, which should be anytime now, considering I've had nothing to eat or drink on top of being deprived of sleep, somebody is going to come in and finish the job.

Not somebody. Lucas. I'm sure Quinton will argue he should have the job, but Lucas will find a way to win. Because I didn't only betray Aspen, which for Quinton is bad enough.

I wish he would get it over with.

At least somebody came in and took off my handcuffs, probably a couple of hours after Lucas left me here. By that time, the burning agony in my ass had dulled to searing pain. I was able to clean myself up at the sink, but when I went back to cup some water in my palm later, nothing came out of the tap. It's been dry since then.

My stomach clenches, and I curl into a tighter ball. God, I'm so hungry. So thirsty. The urge to cry almost overwhelms me, but that would mean dehydrating myself even more.

Sometimes I remember my normal life. Times when I thought I was hungry. I used to say I was starving, even. What a fucking joke. Sure, there were times when we had to tighten our belts, as my aunt used to say, but what did that mean? No ordering a pizza on a Saturday night, but heating a can of flavorless chili or spaghetti instead. Big deal.

I had no idea what real hunger was like. How desperate a person can be when they barely have the strength to move because they're so famished. I grit my teeth and swallow the saliva in my mouth, pretending it's water.

I close my eyes in a desperate attempt to will away the hunger pangs. Maybe it hasn't been as long as I thought since there are still pangs to struggle with. They won't last much longer—but neither will I unless I get something to drink soon. Thirst kills quicker than hunger. I remember that much.

For some reason, there's still a tiny part of me that wants to live. Am I that sick in the head? It's not like I have anything to live for.

Somebody pounding at the door makes my eyes fly open again. "Fuckers," I whisper, grinding my teeth together until it hurts. Silly me, closing my eyes. What was I thinking? Maybe the camera is hidden in the lights. The lights they never, ever turn off. The lights I can see from behind my eyelids.

There's a clicking noise that I realize is coming from the door. Somebody slid a key into the lock. Now, they're turning it. I roll over, facing the wall, and hope whatever's going to happen will happen fast.

Screeching hinges signal the door being opened. I brace myself, now fully awake and clear-headed, thanks to adrenaline pumping through my system.

A set of footsteps marks the entrance of the guard...

... before a second set of footsteps rings out. I listen hard, dread building in my chest. I'm sure there's only one person Lucas would allow to visit besides one of the guards, and it's himself.

"Get her on her feet," he growls. I was right. I don't bother putting up a fight when the guard takes hold of me, pulling me to my feet before spinning me in place so I can face the headmaster.

I keep my gaze low, around his knees. I don't want him to start bitching that I made eye contact before I was invited to. Or maybe I'm just too scared to look at him, too scared of what it would make me feel.

"You look like hell."

I don't react. I mean, I'm sure I look like hell. Is that supposed to hurt my feelings?

"So you're going to ignore me now, is that it? Is your tongue tied again?" His laughter is like the sound of nails on a chalkboard, and I can't keep from shivering.

"You had a lot to say the last time I was with you. I wonder what's different now?"

That's right, buddy. Get it all out of your system. I can't bring myself to care when the struggle to stay on my feet already takes up so much of my concentration. I can't help but sway back and forth a little. Or is that the room swaying?

"Wake up." His sharp words stir me out of my stupor. So much for adrenaline. I guess even that can only go so far. I can't stop the shiver that skates down my spine.

"Look at me." I am looking at him, but I know what he means. I won't even give him the satisfaction of smarting off since he'll only use that as an excuse to smack me around. Or worse. It's not like he's never done worse.

So I lift my gaze, forcing myself to connect with his eyes. The endless darkness inside his vicious stare takes my breath away. He doesn't look like himself. He doesn't even look like a person.

I've never seen anyone so cold. Not even Rossi, which is saying something. There were moments back in that freezing cold cell where I thought for sure he wasn't even human. That he was a demon or something.

But this is a whole other level. Because this man has been inside me. He used me. He's also very gently, almost tenderly, cleaned me up afterward. For fuck's sake, he tried to introduce me to classic cinema. We aren't strangers. Yet that's what it feels like now.

"There she is," he murmurs. "There's the lying little slut."

Don't react. Don't give him the satisfaction, dammit.

"What? No smart-ass answer? No cutting remark? I'm surprised." He folds his arms, eyes narrowing. "You haven't been here all that long. I thought you were stronger than this. I'd say I'm disappointed, but you can't disappoint me any more than you already have."

I can't do this anymore. I can't stay on my feet... too tired. Before I know it, my knees give out, and the floor rushes up to meet me. I brace myself for my body to hit the unforgiving ground, but instead, my head lands against a firm chest. Strong arms wrap around me, giving me the support I so desperately need to stand.

For a single moment, I close my eyes and pretend I'm somewhere else. I'm in Lucas's apartment, and he is holding me on the couch, whispering sweet nothings in my ear.

For that short moment, I'm safe. I'm happy. I'm loved.

"On your feet," Lucas snarls, shoving me away like I'm nothing to him. I stumble backward, surprising myself by not falling on my ass as soon as he lets go of me. "You will stand in my presence. Do you understand?" I barely dip my chin, blinking hard to try to wake myself up. I take a few deep breaths, too, hoping for the oxygen to clear my head.

"So that's what it takes, huh?" Lucas muses aloud. He sounds like he's having fun. "That's where they fell short before. They should have made it so you couldn't sleep. Well, Quinton is young. He doesn't have the experience that I have. I'm sure he's never tortured anyone to death."

No, but he's definitely killed. Many times. A sinister bubble of laughter escapes me.

"Is there anything funny about what I said?" he demands, cupping my chin and lifting my head until our eyes meet again.

He leans in close, and for one completely insane moment, I think he's going to kiss me. Just goes to show what happens to a person's brain when they haven't slept in days.

His eyes dart over my face, his lips twisting in a smirk. "How's it feel, knowing your little plan went to shit? Did you honestly think you could get past Quinton? I'm sure you did because you wouldn't know what it's like to be loved."

Don't react. Whatever you do, do not react.

"I suppose it shouldn't come as a surprise," he continues in a deceptively quiet, smooth voice, like ice skittering over my spine. "I can't even hold it against you. From the minute you were born, I'm sure people have told you you're worthless. Useless. A burden. So how could you help but fail in your little plan?"

Stay strong. You're better than this. I know he only wants to break me down. He wants the satisfaction of making me cry, and with a guard in the room, he's less likely to pull my pants down and fuck me. So he has to use another method. But I'm not going to let him win.

Nothing in the world has ever mattered more than not letting him win.

"I guess you wouldn't know there's nothing a person won't do to protect their loved one." His gaze hardens and intensifies. "You wouldn't know because you are not actually worthy of love. The same goes for your little partners. Marcel, and whoever he was working with on the outside."

So that's it. That's the endgame. He wants a name.

"Who is it?" he whispers. "Come on. You have the chance to do something right for once. You can make up for a little bit of the harm you've caused. Do the right thing. I'll take care of the rest."

"Are you finished yet?" I croak. "Or aren't you tired of hearing yourself talk?"

His grip tightens an instant before he throws me back. I glance off the cot and scrape my tailbone against the frame. Pain radiates up my spine. I'm still whimpering in pain when I'm yanked to my feet again.

"I should have known. You can't even make the right choice, the only choice that will help you in a situation like this. Where it's obvious nobody gives a fuck what happens to you. Did you give that a moment's thought before you began putting your plan in motion? You are expendable. You're a pawn. The person behind this will sleep well tonight, not giving a damn about what happened to you. And you're still going to protect them?"

"I'm not a rat," I whisper, and this time, I don't need his help lifting my chin. I can do it myself.

He lifts his brows. "Am I supposed to applaud? Should I respect that? Because from where I'm standing, you're a fool. A liar. You might as well be a rat because you've already betrayed me. Someone who tried to do well by you."

"Do well by me?" For some reason, out of everything that's come out of his filthy mouth, that's what finally does it. I can't stay quiet. "Since when have you done well by me? What, because you didn't kill me before now, I'm supposed to be grateful? Because you've only used me a few times like I'm not even human, I should break down crying from shame? Because I betrayed you?"

Now, I'm awake again. Now, I don't care if it makes me look weak to react. I can't help myself. "Tell yourself all you want that you're the good guy," I mutter through clenched teeth, "but we both know the truth. All you want to do is grind me down so you feel superior to at least one person in this school. Well, fuck you."

"I'd watch what I say if I were you," he whispers. "Next time, I might come back alone. And I think we both know I can't help myself when I have you alone."

Maybe it's the stubborn streak in me that keeps me from blurting out what pops into my head. *Sure, that's probably the only way you can get it up.* I want to die, but I'm not that desperate to take my last breath. And I know I would if I said that. He'd probably snap my neck without thinking about it.

When I don't react, he shakes his head and clicks his tongue. "That's all right. I'm a patient man, Delilah. Those of us who are free to eat, drink, and sleep whenever we please can afford to be patient. You'll come around." I wish he would hold his breath until the time comes, but I'll settle for him getting the hell out of my face. He does, followed by the guard, who locks the door as always.

I collapse onto the cot, curling into a ball, facing the wall again. This time, when tears threaten to fill my eyes, I don't bother fighting them back. I don't have the strength now.

You're unlovable. You're worthless. You're a failure. Nobody has ever loved you. Because you're broken.

I'm not so sure I want to die anymore. Now I want to live. Now I have a reason to.

I'm going to make him pay. I'm going to make them all pay if it's the last thing I ever do.

This time, when I close my eyes, nobody pounds on the door. Whether that's because Lucas decided to back off a little, or I just got lucky, I don't know. Sleep overtakes me before I can decide what's more likely.

34

LUCAS

My inbox is full. There are a dozen voicemails waiting for me to give them my attention.

But here I am in my apartment, nursing a Scotch, too sick in what's left of my soul to do more than swing between rage and self-loathing. That's been the rhythm of my days since leaving Delilah in that cell. Since I almost lost my daughter so soon after I found her.

My fault. My fucking fault. I told myself I was keeping her here for Aspen's sake, yet I couldn't have made it easier for her to go behind my back. Hindsight is 20/20, right? I've spent every waking moment since that night going over the many times I could have chosen differently and avoided what eventually unfolded.

I could have kept her locked up here, so she couldn't have sneaked out. No leaving the guest room unlocked, no letting her walk around like she owned the apartment.

I could have stuck to my word and refused any sort of sexual contact between us.

I could have kicked Marcel out of school for some reason, any reason. I should've known, should've seen there was something brewing.

I sure as hell should have made sure Delilah and Aspen never spent time together. That might be the most regrettable mistake of all. Why didn't I see through Delilah? I should have forbidden her from getting to know my daughter. I shouldn't have allowed them to spend time together, even supervised. The girl is clever, sharp. I should've known she'd find a way to get around Quinton and have a few private moments with Aspen.

But I was too busy telling myself I had everything under control. That so long as I made sure the girl knew who called the shots, everything would hum along like a well-oiled machine. Who the hell do I think I am? My pride almost got Aspen kidnapped, murdered, and who knows what else.

There's a reason she was kept from me. I have to laugh at myself as I pour another Scotch since the first one didn't do the trick. I doubt this one will, either. I don't know if there's enough left in the bottle to wipe out the depth of my self-hatred. Charlotte knew I wasn't fit to be a father. Hell, everybody did. There's something inside me that's too broken, too twisted. I can clean up my act all I want. That doesn't change anything.

When my phone rings, I snarl at it. The world is still turning. Fuck the world. It can take care of itself for a little while. The ringing stops, and I let out a sigh of relief—before it starts again almost immediately.

Something about that makes my blood boil. I cross the room, pick up the phone, and my stomach sinks when I see it's Nic calling. Of course. No one else would keep ringing until they pissed me off enough to make me answer. I don't know if I have it in me to sound glad to hear from him, but then we've never much relied on formalities anyway.

"Yeah?" I ask on answering, shaking the ice in my glass.

"I hear we're already well into the liquor cabinet this evening."

"We are," I growl. "Is that against the law now?"

"You know it isn't. Just take it easy. You can't run a school when you're half in the bag all the time."

"Who says I'm—"

"No one. Christ. I'm busting your balls."

"You'll have to forgive me, but I'm not in the mood for my balls to be busted."

"Who is?" He lets it go, moving quickly to another topic. "I found something I knew you'd want to know. I couldn't help but dig deeper into the trust. Something about it didn't sit right with me."

It's still barely enough to grab my interest in my half-drunk state. What does any of it matter anymore? Nothing he says is going to exonerate the girl in the cell. "That makes two of us. What did you find?"

"It's all about the fine print. The money is in her name, yes, but it's not that simple."

Dammit. Just like that, I care again. I'm barely breathing as I sit down with my drink. "Go on."

"For one thing," he continues with a sigh, "the bank wouldn't allow her to access the money unless either Matteo or Rico were present at the lawyer's office when she signed the paperwork."

"Jesus Christ." I should've known from what she told me that Dick wouldn't make it easy.

"And in the event of their deaths, meaning neither of them would be available when she attempts to claim what's hers, the money is automatically transferred to an offshore account."

The full picture is clear now, and it sickens me. "He was putting together an emergency plan. Once he knew what those fuckers were going to do to Aspen, he wanted to be sure there was escape money in place for when the Rossi family came knocking."

"So if his sons died, the money was still accessible. Which was all he cared about. It had nothing to do with Delilah. I'm sure he had no intention of her ever seeing a cent, even if things blew over and everybody lived."

"If he survived and the boys didn't, he'd have plenty of cash to haul ass. Rather than put plans in place to protect their lives, he made sure to set himself up."

"Fucking prick."

"It tracks with everything she's said about him. He cared about his boys more than he ever did about her, but ultimately, he cared about himself most of all."

"At least you know she was telling the truth about that much."

"Not that it does much good. She had to go and destroy herself."

Nic makes a thoughtful noise. "Is that what she did?"

"How can you ask me that? She almost got Aspen killed. You think she deserves to live after that?"

"It's not me we're talking about here. It's you."

"What the hell is that supposed to mean?" I gulp the rest of my drink, but the anger brewing in my chest is hotter than the path the liquor carves as it goes down my throat.

"I don't know what it's supposed to mean. I know that no matter what happens, you're going to do what's right for you and your kid. At the end of the day, that's all any of us can do. We protect what's ours."

But that's the problem I have to face after getting off the call. Sitting in my silent apartment, staring at the wall, considering pouring another drink. I didn't protect what's mine. I came in after the fact, once the protecting had been done. I had to be roused out of bed by a fucking guard. I wasn't there when Aspen needed me once again. All I did was clean up the loose ends—and even then, that's not been completely done since Delilah still sits in a cell. So long as she continues to live, that end has not been tied up.

Where is that dark side of me now? The side that found it so easy to punish her until she screamed? I could use him right about now. He would make it possible for me to finish this, as I know it needs to be finished.

It doesn't help that everything I set eyes on in this place brings up a memory of her. Having dinner, watching a movie, and even sitting in silence while we both worked. And of course, the bedrooms carry their own memories.

Even if I kill her, I'll never be rid of her. And that's on me. That's my weakness, my stupid mistake. I allowed her to get too close, so close that her betrayal struck me to my core. I lost perspective because I lost my grip on myself. Time and again, I went against what instinct told me was right in favor of what I wanted at the moment.

And always, I told myself I had it under control.

There's only one thing I can do. What I should have done from the beginning. Rather than pour another drink, I go to the guest room and pull out a set of clean clothes. I add a clean blanket to the pile and pin two bottles of water under my arm, then head out for the holding cells. It's late enough that the halls are virtually empty, and anyone who happens to see me in passing doesn't exactly take pains to start a conversation. I can only imagine how I must look. One thing I've always been able to do is put on a foreboding image. The mood I'm in, I don't have to try. It radiates from me.

This time, when the guard unlocks the door, I tell him to wait outside. This is a conversation we need to have in private.

She's curled up in the corner of the cot, facing the wall. I tell myself not to pay attention to that, dropping the pile at the foot of the bed. "These are for you," I mutter before backing away.

She finally dares to glance over her shoulder. Once she's confirmed I'm alone, she looks at what I've brought her. I don't expect thanks, and I don't get any. "I was kind of hoping for a steak."

"As it turns out, the kitchen is fresh out of steak for people who scheme to get other students killed."

She turns her face toward the wall again, her shoulders rising and falling as she sighs. "Anything else? Did you want to fuck me until I bleed this time?"

"Not this time. Not ever. That's never happening again."

She snorts. "So you've said before."

"This time, I mean it. This time, I'm going to do what I should have done all along. I'm going to stay away from you. You're on your own now, Delilah."

A half-hearted chuckle falls from her lips. "I've always been on my own, Lucas. Don't you get that?"

"No, it's you who doesn't get it. You could have had something good here at Corium. You could have had a friend... maybe even more. You were the one who threw it all away."

Her breathing hitches, betraying her. Not that I didn't know this was all an act. She's suffering, no doubt about that, no matter how she tries to pretend otherwise.

Finally, she rolls over, and I can't shake the stirring in my chest when I see how haunted she looks with her big eyes and sunken cheeks. It's only been a few days that she's been kept without food, but the effect is visible. "So that's it?" she whispers. "I can go?"

"When did I say that? No, you will remain at Corium. I let the council decide what to do with you. This is the last kindness I will extend to you." I nod at the pile of clothes.

"No. No, please." She sits up, shaking, as the last of her pride falls away. "Please, don't leave me down here. I didn't hurt her. I wasn't going to; I told them I wouldn't be able to do that."

"Told who?"

She presses her chapped lips together into a tight line. I let out a frustrated sigh at her unwavering unwillingness to talk.

Her voice rises in pitch and volume when she repeats, "I didn't hurt her!"

"You had your chance, and you chose to turn your back on it."

"Please, Lucas. Please, don't leave me alone." Her voice catches an instant before a single tear cuts a line down her cheek. "I won't ever try something like that again. I won't go near Aspen. I swear!"

"Do you know what the worst part is?" I ask, keeping my distance no matter how much I want to go to her. "I don't know whether anything you say is true or not. This could all be an act."

"It's not!"

"Just like it wasn't an act when you went out of your way to befriend Aspen?" Her shoulders slump when the truth of that hits home. "I can't believe you, and I won't anymore. You've burned your last bridge."

She covers her face with her hands, shaking her head. "Please…"

"I won't be coming back down here again." I can't stand to look at her anymore. I have to get out of this cell, away from her, and put this shit show behind me.

Yet even as I step outside and listen to the lock click as it engages, I know it won't be that easy. Not with the sound of her brokenhearted weeping still ringing in my ears.

35

DELILAH

He didn't mean it. He'll be back. That was just another one of his threats, a way of breaking me down so the next time he visits, I'll do whatever he wants.

And at this point, I will. No matter what it is, I'll do it. He can take any hole he wants. I'll grovel, I'll beg, I'll lick his shoes if I have to. Anything, so long as this ends. I don't know how much longer I'll be able to stay in this cell by myself, totally disconnected from the rest of the world.

At least I have some water and clean clothes, right? The half-crazed laughter that bubbles out of me at the thought is worrisome. I'm losing it. I've tried so hard to hold myself together, but it's only a matter of time.

I almost wish he would have announced it was time for me to die. It doesn't matter how strong I am. If he's leaving me on my own, washing his hands of me, I'm as good as dead anyway. And he knows it. Now, I'll have the fun of anticipating it.

I'm still betting on Quinton, but who knows? He might decide to outsource. Maybe he'll enjoy it more if he gets to stand back and watch.

I'm about to fall asleep—it's the only thing to do around here— when a sudden click from the lock startles me. I sit up, my heart in my throat, hands clasped between my knees to keep them from shaking. Is this it? Is this when it happens?

Or did Lucas decide he hasn't finished with me after all?

As it turns out, the person who walks through the door is the last person I ever expected to see. "Aspen."

"Hi," she murmurs before giving the guard a pointed look. He's probably my least favorite of all of them, though at least none of them have put a hand on me or threatened me.

He takes her look for what it means and leaves us alone. "So," I croak once it's just the two of us, "They sent you to do it? Or did you feel like you deserved to do it?"

"What do you mean?"

"Don't play with me now, please. Did you come to kill me? If so, I wish you would get it over with."

"No, I didn't come to kill you. Why would you even think that?"

"Like I said, I'm not in the mood for games. If you didn't come here to kill me, what did you come for?"

"I only wanted to know..." She looks at the floor, hair falling on both sides of her face. "I wanted to know why. I never did anything to you. I even lent you my clothes. I tried to be your friend. I saved your life."

So this is it. She wants a little closure before I'm gone. Because everything is about her, isn't it? As always. "You really don't know? Have you already forgotten what you did?"

"I don't know what you're talking about."

"Nash. I'm talking about Nash."

Her head snaps up, eyes wide, and now a flush creeps up her neck. "I was defending myself."

"It took you that many stab wounds to defend yourself? From what I heard, it was overkill."

"He was going to rape me."

I want to flinch away from her ugly words. Instead, all I do is scoff. "Says you. Isn't that convenient since he can't defend himself now?"

"Maybe you didn't know him like I did. He hated me. There was some sick, twisted thing in his head, and he turned it against me. After that night, he taunted me. Even though he wasn't in the video, he knew about it. Because he was there, he took the video."

Nash was fucked up, far beyond any help, but he was all I had. The only person who seemed to give a shit about me.

"Of course he did. And when you snapped, as you say, you took away the only person who ever gave a shit about me." I hate the way my chin quivers, but I can't help it. Even now, after all this time, the pain is so fresh. "Did you know we were going to be married? I was finally going to have a life."

"I didn't know that," she whispers.

"Nobody ever cared about me. I was forgotten. I was shunned by my own family. He was the one person who ever took an interest. He was going to be my husband. Now I have nobody, and you have everything. So yeah, I set you up because you killed the only person I ever loved."

She falls back a step, hitting the wall. Folding her arms, she leans against it. "I didn't know that, either."

"Now you do."

"I did it because he could have killed me easily, and he did kill part of me... he was the one who drugged me that night. That's what he told me when he attacked me. He gave me the drug that caused me to lose my baby."

"Baby... I... I'm sorry."

"I'm sorry that you lost someone you loved, but I'm not sorry that I defended myself."

"I know he wasn't a good person, but he was the only person I had."

For a few minutes, a heavy silence hangs between us. I don't want to believe that Nash went that far, but deep down, I know he did it. I always knew he was capable of terrible things. I just chose to look past it because I was so desperate for him to love me.

When I look back up, Aspen screws up her face like she's concentrating hard. What is she doing? Probably thinking about how to end me.

"Okay. We have to get you out of here."

"Oh, sure. I was just thinking the same thing." I roll my eyes. "Let me guess, by getting out, you mean to kill and throw my dead body out?"

"No. I mean it. You're leaving, as in walking out of here. Now."

The thing is, she looks serious. I was already starting to wonder if she was playing with a full deck, the way my aunt used to say. It was one thing when she was so desperate to be friends with me. But this is a whole other level of crazy. "Why?"

"Because I believe in giving people second chances."

"I thought I already fucked up my second chance."

"Okay, maybe a third chance... Look, I don't know why I see this good person in you, but something tells me it's there and that you are worth giving a real chance. One away from all of this."

"How exactly do you think that's going to work?"

She looks me up and down. "I stashed a coat and hat in a closet near the entrance. There's some cash in the pocket. You need to take the helicopter to Takotna, then get on a plane. Once you get to North Woods, you can use it to go wherever else you need to go."

My mouth falls open. Either she is playing a cruel joke on me or I'm hallucinating.

"Wait a second. You were already planning on this?"

"I only wanted to talk to you first. I just had to know why you tricked me. Now I do."

"And you still want to help me?"

"Come on. We're wasting time." She checks her phone, frowning. "I came down here specifically at this time because the guards change shifts in around two minutes. They always bullshit for a little while, catching each other up on whatever happened during the day. That should give us time to get upstairs before anybody knows you're gone."

"Hang on, just wait." I stand, trembling with excitement but also skeptical as I've ever been. "How do I know this is for real? What if you're going to sneak me out of here because your husband and his friends want to beat the hell out of me and leave me bleeding out in the snow?"

"I guess you're just going to have to trust me, aren't you?"

"No offense, but that's not so easy to do."

"I'm not the one who has lied. I'm not the one who pretended to be your friend just so somebody else could hurt you."

"Ever heard of such a thing as revenge?"

"Yeah, I know all about it. And I know what a waste of time it is." She checks the time again, and her frown deepens. "Come on. We don't have much time. Are you in or not?"

On the one hand, I'm still pretty sure this is all a ploy for Quinton to kill me.

On the other hand, what's the alternative? Waiting even longer for the inevitable? Besides, even though I shouldn't, part of me believes her. Maybe my brain's going soft after being isolated all this time.

She stands by the door, staring at her phone, waiting for the right moment. "Are you ready?" she whispers.

I nod, hoping nobody is checking out the security feed just now. "I hope you're right about this," I whisper back.

"I am. Just follow me, and don't say a word." She opens the door just far enough that she's able to peer out into the hall. Once she's satisfied, she opens it another few inches before slipping through the gap and waving me out behind her. It's now or never.

I step out of the cell. Finally, I'm out.

And now I'm in more danger than ever, as Aspen closes the door, then takes me by the hand. I'm hardly strong enough to run, but I have to do this. I have to make it out of here. Once I'm in North Woods, I can finally get to the house Nash told me to find. The address is burned in my memory. If there's enough cash in the coat pocket to get a cab from the airport, I'm home free.

But not until we make it up and out of here.

Rather than take the elevator, she leads me to a stairwell. "You're not seriously expecting me to be able to do this, are you?" I ask, exasperated at the idea of having to climb all those stairs in my condition.

"You don't have a choice. Let's go. Move your ass." She takes off ahead of me, and I curse her under my breath before pushing myself to follow. I can't let a little fatigue and weakness get in the way now. Not when the rest of my life depends on it. There will be plenty of time to rest once I'm free.

By the time we get to the last flight, I almost have to pick my legs up using my hands to get from one step to the next. "Just a little farther," she whispers, encouraging me from up ahead. "Hurry. I made sure the helicopter would be waiting."

"What's in this for you?" It's better than dwelling on my almost numb legs and the fact that I might throw up even though there's nothing in my stomach.

"I don't know. I just don't feel right having you locked up like that." She holds up a hand, and I fall back a step before she opens the door to make sure the coast is clear. My heart's pounding in my ears as I wait—and when she waves me through, that pounding turns to thumping that I'm sure will kill me before I ever reach fresh air.

We stay close to the walls, darting down the wide passageway leading to salvation. Before we reach the doors, Aspen pauses to duck into a closet. She comes out holding a puffy coat, which I quickly pull on, along with the knit cap she offers. I plunge my hands into the pockets and close my fingers around a wad of cash. If this is all some elaborate trick, she really pulled out all the stops.

"Come on. Hurry!" She leads the way again, and before long, I'm out in the cold, clean air. It's enough of a sudden change to shock my system, but if anything, it gives me the added incentive to haul ass to the helipad.

"I can't pay you back," I remind her as we run.

"I'm not asking you to. Whatever happens after this, that's on you. At least now you have a chance." We reach the helicopter, and the pilot opens the door. Aspen hangs back while I climb inside. Once I'm seated, I look out at her. She's shivering, and I wonder if this is her coat I'm wearing.

"Thank you." It feels empty, meaningless, but it's the least I owe her.

"You're welcome." She turns tail and runs, probably trying to make sure she's not missed once they raise the alarm that I'm gone.

This feels too good to be true. Nobody jumped out and grabbed me. Nobody dragged me back to my cell. The pilot gets the engines fired up, and within moments, we're lifting off the ground.

I can't believe it. A surge of emotion hits me all at once, but I can't decide if I want to laugh or cry. I'm never stepping foot in that place again. I'm putting it all behind me. From now on, my life belongs to me alone.

To think, I have Aspen Rossi to thank for it.

THIS ISN'T what I expected.

"This is the place?" My cab driver cranes his neck, peering through the windshield at the rather rundown-looking building. It's not the sort of place I expected Nash to send me. Here I was, feeling proud of myself, proud that I finally did what he instructed. I could barely sit still on the plane, so eager to finally arrive.

Now? I'm wondering if I got the address wrong, after all. Wouldn't that be the cherry on top of the shit sundae my life has become?

"Well? Are you getting out or not?" I'm keeping the guy from picking up another fare. I guess if I got it wrong, I can always try again. For now, I hand him the cash and hurry out of the car. I'm still weak and shaky, but more than anything, I want to get inside so I can finally rest. That thought alone is enough to keep me moving along the brick walkway leading up to a barren front porch. There's no sign of life behind the windows, but this is supposed to be a safe house. I guess they can't exactly hang a sign advertising that.

Here goes nothing. I knock on the door and hope this is the right place because I'm so tired I don't know if I can stand any more traveling. There has to be a hotel somewhere I could stay for the night if I'm totally off base. Somewhere I can get my head together.

As it turns out, I don't need to worry about it. A middle-aged woman dressed in casual but expensive-looking clothes opens the door. The woman is not shopping at Goodwill, that's for sure, and she's groomed perfectly. In other words, she doesn't fit in with her shabby surroundings. "Yes?" she asks, wearing a patient smile.

"Um, Nash Brookshire sent me. I was supposed to be here weeks ago."

"Are you Delilah?"

Tears fill my eyes, followed by a lump in my throat. I can only nod hard since emotion seems to have stolen my voice. "You poor thing," she murmurs, reaching for me and pulling me inside. But she's gentle about it, caring. "I'm sure you've been through so much. But don't worry. You're safe now."

"Thank you," I manage to blubber before sobbing harder than before. It's over. It's finally over. I'm finally safe.

"First things first. You need a shower badly. No offense." She pats my arm, still smiling, her eyes crinkling at the corners. "Once we get you settled in a room, you can get some sleep. You seem worn out."

"I am." Though even with my head spinning like it is, the sound of female voices coming from overhead sinks into my awareness. I look up, curious.

"Come on. You can use my things for now until you can get some of your own. You might want to be quick about it—sometimes the hot water goes in and out depending on how much usage there's been during the day."

Once we're upstairs, I'm greeted by a line of closed doors. The only one that's open leads into a white tiled bathroom with a clawfoot tub. Along the way, passing all those doors, I hear more voices. This time, some of them are male, too.

"I'm sorry," I finally have to say once we reach the bathroom. "Nash never gave me any idea what kind of place this was. Are there a bunch of people staying here?"

"We sort of have a revolving door," she explains with a tiny shrug, going through the cabinet under the sink and pulling out shampoo and body wash. "But don't worry. There's a room available for you. Three doors down on your right. I'll make sure everything is in place while you wash up."

I'm so grateful I could start crying again. Right now, I don't care what kind of place this is or who walks through the revolving door. So long as it's not anybody with a grudge against me, I'm fine.

I can hardly believe it. I got away. I really made it. I don't even care that I have to hurry through showering if I want any hot water or that the towels left for me on the sink are sort of scratchy and cheap. It doesn't matter. I'm free.

With one of the towels wrapped around me and the other around my hair, I grab all my clothes and hustle down the hall before anybody can step out of a room and see me like this. My hostess is waiting for me in the room, which is small and cramped and only has one tiny window, but it's a huge step up from where I've been lately.

"I'm so sorry," I offer with a tiny laugh. "I didn't get your name. I want to thank you, but I don't know what to call you."

"You can call me Grace. As for thanks, none are needed. Nash knew what he was doing, sending you here."

"Yes, I think he did."

"There are clean clothes here on the bed." She pats a small pile. "You get some rest, and later, you'll have dinner brought up to the room."

"That's great. I'm starving." I ate some food on the plane, but I don't think I'll ever get enough to make the empty feeling in my stomach go away completely.

"Not to worry. We won't let you starve here." She goes to the door, waiting until she's in the hall to add one final thing. "Don't think about making friends with the other girls. It never ends well."

I turn around, ready to ask what that means, but she's already gone. The door is closed.

And to my horror, there's the click of a lock.

I take one slow step after another, dread building in my gut. No way did I just hear that. I have to be imagining things—I'm so tired and hungry. Yet when I reach out and close my fingers around the knob, it won't budge. She locked me in.

"Hello?" I knock on the door, panic in my voice. "Why did you lock me in? Come back! What the hell is going on?" When that doesn't get me an answer, I go from knocking to pounding with the side of my fist. "Hello!"

There's nothing. Only soft noises coming from the rooms on either side of the one I'm now locked in.

I back away from the door, staring at it. Where the hell did Nash send me? He never did say, only that I would be safe here. He must have gotten his signals crossed because how could I be safe somewhere I'm locked in? Hell, if there was a fire, I don't even think I could fit through the window to get out.

I go to the bed, quickly putting on the clothes left for me—a thin nightgown and a pair of panties.

Is this really happening? Again? My chest hurts to think of it, so I have to stop doing that. Obviously, something's not right about this. I'm going to have to leave the second I get the opportunity.

When the lock clicks again, I grab the coat, prepared to flee if I have to. There's more than enough money to get me someplace else. I only need to get out of here. I don't know what this place is or why Nash sent me, but I don't think he would mind me leaving now that I'm getting such a bad feeling about it.

The sight of Preston makes me almost collapse with relief.

"Oh, my god! I'm so glad you're here. There must have been some kind of a mistake."

He doesn't say anything at first, closing the door behind him and leaning against it with his arms folded. "So you made it. Honestly, I wasn't sure you'd be able to. Especially after the way my plan went to shit."

I blink hard, staring at him. "Can we not talk about that right now? I'm a little more freaked out by what's going on. Why did she lock the door on me? Where am I?"

"No, I guess he wouldn't have told you." He strokes his jaw, grimacing, and I can't help but notice all the ways he and Nash look so much alike.

"Told me what? What am I missing?"

"Sweetie, this isn't a safe house."

"Okay, what is it? A halfway house or something?" That would explain why there are so many other people here.

"More like... well, let's just call it what it is. It's a brothel and a very profitable one. Some of the girls stay here all the time, while others pass through on their way elsewhere."

No, this can't be. "And Nash knew about it?"

"Why wouldn't he? The family runs it. We have a lot of little businesses like this."

"But why would Nash send me here? Of all places?"

He tips his head to the side. "Wow. I always heard you were sort of dim, but I didn't know you were flat-out fucking stupid."

I can't help but recoil in horror. "Excuse me?"

"Excuse me?" he taunts before laughing. "My brother knew what he was doing. He told you to go here so you could earn the family money. What, did you think he actually gave a shit about you?"

"That's not true," I insist, but he only laughs louder. "It's not!"

"Sure. Whatever you need to tell yourself. Anyway, you're here, so you might as well get used to it."

"No way. I'm not staying here!"

"That's where you're wrong. You are staying here. This is where you live now, and this is where you will service any and all men who come through this door. But don't worry about it," he adds, snickering when I gasp. "Sometimes, some rich guy comes through and decides he wants to buy one of the girls to be his personal sex slave. It could be a step up."

He reaches for the doorknob, looking me up and down. "Get some sleep. You look like shit. Nobody is going to be willing to pay for you when you're like this." With that, he leaves me alone, and I'm too stunned to rush to the door before the lock is engaged again.

It can't be true. It can't be. Nash loved me, and I loved him. He wouldn't have done this to me on purpose.

Would he?

I slide down the length of the door, landing in a heap on the floor as the world comes crashing down around me.

36

LUCAS

This is a goddamn nightmare. Just when I think I have everything in place, somebody has to come along and throw me a fucking curveball.

In this case, the somebody in question happens to be the daughter now facing me with defiance. "Do you want to tell me why there's footage of you helping her escape?" I bellow at my daughter. I can't control my anger, faced with the knowledge Aspen was the one who made this happen. "She was locked up for your sake!"

"That's not true."

"And do you think you're in any position to know whether or not that's true? I put her in that cell because of what she did. She set you up. You would be dead by now if things had gone according to plan!"

"But she doesn't deserve to be kept in a cell like an animal. That was why I helped her. And honestly, if I never had to see her again, I wouldn't mind. I don't need somebody else's death on my conscience, either, and we both know that would eventually happen if she stuck around here long enough. Rules or no rules." She folds her arms, jutting her chin out in a way that's far too reminiscent of my family.

"You had no right to do that."

"I think if she was locked up because of me, I'm the only one who did have the right."

She's too smart for her own damn good. "You know what, I can't even see you right now. Go back to your room." I'm afraid I'll say something I can't take back, and that's the last thing I want to do. Especially when we've already come so far.

But goddamnit, I've never been so fucking furious in all my life. I truly cannot remember a time I've been this close to losing my shit.

She's gone. She actually got away. All thanks to Aspen's conscience, which she certainly could not have inherited from me. This isn't the end of our discussion. We will definitely revisit this, and soon.

Right now, I have bigger problems like a fugitive on the run. That's the only way I can think about her now. I need to find her. No way am I letting her go. Why does she get to be free after what she's done?

How could I let her go free after what she did to me?

There's only one person I can call, the only one who makes any sense in a situation like this.

"I have a problem," I tell my brother, pacing my apartment now that I'm alone. Like a caged tiger, unable to do what comes naturally. In this case, that would mean tearing somebody's fucking head off. Starting with the pilot who took her out of here in the first place. He had no such orders from me.

"Another one?" Nic asks with a short laugh. "What is it this time?"

"For starters, there's an escapee on the loose. And I need to find her immediately."

Heavy silence greets me, and every second of it is like a blade inching deeper into my chest. I can only imagine how he must be judging me. How disappointed he must be in his fuck-up of a brother. I couldn't get this right. I haven't changed at all.

"Let me guess. She snuck out, and now she's somewhere in North Woods, most likely."

I come to a stop, staring at my reflection on the TV screen. "You already knew before I called, you bastard."

"What would ever give you that idea?"

"Don't fuck with me. You aren't the least bit surprised."

"No. You're right." He sounds sympathetic, but that's not what I need from him right now. I don't need anybody's sympathy, not ever. "I'm not surprised because I got word of a single student getting on the plane to North Woods. Alone. Unscheduled."

"How the hell would you know that?"

"Do we really have time to go into this?"

"Right now? I didn't think we did, but I'm starting to reconsider. Tell me," I bark.

"Fine. We'll do it your way." He sighs, and I hate the sound. The exasperation in it. "Did you think I wouldn't make it a point to keep a close eye on her? That I wouldn't make sure my contacts knew to watch for a girl of her description with long, auburn hair?"

"What would make you do that?"

"For starters, the fact that you fucked her in your office, Lucas."

It hits me with all the force of a cannonball, rocking me back on my heels. "How the hell—"

"Think about it."

I don't have to think for long, and now I don't know who I'm more furious with. "My new secretary. Son of a bitch, I should have known. You had her spying on me all this time."

"Keeping watch over you on my behalf," he corrects. "And can you blame me? Now we both see I had every reason to be concerned. Don't take it personally. We all have our weaknesses, don't we?"

"You need to watch what you say."

"Who says?" he counters. If it wasn't for the laughter in his voice, I'd think he was just as pissed as I am. "It was clear from the beginning you were too wrapped up in her. The fact that you were unwilling to take my advice. Remember that? Remember when I told you how this could be avoided?"

"I don't have time for you to dog-walk me past every fucking mistake I've ever made, all right? Can we do that later? I need to find this girl."

"Do you, though? Do you really?" There's no more laughter. His voice is softer now, low, heavy. "Or should you let her go? That might be for the best, you know. There's no reason for her to stay there now. She's far away, Aspen is safe, and now things can fall into some semblance of a normal pattern."

The thing is, I know he's right. The best thing in the world would be to move past this. Acknowledge the fact that she got away and let it go. She's been nothing but a curse since the moment I set eyes on her.

"She got away from me," I mutter, speaking more to myself than my brother. "How am I supposed to let that go? How do I live with that?"

"Time heals all things."

"We both know that's a bunch of bullshit. Don't pretend you haven't let shit fester inside you for years and years."

"And what good did it ever do me? Just like, what good would it do you? It's time to start focusing on the things you have, all the good stuff you've got going for you. That's what matters. Not some stupid kid who managed to jump from the frying pan into the fire."

Something about his choice of words makes the hair on the back of my neck stand up. "What are you telling me?"

"Fuck me and my big mouth," he groans. "Are you sure you want to hear this?"

"Yes, for fuck's sake!"

"Fine. Like I said, I've had eyes on her. As soon as she got off the plane, I had someone follow her cab. She got out at a building owned by the Brookshire family."

"No big surprise there."

"Lucas. It's a brothel."

My stomach drops. "It's what?"

"Some of the girls working out of the house live there full time. Others are dropped there, waiting to be picked up by whoever's taking them to their next destination. Sometimes they cross into Canada; other times, they move on to Russia. From there, who knows?"

I hear what he's saying, but I can't piece it together. "Why would she go there, though? That doesn't make any sense."

"If she knew about it, somebody must have given her the address. Maybe that's where she was trying to end up when Quinton first found her on the street. Maybe she thought she'd be safe there."

"But who'd give her that idea?"

"You would have to ask her yourself. But I'm guessing since it's affiliated with the Brookshires, she got the address from Nash."

Why would he send her there? That's what I can't wrap my head around. "There had to be plenty of places he could have told her to hide."

"Exactly. But he chose that particular location."

"He didn't care what happened to her there," I conclude. Why does the idea make me hurt for her? There she was, promised to this piece of shit. According to Aspen, she believes she loved him—and he loved her. She said as much in the cell before Aspen helped her escape.

All this time, she had no idea he tried to send her to a brothel where traffickers come and go all the time. For all I know, by now, one of them could have decided to take her along with them on the next leg of their journey.

Nash never gave a damn about her. Nobody ever has.

"You still with me?" Nic asks. "Listen, I was only trying to look out for my little brother. Don't take it too hard, okay? You can hate me all you want. Just don't do it forever."

"I don't have time for any of that right now. I need to figure this out."

"You still think there's something to figure out?"

"Am I supposed to leave her there?"

"Considering you kept her locked in a cell for days? Is it really so much worse?"

In all honesty, he has a point. And really, I don't owe her a fucking thing. Time and again, she turned her back on every little bit of kindness I tried to show. The little bit of respect I tried to give her.

No, it wasn't all the time, but I made allowances left and right, and she made a fool of me as a result.

Maybe this is exactly what she deserves.

But truly, does anybody deserve the sort of fate I'm imagining now?

How many men are going to fuck her there?

"What do you want me to do?" Nic asks. "I've got one of my guys keeping an eye on the place just in case they try to take her to another location."

Part of me wants to tell him to leave her there. That she can rot with a stranger's cock up her ass for all I care. I don't owe her shit. She's made her choice.

Then there is another part that wants to tell him I'll be on the first flight to North Woods. That I'll be the one to rescue her from that place. That I'll kill anyone who dares to lay a finger on her because she is mine.

I want to tell him both.

I just don't know which one I want more.

≈

To be continued in Reign of Freedom

If you haven't read Quinton and Aspen's story yet, catch up on them in King of Corium

ALSO BY THE AUTHORS

***

DARK ROMANCE

The Blackthorn Elite
Hating You
Breaking You
Hurting You
Regretting You

The Obsession Duet
Cruel Obsession
Deadly Obsession

The Rossi Crime Family
Protect Me
Keep Me
Guard Me
Tame Me
Remember Me

The Moretti Crime Family
Savage Beginnings
Violent Beginnings
Broken Beginnings

The King Crime Family
Indebted
Inevitable

The Diabolo Crime Family
Devil You Hate
Devil You Know

Corium University

King of Corium
Drop Dead Queen
Broken Kingdom

***

STANDALONES

Convict Me

Runaway Bride

His Gift

Two Strangers

This Christmas

ABOUT THE AUTHORS

J.L. BECK AND C. HALLMAN ARE
USA TODAY AND INTERNATIONAL
BESTSELLING AUTHOR DUO WHO
WRITE CONTEMPORARY AND
DARK ROMANCE.

FIND US ON FACEBOOK AND
CHECK OUT OUR WEBSITE FOR
SALES AND FREEBIES!

WWW.BLEEDINGHEARTROMANCE.COM

Made in the USA
Las Vegas, NV
02 August 2022

52526171R00199